THE UNDERSTUDY

For information, contact henrygraypub2022@gmail.com.

Publisher's Cataloguing-in-Publication Data
Names: Peters, Charlie 1951-.
Title: The understudy / Charlie Peters.
Description: Granada Hills, CA : Henry Gray Publishing, 2023. |
Identifiers: LCCN 2023902348 | ISBN 979-8-9866805-3-8 (pbk) |
ISBN 979-8-9866805-5-2 (ebook)
Subjects: LCSH: Crime -- Fiction. | Consolidation and merger of
corporations -- Fiction. | Hacking -- Fiction. | Kidnapping -- Fiction. |
New York (N.Y.) -- Fiction. | BISAC: FICTION / Crime. | FICTION /
Thrillers / Crime. | FICTION / Thrillers / Suspense
Classification: LCC PS3616.E84 U53 2023 | DDC 813 P48—dc23
LC record available at https://lccn.loc.gov/2023902348

Library of Congress Control Number: 2023902348

Cover illustration by Robb Bradley, © 2023 Robb Bradley

Made in the United States of America.

Published by Henry Gray Publishing, P.O. Box 33832, Granada Hills, California 91394.

For more information or to join our mailing list,
visit HenryGrayPublishing.com.

THE UNDERSTUDY

CHARLIE PETERS

HENRY GRAY
HG
PUBLISHING

Granada Hills, CA
"Select books for selective readers"

MARTIN NEWMAN'S DIARY

I've turned a corner. My wife's death isn't hanging over me like it did for the last year. I'm still sad about what happened to her and of course I miss her, but not as much as before. I decided that soon I'm going to move out of the place I rented after she died and move back into our apartment. And I'm going to spend more time at Boundary, too. They were kind to let me work from home after what happened to Sophia.

Last week I bought a bunch of new clothes, joined a gym and decided to cut back on fast foods. I'm going to try out for the Boundary softball team, too. I did pretty good playing second base for them a couple of seasons ago. I picked up my guitar again and I even signed up to go rock climbing in Canada next month. Who knows? Maybe I'll meet someone new there, like I did when I met Sophia.

MONDAY

Ronnie Hewitt sat at one of the outdoor tables of a coffee shop in lower Manhattan's financial district. She was there every morning drinking a plain black coffee, watching the same people walking quickly in and out of the shop, holding their drinks in cardboard cups, all eager to get somewhere important. The building that housed Boundary, the hedge fund where Ronnie worked as personal assistant to its CEO, cast its shadow on Ronnie's table. At Boundary's entrance across the street was a demonstration, a small, well-behaved one comprised entirely of women. A couple of the demonstrators held signs. Others pushed strollers. This was not unusual for Boundary or any investment firm like it. They all pissed somebody off.

On Ronnie's table sat a small box of Paul Smith socks that her boss had ordered. But neither her boss nor his socks were on her mind now. Ronnie was waiting for a call from Miriam Dennis, director of Jerrold House, the public nursing facility in Queens from which her mother had escaped earlier that morning. Carlotta Hewitt had been spotted on the street barefoot and in her bathrobe by one of the facility's janitors on his way home from the night shift.

Ronnie's mother suffered from the effects of a stroke and showed mild symptoms of dementia, but she'd still managed to walk herself out of the facility twice over the last month. And who could blame her? Jerrold House was a shit hole.

Ronnie went to the facility early that morning to calm her mother. Mornings there were especially bad. Orderlies ended and began shifts. Waking patients clamored for food and attention. The halls were mopped with an antiseptic that, as awful as it stank, was preferable to what it hid. A TV hung from the ceiling of every room like huge IVs that the patients stared at mesmerized. Ronnie spoon-fed her mother breakfast, a cereal made of brightly colored pieces of something from a box covered with manic cartoon characters. The cereal had turned the milk in the bowl a shade of light blue.

The last thing her father had asked Ronnie to do was to take care of her mother if anything happened to him. Something did happen to him. He died when Ronnie was fifteen. Carlotta had no work experience so she took a sales job at the glove counter on the first floor of Bonwit Teller. Sometimes after school Ronnie would secretly watch her mother working there, hating how the customers treated her. But her mother never complained. In twenty-three years she never missed a day of work. And Jerrold House is what she got for that.

If the condition of the nursing home wasn't enough to contend with, the facility's director Miriam Dennis made it clear that she didn't like Ronnie or her mother. Carlotta was English and even though she'd lived in America for more than forty years, her accent lingered, prompting Ms. Dennis to ask Ronnie, "What's a woman like your mother doing here anyway?" It was more an accusation than a question because, like many Americans, Ms. Dennis thought Carlotta's accent meant that she'd lived a life of tea and crumpets served by suited butlers in ornate BBC sets. She had no idea that Carlotta Hewitt's father and grandfather were coal miners in West Yorkshire and that her childhood made Ms. Dennis's youth in working class Harrisburg, Pennsylvania look like *Sesame Street.*

Ronnie thought about what she'd say when—and if—Ms. Dennis finally called. And if her boss asked Ronnie why she was late this morning she'd tell him that she'd gone to the boutique on Bleeker Street to pick up his socks even though she'd gotten them Friday afternoon. He wouldn't know any different.

Still, she had to be careful because in the last few weeks her normally predictable boss, Barry Kestrel, had become more difficult to read. That was because word on the street was that Salient, one of the country's biggest hedge funds, was going to make an offer for Kestrel's company Boundary whose smaller size made it perfect for a mega-player like Salient to snatch up.

No one knew how Kestrel would respond if and when the Salient offer was officially made. Would he take the money and relinquish Boundary? Or would he hold onto the company he'd built, like a child holds onto their toys even though they've become bored playing with them?

As Ronnie considered this, the call she was waiting for came.

"This is Director Dennis."

Ronnie put a broad smile on her face so that her voice would sound more pleasant, a trick she'd learned while working cold sales jobs in college. "Ms. Dennis, hi, this is Ronnie Hewitt. I was there this morning."

"My staff told me." The woman was important; she had a staff.

"You probably heard that my mother got out again."

"So I was told."

"I know your job is very difficult—"

"Good of you to say that."

"—but I don't understand how a woman like my mother who can barely walk keeps escaping."

"As I told you, we could put her in the security ward, but you didn't seem interested."

The week before Ms. Dennis had given Ronnie a tour of the security ward, where Jerrold House's most dangerous patients were kept. Many were violent; all were sedated. Life there for Carlotta Hewitt, a woman who'd never used the word "shit" once in her life, would be like, in the words of one orderly, "being eaten by a wolf and shit off a cliff."

"There's a waiting list to get into Jerrold House, Ms. Hewitt." This was Ms. Dennis's favorite threat.

"I appreciate how hard your job is, Madame Director," Ronnie said, trying to flatter the bitch, but before Ronnie could say anything else she heard what sounded like a door slamming. Or was it a gunshot?

"There's been an incident," Ms. Dennis said and she hung up.

Ronnie put her phone away, more determined than ever to get her mother out of Jerrold House and into Ledgewood Gardens, a private facility in the Connecticut countryside, a million miles from Union Turnpike in Queens. But Ledgewood was expensive and what Ronnie made as a personal assistant wasn't nearly enough to keep her mother at a place like that.

When she wasn't doing errands or fielding calls for Kestrel, Ronnie worked with Jubilee, an improvisational theater company she'd cofounded with her partner Alex and a dozen other performers. Jubilee was notorious for its political material. It had no favorites, left, right or center, which meant that their material managed to piss everyone off at one time or another and Ronnie prided herself on that. Like most small theatres, Jubilee's shows barely made enough to pay for rent and publicity. Their day jobs—hers working for Barry Kestrel at Boundary and Alex's with a computer company called Nerd Nation—paid for food, rent and other essentials, leaving nothing to move her mother to private care.

Ronnie considered calling the agents who saw her work at Jubilee and were eager to submit her for the writing staffs on the late night talk shows. Women comedy writers, they told her, were in big demand now. But Ronnie preferred the freedom that Jubilee gave her. The networks, even the cable stations with characters that swore endlessly and had color, diversity and nudity coming out their asses, were beholden to big money. Let's be honest. They were big money.

She'd get the money she needed another way.

Ronnie could feel the tension as soon as she walked into the Boundary lobby. It was like a fog that had rolled in two weeks earlier with rumors of the Salient offer and it grew thicker every day. Since she was the CEO's personal assistant, everyone who worked there stared at her like a barometer, as if there might be something about her walk, her expression, her clothes, her make-up, anything that would give them a hint whether the deal with Salient was going to happen and if they'd still have a job if it did.

"Good morning, Ms. Hewitt." The guard, Pete, was in his fifties and old school so he never called her by her first name. She hoped that Pete would keep his job if the Salient deal came through.

Ronnie headed to the farthest elevator in front of which stood a younger guard in an expensive black suit. This elevator was private and it took you to the south wing of the fifth floor where Barry Kestrel's and the other board members' offices were.

"Morning, Ronnie," the guard said.

"Hey, Hector."

Hector, who had a small tattoo of a key on his neck, mimed holding the elevator door open. "You know if the man's gonna take the deal or not?"

"What deal?" Ronnie said, grinning.

Hector let the door close and the car began its rise.

Ronnie got off on the fifth floor. She went to her desk that was directly outside Kestrel's office.

Across from her sat Heidi Schulman who Ronnie met at NYU when they were both theater majors. Heidi had plans to become a Broadway stage manager, but like most of her classmates she quit the theater when she realized that what she wanted even more than a Tony Award was a steady salary, health care and an apartment with a bedroom. Heidi was Barry Kestrel's executive assistant for the last seven years.

Shelby Mason, Heidi's assistant, sat at a desk close to Heidi's. Shelby was petite, pretty and very pregnant. She came from the "deep south" which to most New Yorkers meant anywhere below Newark on I-95. Given her teenaged looks and "aw shucks" demeanor, Shelby could be surprisingly effective at her job.

Shelby was speaking on her headset when Ronnie sat at her own desk. "I told you, sir, I'm not able to do that," Shelby said to the caller. She looked at Ronnie and mimed shooting herself in the head with her finger.

Ronnie gestured to Shelby as if to say, "What's the problem?"

"Please hold a moment," Shelby said and put the caller on hold. "This guy's called twice already demanding that he speak to Kestrel."

"Who is he?"

"He won't say."

"Tell him Kestrel's unavailable and he's definitely not gonna talk to anyone who doesn't give his name."

"I told him that, but he won't listen," Shelby said. "And he's talking through one of those things."

"One of what things?"

"Those things that make you sound like Darth Vader."

"A voice modulator?"

Shelby nodded. "That."

"Then you don't know if it's a guy."

Shelby hadn't considered this. She frowned. "Is that sexist of me?"

Heidi laughed at Shelby's question and said, "I'll bet you anything it's Jeremy Posner. He's such an asshole."

"Give him to me," Ronnie said and Shelby transferred the call to Ronnie who grabbed the receiver on her desk. "This is Veronica Hewitt, Mr. Kestrel's personal assistant. How can I help you, Mr.—?"

"I told the other girl I need to speak to Mr. Kestrel, not one of his secretaries." The person was speaking through a modulator like Shelby had told her. What they said and the way they said it led Ronnie to think the caller was a man.

"First of all," Ronnie said, "the person you were speaking to is a woman, not a girl, and I'm not a secretary, sir. I'm Mr. Kestrel's personal assistant."

"Wow." The voice modulator didn't hide the caller's sarcasm. "I'm impressed."

"Whoever you are," Ronnie said, "Mr. Kestrel will not speak to anyone unless he knows what it's regarding."

"Then shut up and listen to me," the voice said through its modulator. "Tell your boss that I have one of his employees."

Ronnie paused. What did the caller mean? Was this call real or a joke?

"Did you hear me?"

"If you don't identify yourself I'll have to report this call to security," Ronnie said.

"I'll state my demand once. That's all. Maybe you want to write it down in case it's too long for you to remember. We have an employee of Boundary's in our possession and I will call Mr. Kestrel at 10:45 to discuss the terms for his safe release."

As upset as she was, Ronnie had the wherewithal to say, "Use Mr. Kestrel's private line." She gave the caller that number and he hung up.

Ronnie stood in place. Shelby saw the expression on her face and asked, "Did he say something dirty?"

Ronnie didn't answer, but instead walked quickly to a heavy, locked door that separated the board's offices from the security offices on the same floor. She punched a code into the door's lock, walked through it and closed it behind her.

— • —

Barry Kestrel looked down from his fifth floor office window at the demonstrators circling the building's entrance. They were all women, a few pushing children in strollers that probably cost as much as a used car.

"Who are they?" Kestrel asked Joshua Rosenberg, Boundary's corporate lawyer, who stood next to him also watching the demonstrators.

"Angry mothers, Barry," Rosenberg said.

"The only thing more frightening than mothers: mothers with lawyers," Kestrel said.

In the room with them were Natalie Jenkins and Walter Shaw, Kestrel's two partners on the Boundary board. Ten years earlier Boundary was sued by an employee claiming that she was passed over for a promotion because she was a woman. The case was settled out of court but, hoping to put other suits like it to rest, Kestrel made Natalie Jenkins Boundary's CFO and his de-facto partner. She was excellent at the job.

Natalie looked at the protestors below, too, all of them dressed in casual but expensive clothes. She wondered if any of them were single mothers like her and, if so, how they managed? Were they as overwhelmed as she was? As depressed? Did they have husbands? Or, like Natalie, were they single and had found their child's father in a high-priced sperm bank?

Walter Shaw wasn't interested in the protestors. He was a numbers man and things like protests didn't interest him. No one could figure how old Walter was. His tastes and manner suggested he was far older than anyone else in the room, from another generation really. But his chubbiness smoothed any wrinkles on his face and he had thick white hair that was, in Kestrel's opinion, wasted on a man like Walter.

Kestrel was happy to let Jenkins and Shaw run Boundary's day-to-day operations. Only the most crucial decisions were made by Kestrel, decisions like whether to sell the company to Salient. He looked at the protestors and turned to the lawyer Rosenberg. "What do these women want?"

"They're demanding that we pull the catalogue."

Boundary had purchased a German conglomerate six months earlier. Included in the sale was the venerable New York store that had once sold fishing tackle and hunting gear to the upper class sportsmen of *Mad Men's* world. It now sold clothes to porno-drenched teens and middle-aged men and women desperately hoping to be mistaken for one. The protesters downstairs claimed that the latest edition of the store's catalogue, filled with semi-nude teenagers in provocative poses, was child pornography.

"How bad can it be?" Kestrel asked.

Rosenberg handed the catalogue to Kestrel. He opened it to a page on which a nearly topless teenaged girl sucked Lolita-like not on a lollipop but the tip of another girl's running shoe.

"My father used to buy trout flies in that store," Walter Shaw said.

"The protesters claim that it's pornography," Rosenberg said of the catalog.

"What the hell is pornography anyway?" Kestrel asked.

Rosenberg took the opportunity to paraphrase Justice Potter Stewart's famous remark. "The Supreme Court says they can't define it, but they know it when they see it."

"That's how I feel about a vagina," Kestrel said. "I couldn't define one for the life of me, but I know one when I see it."

"For God's sake, Barry," Natalie said.

Kestrel flipped through several more pages of the catalog. "It's true. Any man who tells you he knows how a vagina works is lying. All we know is that it's full of tubes and eggs and stuff. Like a magic refrigerator."

"Wonderful, Barry," Natalie said. "Now I'm an appliance."

"But a major one," Kestrel said and flung the heavy catalogue into a steel wastebasket, nearly causing it to topple over. "Pull the catalog, counselor, and send out a press release apologizing to all mothers throughout history. Except mine."

"Capitulation is very unlike you, Barry," Rosenberg said. "Would this have anything to do with the takeover rumors flooding the street?"

Kestrel ignored the question. "Do it."

"As you wish, sir," Rosenberg said, bowing with mock reverence and leaving the room.

Kestrel gestured at the protestors below. "The last thing we need right now is a bunch of pissed-off mommies messing up this deal."

Kestrel had a mole at Salient who'd told him that their board was split about acquiring Boundary. Some were eager to make the purchase; others were against it. Normally, Kestrel would tell Salient to go fuck themselves. But he'd become bored with running Boundary. And when his connection told him how much Salient was thinking of paying for Boundary any qualms he had about selling the company disappeared.

He told Jenkins and Shaw about the likely price in case they wanted to put a group together and buy Boundary themselves, but neither did. Natalie would be happy to take her millions and raise her daughter with other overprivileged children. Walter would take his money and spend his days immersed in his hobby: building miniature replicas of medieval cities, full of cathedrals and forts and knights on horseback. All three of them wanted very much for the deal to happen.

"So you really think Salient's going to make the offer?" Walter Shaw asked.

"Yes, Walter, I think they are," Kestrel said like a parent annoyed by a child in the car's backseat.

But Walter's default emotion was insecurity. "I hear that there are people on the Salient board who are against buying us."

"Christ's sake, Walter," Kestrel said. "You're going to be a very rich man soon. Granted, a rich boring man. But enjoy it for five minutes, will you?"

— • —

Louis Pike sat in Boundary's security office kitchen finishing the third chapter of a paperback copy of *The Picture of Dorian Gray*. The rest of the company's security staff was downstairs at the building's entrance dealing with the protesters.

Pike was Barry Kestrel's driver. He was forty-eight years old, Black, and, as an ex-NYPD detective, licensed to carry a gun. So he doubled as Kestrel's bodyguard even though over the two years Pike held the job no one had threatened his boss. Kestrel wasn't flashy enough for most people to notice, forget recognize. So Pike drove him to and from work every day and sometimes to meetings, meals, his country home in Dutchess County upstate and the rare party.

Kestrel was polite to Pike, but rarely spoke to him. Pike wasn't offended. He preferred it that way.

The name on Pike's birth certificate was Romulus Louis Pike. Only his mother had ever called him Romulus. Only a mother would. In his four years in the army Romulus became "Mule" and for most of his years as a New York City cop his colleagues called him "Romy" until he married his surprisingly attractive wife, Claire, after which they called him Romeo. Claire, a dancer with Alvin Ailey, died from brain cancer three years after their marriage. Detective Second Class Pike retired after his twenty-first year on the force. At Boundary everyone called him Pike.

Currently he was taking a "Great English Novels" course at the New School. He loved reading. But only fiction. Nonfiction he didn't trust. His years as a cop taught him that everybody lies and, worse, most believe their lies. Talk to a witness long enough and they'll convince themselves—and maybe even you—of anything. Given the chance, Pike would happily spend the rest of his life doing nothing but reading. His current job was perfect for that and, as proof, he sat in the small kitchen at 10:20 on a Monday morning reading the Oscar Wilde classic when he looked up and saw Ronnie Hewitt enter the security offices.

Because his wife Claire had introduced her detective husband to a new world of independent movies, art galleries and Off-Off-Broadway theaters, including Ronnie's company Jubilee, Pike had seen Ronnie's work even before he'd officially met her at Boundary. He told her that he liked what he'd seen of it. She asked him to keep that part of her life between the two of them and not tell anyone else at Boundary about it. Pike did as she asked. He still went to see Jubilee's shows even though Claire was gone. Ronnie and Pike had become friendly over the last two years.

When Ronnie saw him she walked quickly into the kitchen.

"What's up?" he asked.

Ronnie looked around to make sure there was no one else who could hear what she said. "Someone called and said they have one of our employees."

"What do you mean 'have' him? "

"Like in a kidnapping." She was uncharacteristically rattled. "They want money for him."

"Did they say that?"

Ronnie thought. "No, wait, I don't know. Maybe they didn't. I can't remember."

Pike pulled up a chair for her. "Sit down." She sat. "Take a breath." She did. "What did he sound like?"

"I don't even know if it was a man or a woman. They were using one of those things you hear in the movies."

"A voice modulator?" Pike asked and Ronnie nodded. "Okay," Pike said, "let's assume for the moment it's a man." From experience he knew that there was a better than 99% chance the caller was a guy. "It's probably a joke."

Ronnie shook her head. "I don't think so. Kestrel gets prank calls all the time. And haters, too. But I never got one like this before. It was different."

"How?"

"It just was."

"What else did he say?" Pike asked, casting the caller as a man.

"He demanded to speak to Kestrel personally."

"What else?"

"He said he'd call Kestrel back at—" she looked at the wall clock over Pike's head – "10:45."

She bit her bottom lip reminding Pike that, like Claire, Ronnie was slightly gap-toothed. "Everything's gonna be fine," he said. Twenty years ago he might've called her "sweetheart" only to reassure her, but you couldn't say anything like that now. "Let's go see Mr. K."

Ronnie smiled weakly as Pike led her out of the kitchen and through the security office. In case this abduction turned out to be real, he was already making a list in his head of people he knew to call in both the NYPD and the Manhattan FBI office. When Pike and Ronnie got to the security door Ronnie punched in the code. But she made a mistake and swore.

"Relax," Pike said to her.

She punched the numbers in again and the door unlocked. When they got to Kestrel's office door Ronnie asked Heidi who was in there with him.

"Jenkins and Shaw," Heidi said. "Why?"

Shelby saw Pike with her and asked, "Is everything all right?"

Ronnie nodded. "Fine."

— • —

Kestrel was surprised when Pike entered his office with Ronnie. He went quickly to the window and looked at the street below. "Something happen with the protesters?" he asked.

"It's not them," Ronnie said.

"Then whatever it is can wait."

When Ronnie hesitated, Pike said to Ronnie, "Tell Mr. Kestrel."

"Tell me what?"

Ronnie looked at Pike before turning to Kestrel, "Someone called me just now."

"So?"

"They said they have one of our people."

"Have him where?" Kestrel asked.

"It could be a kidnapping threat, sir," Pike said.

Walter stood up. "Good God."

Natalie was surprised, too, but her reaction suggested annoyance more than concern. "Seriously?"

Kestrel held up his hands. "Relax, everybody. Sit down, Walter. It's a joke."

"I've gotten a lot of crank calls from people who don't like you," Ronnie said, "but there was something about this one that—"

"Trust me, Ms. Hewitt," Kestrel said, "if you were a man you'd understand. How can I talk to this guy?"

Pike turned to Ronnie. "He said he'd call back at 10:45, right?"

Ronnie nodded. Pike looked at the six identical industrial clocks on the wall that showed the time in the world's financial capitals. It read 10:42 above the one that said New York.

"I gave him your 859 number," Ronnie said.

"It's a joke," Kestrel said. "You ladies always overreact to shit like this." He pointed to the New York clock. "In three minutes I'll prove it to you."

They waited.

— • —

It was Heidi who'd told Ronnie two years before that Barry Kestrel, CEO of Boundary, was looking for a personal assistant, essentially an errand girl. Ronnie got an interview.

She expected not to like him. She wanted not to like him. He was, after all, the kind of person Jubilee mocked in their sketches, the one percent of the one percent, the face of a system that produced nothing useful for anyone. All it made was profit, icing for the icing, with no cake underneath. It was the same system that had used her father and humiliated her mother.

But Kestrel surprised Ronnie. He was an enigma, neither the old school, Tom Wolfe-like, seersucker-wearing patrician nor the shaved-headed, workout-obsessed millennial clad in black.

He was staring out the window when she entered his office for her interview, his back to her like it was now. "Do you know why I put my office on the fifth floor instead of the penthouse like every other CEO would do?" Kestrel asked her without turning around.

"Why?" Ronnie said.

"I grew up in the city and if I build an office or buy a home in New York I want to see New York. I want to see the people on the street, real people, walking, eating, smoking, pissing, flirting, begging, spitting, arguing. Only rich Chinese and Russians are stupid enough to buy a place in Manhattan so high that all you can see from it is New Jersey. If I want to look at New Jersey, I'll buy a place in Hoboken."

Ronnie laughed and Kestrel turned quickly to her. Was laughing at him a mistake? She didn't care. There were other jobs. She met his stare and Kestrel grinned. He sat at his desk and picked up her resume. "Theater school. Does that mean you can pretend to be interested in people when they talk to you?"

"How am I doing so far?"

This was a big gamble, but she bet that Kestrel would get it. She was right. He did. He smiled and hired her. Her salary was more than what she'd get doing anything else this easy and, like every personal assistant, she fudged her hours. While on an errand she could read or write or even oversee a rehearsal at the theater. Who would know?

She got to know Barry Kestrel well over the last two and a half years. He was fifty-three years old, never married and childless. He had no pets. He didn't even have plants. People made the mistake of trying to hug him only once. He could be funny, but he almost never laughed. He was unfailingly polite and unlike his younger colleagues who used the word "fuck" like a comma, he swore only when he was angry, something that happened rarely. He never made a pass at Ronnie or said anything inappropriate to her. And it wasn't because of "me too". It was how he was.

Of course she didn't want Kestrel to know about her work with Jubilee. So she'd been writing under the pseudonym Mr. Gladstone for the last few years. It was the name Dustin Hoffman used in *The Graduate* to book the hotel rooms in which he let Mrs. Robinson seduce him.

Ronnie looked at the New York clock. It read 10:44.

Pike absentmindedly flicked the pages of the Oscar Wilde paperback he held while he watched the others in the room. Kestrel leafed through papers on his desk. The others stared at the clock. Ronnie seemed the most anxious. She was, after all, the one who'd spoken to the caller.

Pike remembered the first time he saw her, his first day at Boundary two years before. Ronnie wore her hair very short like his wife Claire. Both women looked smarter when they smiled. A lot of women smile when they're confused. Claire and Ronnie smiled when they got it. And when Ronnie smiled she put her front teeth over her lower lip the same way Claire did.

It was 10:44 and Pike figured no one would call. It was a prank and whoever was behind it had made their point or chickened out. In a few minutes they could all go back to doing whatever it was they did every day which, in Pike's case, was nothing.

Finally, the clock read 10:45.

"Where is this jerkoff?" Kestrel said. He hated when people were late. For another minute no one said anything. And at 10:46 they relaxed.

"Thank God it was a joke," Natalie said just as the phone on Kestrel's desk rang. Everyone tensed.

"Check this out," Kestrel said and punched a button making the call audible to everyone in the room. "Barry Kestrel here," he said. "What can I do for you?"

"Like I told your girl, Mr. Kestrel, I have one of your employees," the caller said.

Kestrel looked surprised by the caller's voice modulator. Pike should have warned him that Ronnie said the person was using one, but he hadn't heard it himself yet. It was disturbing.

"Right," Kestrel said, "and you have Chef Boyardee in the cupboard and Mrs. Butterworth in the refrigerator. If this is you, Jeremy, I'm not laughing."

The voice was calm. "This isn't Jeremy and I'm not laughing either."

The mood in the room changed, but Kestrel tried to keep it playful. It might still be a joke and the last thing Kestrel wanted to do was to fall for it in front of the others.

"Your reaction, sir?" asked the voice.

"Are you talking through one of those voice things?" Kestrel asked.

"No, this is what I really sound like, asshole."

Kestrel tensed, but all he said was, "If you're one of those protesters you can relax."

Walter leaned over Kestrel's desk and spoke into the phone. "We decided to pull the catalogue." Kestrel pushed Walter aside.

"I'm not a protester and I don't give a shit about your catalogue," the caller said. "Like you, Mr. Kestrel, I'm a businessman and I've got a deal for you."

Kestrel was serious now. "What's that?"

"I've got one of your employees."

"Who?"

"His name is Martin Newman and unless you pay two million dollars for his release we will not be responsible for anything that might happen to him."

Pike had heard things like this before, but the others hadn't. They looked at one another, unsure how to react. Ronnie quickly walked to a small desk on the other side of the office and booted up the computer on it.

"Did you hear me?" the kidnapper asked.

"Two million dollars is a lot of money," said Kestrel.

"That's why I suggest you do exactly what I tell you to."

Kestrel spoke cautiously, trying to gauge the person he was speaking with like he did whenever he was making a deal. Pike had heard him do this in the car countless times. "Why would I do anything else?"

"Because I know how men like you think."

"You don't know anything about me."

"I know you enjoyed your sirloin at Smith and Wollensky's last night."

Kestrel swore under his breath. The caller had followed him to the restaurant where Pike had driven him to eat.

"Too much red meat," the caller said, "can't be good for a man your age."

"You don't scare me, you little shit."

The caller laughed. He'd gotten to Kestrel and he knew it. Kestrel knew that the caller knew it and that angered him even more.

"I'll let you think about it and I'll call tomorrow morning to discuss the payment," the caller said. "One other thing. My colleagues and I are all over your company's Internet system. Your personal accounts, too. We know everything you do. In fact I know that you're looking at Mr. Newman's file right now."

Ronnie said, "Shit," and stood up and backed away from the computer.

"That's okay," the caller said as if he'd just seen Ronnie's reaction. "Read his company file all you like. But if anyone investigates more deeply about him we'll know. And Mr. Newman will suffer the consequences." The caller paused. "We'll call you tomorrow morning, Mr. Kestrel, same time, same place."

"You do that," Kestrel said and punched the button on the phone. He kicked the wastebasket that held the discarded catalogue. "Sonofabitch," he said. "Of all the times to kidnap someone."

"When is a good time to kidnap someone, Barry?" Natalie asked.

"Not today, that's for damn sure." Kestrel sat at his desk. "Can we trace his phone?" he asked Pike.

"He's gonna be using a burner," Pike said.

"It could be a she, couldn't it?" Kestrel said. "Maybe that's why they were using a voice thing, so she sounds scarier than if she were just a woman."

Pike nodded. It was a clever reaction on Kestrel's part. "That's possible," Pike said.

Walter turned to Pike. "Will you call the police, Sergeant Pike, or should we?"

Ronnie looked up from the computer screen. "I can get the police on the line for you, Mr. Kestrel."

Kestrel shook his head. "No."

"What do you mean 'no'?" Walter said.

"No means no," Kestrel said. "Can't you see what's happening? We're between a rock and a hard place. If we go to the cops with this it'll be all over the street in two minutes. The Internet would eat this shit up."

"So?" Walter asked.

"So it'd kill the Salient deal."

Walter frowned. "You said the deal was solid."

"Until something like this happens it is. Salient's board is already split down the middle. All the doubters over there would need is this and the deal's dead in the water." Kestrel was right. Everyone in the room knew it.

"So what do we do?" Walter asked.

Pike was eager to hear Kestrel's answer. They all were.

"We pay the ransom," Kestrel said.

Natalie was surprised. "Out of our own pockets?"

"Out of our own pockets. By week's end if everything goes as planned you're both gonna be worth at least thirty million. Maybe more. So don't be so damn cheap."

"What if it's not real?" Natalie said.

"I think it is real," Walter said.

"It doesn't matter if it's real or not," Kestrel said. "That's the thing in this social media world of ours. If someone says something's real, it's real."

Pike silently agreed with this. They all did. How could they not?

"The three of us can dig up a million cash no problem, right?" Kestrel asked Walter.

"They asked for two million," Walter said.

"I can get them down."

"You don't negotiate with kidnappers," Walter said.

"This is America. I can negotiate with whoever I want."

Walter shook his head. "This is not moral."

"Fuck moral." Pike had seen Kestrel angry enough to swear like this only once or twice before.

Ronnie interrupted. "Here he is." She pointed to a photo on the computer screen. He was a young white man in his thirties. There was nothing especially noteworthy about him. "This is Martin Newman," she said.

Walter turned to Pike. "The caller told us not to investigate, didn't he?"

Before Pike could answer, Kestrel said, "He said we could look at his Boundary file." He pushed Ronnie aside and stared at the man's photo. "What's his name again?"

"Martin Newman," Ronnie said.

The man's face filled the screen and the others circled the desk to get a better look at it. Pike stood behind the other four, as interested in them as they were in the man on the computer screen.

From the look on his face, Pike saw that Kestrel had no recollection of the man, but he probably couldn't recognize more than half a dozen of his employees.

"Never heard of him," Kestrel said. He looked at Natalie and Walter. "You guys?" They shook their heads. Kestrel turned to Ronnie. "You?"

"Not that I can recall, sir, no."

Kestrel looked at Pike. "What about you?" Pike said he didn't recognize him, either.

Ronnie began to read the man's file. "Martin Reginald Newman. Thirty-three years old. He's worked here for seven years."

"Which department?" Kestrel asked.

"Research trader."

Kestrel frowned. "One of those assholes."

"Is he married?" Natalie asked.

Ronnie answered her, "No."

Walter pointed to the screen. "It says he's a widower."

Pike noticed that Ronnie seemed surprised when Walter said this. "It does?" she said and looked more closely at the file.

"It says it here. See?" Walter said pointing to the screen.

Ronnie saw it and nodded. "Right."

"It says he has no children," Natalie said.

Kestrel said, "That's good."

"Why is that good?" Natalie asked.

"I don't know," said Kestrel. "Where does he live?"

"259 East 66th Street," Walter said.

"Really?" Ronnie asked, seemingly surprised by this information, too.

"Is something wrong?" Pike asked her.

"It's all so upsetting," she said to him.

"That's the Maxell, those executive apartments," Natalie said. "We rented some for the Tokyo executives when they came here last year."

Kestrel pointed to the screen. "He graduated from Princeton."

Walter looked more closely at Newman's photo. "Princeton? Wait a minute. I think I know this guy."

"You do?" Kestrel asked.

"He worked on the Hyperion merger with me," Walter said. "I'm sure of it. He's quiet." Walter remembered more about Newman as he spoke about him. "And he's got a limp like he has a short leg or maybe a war wound or something. He's the kind of guy who stays in the background."

"Wait a minute," Natalie said. "He has a limp?" She leaned over Ronnie's other shoulder and looked at Newman's face. "You're right, Walter. I remember him, too. He was quiet. I mean he is quiet," she said, correcting herself. "He didn't say much, but when he did he made his point."

Kestrel asked Ronnie if she recognized Newman. She looked at his photo. "I might've seen him around, too. In the cafeteria or somewhere. But he looks like a lot of the people here."

"What did they take him for?" Kestrel said. "He's a nobody."

"Exactly," Pike said.

Kestrel turned to Pike. "Meaning?"

Everyone was looking at Pike now. He had to be careful what he said. "It's a low-level kidnapping," he said. "Two guys sit in a car outside a private school. They grab a kid, call the parents and ask for five hundred dollars."

"That little?" Kestrel said.

"That's the point. Enough to score a hit of oxy or meth. What parent's going to bring in the cops and risk their kid's life for the cost of theater tickets?"

Natalie grabbed Pike's arm. "Tell me you're joking."

Pike shook his head. "So the parents pay 'em. No cops, no danger, nothing. Happens all day every day."

"Pretty smart when you think of it," Kestrel said.

Natalie had already crossed the office and begun digging through her handbag. "I can never find my fucking phone," she said before pulling it out of her bag and punching in a number.

"What are you doing?" Kestrel asked.

"Checking on Courtney."

"Your kid's fine, Natalie."

But Natalie had already reached her daughter's nanny. "Consuela," she said too loudly into her phone. "Donde esta Courtney?"

"Hang up," Kestrel said.

Natalie ignored him. "Llevala a casa. Right now."

"I said hang up," Kestrel said and grabbed the phone from her. He ended the call and handed her phone back to Natalie. "Your kid's fine."

Everyone looked at Natalie. "I'm sorry," she said. "I overreacted." She looked at Ronnie as if she, the only other woman in the room, would be the one person who'd understand what she'd just done.

Walter turned to Pike. "So you're saying that if we pay them then nothing bad will happen to Mr. Newman?"

"That's not what I said, Mr. Shaw. Only how it sometimes works."

"Two million is not five hundred bucks," Kestrel said.

Talk of money refocused Natalie again. "Especially if we're paying it."

"I could make inquiries," Pike said.

"No inquiries," Kestrel said and pointed to the phone on his desk. "You heard what he said. So here's what we do. This does not leave the room. Not a word to anyone until we know more. And when this asshole calls back tomorrow morning I'll offer him one million bucks."

Walter was confused. "Why don't we just give them the two million they're asking for?"

"I have to show strength, that's why. If I don't, it could put this guy in more danger." Kestrel looked at Pike. "Right?"

Pike shrugged. What Kestrel said only proved that he'd seen too many movies. "It's possible," Pike said.

"And they don't expect us to pay them the two million anyway."

"How do you know?" Walter asked.

"Because I know people. I know how they bargain. They get their million, they release Newman and the Salient deal goes through," Kestrel said. "No harm, no foul."

Natalie's conscience made a late appearance. "That's not how this kind of thing is done, Barry."

"Who says? Martha Stewart? If what the detective here says is right," Kestrel said, "then one million tax free is this scumbag's dream come true." He looked at Pike. "What do you think? Does one million sound good to you?"

"I don't have an opinion, sir."

"I'm paying you for your opinion."

"I would tell the authorities," Pike said.

Kestrel waved away that idea. "That's not gonna happen."

"I agree with Detective Pike," Natalie said. "We have to tell them, don't we?"

"We don't have to do anything," Kestrel said. "If we pay the money then our guy is safe. You said so yourself." Pike had said nothing like that, but Kestrel kept talking. "So we're agreed. This stays between the five of us in this room. If we do this right it'll be like it never happened. The deal goes through and this guy, what's his name—? "

"Martin Newman," Ronnie said.

"Newman," Kestrel said, "will be fine."

"What if someone found out what we did?" Walter asked.

"Then we'd look like heroes. Think about it. We sacrificed our own money for this guy's safety."

"You tried to bargain them down, Barry," Natalie said.

Kestrel ignored her. "So nobody says a word about this. Not to your wife, not to your boyfriend, not to your dog. We've got to do this right because there's too much on the line."

"This man's life is in our hands," Walter said.

"That too," said Kestrel. "What's his name again?"

"Martin Newman," Ronnie said.

"Right," Kestrel said, dismissing them all with a hand gesture. As Ronnie stepped out the door, she heard Kestrel add, "And don't forget to pick up my suit at Zegna's."

— • —

When Ronnie and Pike came out of Kestrel's office Shelby asked, "Was it Mr. Posner?"

Ronnie looked at Pike before nodding and saying to Shelby, "Another one of his stupid jokes."

Shelby pointed to the copy of *The Picture of Dorian Gray* that Pike still held in his hand. "How's the great books marathon coming, Mr. Pike?"

Pike forgot that he was still holding the paperback. "I've only got about five hundred more to go."

"I admire you for doing that," Shelby said. "I love to read. I wish I had the time to—oh, wait." Shelby smiled. "Sammy just kicked. You want to feel him?"

Pike didn't want to feel Shelby's baby kick. No man does, but what do you say to an expectant mother who asks you this? You say "yes" like Pike—and every other man—always did and in the process never managed to feel anything that the mother claimed was so obvious to her.

But Shelby's line rang, saving him, and Pike quickly walked to Ronnie who looked for something on her desk. It bothered him to see her this upset. "Don't worry," he said. "It'll work out."

Ronnie walked with Pike to the door that led to the other offices on the floor. "I don't get it," Ronnie said. "Why don't we just give the guy what he wants and get Mr. Newman back today?"

"Two million bucks is a lot of money."

"It's lunch money to those guys." She punched in a code and the door opened.

"Everything'll be fine," Pike said. He was reminded of all the times he'd said that to his wife before she died.

Ronnie shut the door behind him and he walked back to his office.

— • —

Ronnie had eaten only a single bite of her grilled cheese sandwich as she sat in a dark booth of the West Village restaurant, too concerned by what had happened earlier in Kestrel's office to have any appetite.

She recalled the reactions of the others and the looks on their faces as they listened to the kidnapper's demands. She replayed in her head what each person said. She could have predicted what their reactions would be—from Kestrel's concerns about the kidnapping's effect on the Salient deal to Walter's anxieties about Newman's safety, a worry that Ronnie herself had echoed more than once. Natalie took a position somewhere between the two men, eager to appear sympathetic without seeming weak, the contemporary businesswoman's—every woman's—dilemma. She'd made a mistake calling her daughter's nanny in front of the men and she knew it. She wouldn't do anything like that again.

Pike gave little away about his thoughts and those were the ones Ronnie was most interested in.

— • —

Pike normally ate lunch at his desk since he could read there without interruption. But today he left *The Picture of Dorian Gray* unopened and instead read Martin Newman's Boundary file on his computer.

In their company files, employees were encouraged to write about their lives, their families, their feelings, even their complaints about their job. No doubt the idea for this came from some Millennial in HR. The younger the employee, the more they wrote about themselves, most of them believing that everyone was as obsessed as their parents were with them and every single thought they ever had.

Pike read the facts of Newman's life. Martin Reginald Newman was born in Baltimore. His parents were both dead. His father died when he was eleven, the same age Pike was when his own father died. Newman graduated with honors from Princeton. His favorite hobby was rock climbing and the year before he'd traveled to a place called Bhutan to climb a mountain whose name Pike couldn't pronounce. Did a climbing accident account for the limp that Jenkins and Shaw remembered him having? He kayaked, too. And he played second base on the Boundary softball team that played—and lost—in the league championship a couple of years earlier. He was an Orioles fan, his favorite color was orange and he liked dogs, although he didn't have one now. His favorite foods were Italian and Thai. His favorite movies were *The Shawshank Redemption* and *The Godfather.* Pike liked both those movies, too.

Like Pike, Newman was a widower. But there was no indication in his file how his wife had died. All he wrote was that her name was Sophia and that she'd died eighteen months earlier, after which he moved into The Maxwell Apartments. They had no children. Was that fortunate? When Claire died Pike thought it was lucky they hadn't had any kids. He wasn't so sure now. When he saw parents and their children together, even single parents, he wondered what having had a kid would have been like.

There was a recent attachment to Newman's file posted only a day earlier.

I've turned a corner. My wife's death isn't hanging over me like it did for the last year. I'm still sad about what happened to her and of course I miss her, but not as much as before. I decided that soon I'm going to move out of the place I rented after she died and move back into our apartment. And I'm going to spend more time at Boundary, too. They were kind to let me work from home after what happened to Sophia.

Last week I bought a bunch of new clothes, joined a gym and decided to cut back on fast foods. I'm going to try out for the Boundary softball team, too. I did pretty good playing second base for them a couple of seasons ago. I picked up my guitar again and I even signed up to go rock climbing in Canada next month. Who knows? Maybe I'll meet someone new there, like I did when I met Sophia.

Newman's file saddened Pike. In it he seemed eager, almost desperate, to impress the reader with how happy he was. But underneath he sounded lost, and reading it was like reading the diary of a castaway on the desert island that was New York City and, more specifically, Boundary. Pike found nothing in Newman's file that gave any clue why he of all people might have been kidnapped other than the fact that, like Pike had explained to Kestrel and the others, he was completely unspecial.

— • —

The café was nearly empty as Ronnie considered what Kestrel might do now. Would he keep things quiet by paying off the kidnappers with a million dollars? She hoped he would. But how would he react if the caller stuck to his original demand of two million? Or maybe Kestrel would take Pike's suggestion and go to the police.

Ronnie heard a voice behind her, close over her shoulder. It spoke through a modulator like the one used in the phone call that morning. "Don't move," it said.

But she did move, turning quickly, almost knocking over what was left of her iced tea. She looked into the boyish face of the man speaking into the modulator and said, "Jesus Christ, Alex, put that away."

Alex stuck the modulator in his jacket pocket and sat opposite Ronnie in the booth.

"You can't let anybody see you with that thing," she said.

"I know that."

"Do you really?" She wanted him to know how annoyed she was.

"I do." Alex Ryan, her boyfriend, was three years younger than her, but sometimes—like now—he seemed even younger than that. He pointed to her grilled cheese. "Are you gonna finish that?"

"Here." She slid the plate across the table to him and he bit into what was left of the sandwich.

"How'd it go?" he said.

"What was that shit you said about following Kestrel to the restaurant last night?"

"I saw that in a Japanese movie. Wasn't it great?"

"It was stupid. Everyone knows I make his reservations so you can't do anything like that without telling me first."

"You're right. I'm sorry," Alex said. "So what happened? Tell me."

Ronnie took a deep breath. She relaxed. Why shouldn't she? Everything had gone as they'd hoped and as she'd predicted. "Tomorrow Kestrel's gonna offer us a million bucks."

Alex clapped his hands. "That's exactly what you said he'd do."

"We're a long way from this thing working out."

"I know," Alex said in a way that suggested he didn't. He picked at her French fries that were soggy by now.

"Kestrel's more worried about the takeover falling apart than he is about what happens to Newman," Ronnie said.

"That's what you said would happen, too."

"It's pathetic how well I can predict what he's gonna do."

"And he's not gonna report it to the cops?"

"Not unless Pike or Shaw persuades him to."

Alex dipped a French fry in ketchup and ate it. "What about my warning about investigating Newman, did that work?"

"Let's hope. Everything depends on that." On one hand, Alex's enthusiasm made her feel more confident. On the other, it worried her. "Don't you have a rehearsal now?" she said.

"Two o'clock."

"Then you should go. You're never late so you can't be late today. We have to do everything just like we would in a normal week."

"Everything normal. Got it."

"Then get to your rehearsal."

"You worry too much, sweetie. Everything's gonna happen just like we planned." As he bent over and kissed her, she could taste the pickle that he'd eaten from her plate. He left.

Alex and Ronnie met as acting majors at NYU. She was a senior and he was a freshman from a working-class family outside Pittsburgh. After graduating, Ronnie was cast as Masha in an Off-Broadway production of Chekov's *The Seagull*. It was a big break for her. Critics noticed her. *The New York Times* called her performance "complicated and nuanced". She was thrilled; who wouldn't be? But after five months she was bored. She didn't want to say the same lines over and over, not even Chekov's, every night and twice on Wednesdays and Saturdays. Great actors did it and they did it with genius. But it wasn't for her. So with some NYU classmates she started their theater company Jubilee. Alex was part of the original group and she and Alex became lovers. The first year everyone in the company wrote and acted in the sketches, but it was soon obvious that as good as Ronnie was on stage, she was an even better writer. Her voice was sharp and funny and angry. So she ditched acting and, instead, wrote and directed under her pseudonym Mr. Gladstone.

The clock over the bar said 12:30. Ronnie's next stop was the boutique on Vessey Street to pick up Kestrel's suit for what he hoped would be his press conference after Salient bought Boundary. She'd buy him a tie while she was there. He trusted her taste.

— • —

Pike found nothing especially helpful looking at Newman's Boundary file. But the caller had warned that they shouldn't look into anything else about Newman and claimed he had the means to know if they did that. But what if that was a bluff? Even if it weren't, what if the kidnappers did find out that Pike had looked more deeply into Newman online? What would they do? The last thing a kidnapper wants is to harm the person they've kidnapped. They're the only leverage a kidnapper has.

So Pike searched Boundary's digital records which indicated that over the last month Newman had entered and left the building only a couple of days a week. That matched what he said in his file about being allowed to work at home and coming into the office only occasionally. Newman's files also showed that he'd taken a month's leave of absence the year before. That probably coincided with his wife's death.

Pike pulled up video recordings. He watched Newman enter and exit the building on several of them. He was always by himself. He carried a black briefcase and often wore an old-fashioned flat cap. Pike never got a good look at his face and Newman never greeted anyone on his way in or out. He looked like a loner. But in none of the videos did he walk with a limp.

Pike then googled Martin Newman. There were a lot of them. Some were young, others old. One was a beagle. He found one or two men that might have been the Martin Newman he saw on the computer in Kestrel's office. One of them wore climbing gear, but his helmet obscured his face and he looked a lot younger than thirty-three. That was all. It seemed that Martin Newman, Boundary employee, hadn't done anything interesting. But if anyone had Googled Romulus Louis Pike they'd have found nothing either. He'd looked himself up once and most of the links he found referred the user to the co-founder of ancient Rome who, along with his brother Remus, had been, according to legend, suckled by a she-wolf.

As a cop, Pike had dealt with kidnappings. One had happened when a criminal, cornered in the bungled robbery of a liquor store, took the store clerk hostage. A man taking a wife, ex-wife or girl-friend wasn't uncommon. Sometimes the victim was a child, a pawn in a custody battle between parents. But the person on the phone that morning sounded calm and professional, not scattered like a prankster or junkie might.

Why would anyone choose to kidnap Martin Newman? Or *did* anyone choose him? Was the kidnapping a scam that Martin Newman himself was behind?

The only thing that made sense was why he was taken now. The Salient deal was looming and, as a result, Kestrel was willing to do anything to keep the kidnapping out of the news even if it meant he lost a million bucks paying Newman's ransom. The timing meant the kidnappers knew about the Salient deal, too. But so did everyone on the street.

— • —

Ronnie's taxi inched through the traffic. On her lap was a garment bag that held Kestrel's suit from the Vessey Street boutique.

It was her idea to create a fictitious employee called Martin Newman who worked at Boundary. It started when a real Boundary worker had died in a car crash over the Christmas holiday. Kestrel told her to send flowers to the guy's family and write a note that suggested how popular the man was at work.

Kestrel had no idea who the dead man was, so Ronnie pulled up his file. He'd worked as a research trader at Boundary for almost eleven years. He'd written hardly anything about himself in his file so she asked the people in his department about him. His coworkers could tell her almost nothing about the dead man. They didn't know if he'd been married, if he had kids or a pet, what his hobbies were, nothing. Most didn't even put his name to a face until Ronnie showed them a photo. "Oh, him," they all said. They'd probably have said that about any face she showed them.

This inspired Ronnie to create a Chaplinesque character that would symbolize the faceless, cog-in-the-wheel role of the modern finance drone indistinguishable from other employees. He'd be the updated version of Chaplin's tramp, swallowed by the machinery in *Modern Times*. She called him Martin Newman.

Ronnie's Martin Newman was born in Baltimore. He had a heart murmur as a child, but he recovered from that. He was a kayaker now and even played second base for the Boundary softball team. He read mysteries. He was a moderate Republican. His favorite color was orange. He liked dogs. He went to church on Christmas and Easter. He longed to get married and have children. He wanted to become rich and retire before he was thirty-five (who at Boundary didn't?) and he adhered stridently to the American canard that you can be whatever you want to be as long as you work hard enough. Of course it helped if you actually existed.

Alex had studied computer programming on the side and he had a job with Nerd Nation, a company of geeks that helped mostly older people fix their home computers. Ronnie asked him to put Newman's personal file into the Boundary employees' site because it'd make Newman feel more authentic. Alex loved the idea and he easily got into the company's files where he gave Martin Reginald Newman an official seat at Boundary's table.

Ronnie got ideas for Newman from people she saw at Boundary or in cafeterias, on the street, anywhere. Alex added things to Newman's file almost every day, too, and he kept a private diary of the character on his own computer. Ronnie eventually planned to write a series of scenes around the Newman character. Maybe even a short play about him that Jubilee would produce. She and Alex told no one else about Martin Newman, not even their colleagues at the theater company. Newman was invisible; that was the whole point. He'd appear when she and Alex decided.

Ronnie and Alex would change things about Newman on their own, surprising and amusing each other when they'd go online to discover what the other had added. So this morning in Kestrel's office Ronnie was surprised when she saw that Alex had made Newman a widower. And that their imaginary character now lived at The Maxwell Apartments. She didn't remember Alex telling her that he'd made those changes, but it wasn't a problem and they'd helped make Newman even more real.

She couldn't remember when the idea of actually kidnapping Newman occurred to her. At first Martin Newman and his whole artificial life was only intended to be a sketch, or series of sketches, about a missing man whom no one missed. But the more she thought about it, the more she wondered if it might actually work. What would happen if she and Alex actually did kidnap an imaginary employee and demanded a ransom for him? They wouldn't be committing a real kidnapping, would they? And if something did go wrong, Alex could delete everything, leaving no kind of trail that led to them. It'd be so easy.

It'd be perfect justice, too, if the ransom money from Boundary helped rescue her mother. Ronnie's father, Robert, lost his job during the spate of leveraged buyouts in the 1990s and, like thousands of other workers, also lost his pension. Depressed, his health spiraled quickly downward. He died of heart disease when Ronnie was fifteen. Her father's life insurance company hired doctors to prove that, because of his depression, Robert had stopped taking his medicine. The word "suicide" was used. An "expert" psychiatric witness's testimony gave the life insurance company, Star Accessibility, the right to refuse payments. Carlotta sued and lost. But frightened of bad publicity, Star Accessibility gave Carlotta ten percent of what they owed her. It was a pittance that she quickly used up.

All that made the idea of getting money from Boundary by kidnapping an imaginary man even more fun to think about, but it wasn't realistic. Kestrel would never give into any kidnappers. He'd go straight to the cops.

But when the Salient deal appeared, Ronnie saw an opportunity. Kestrel was eager, desperate really, to take Salient's offer. Ronnie figured that, to keep everything out of the news, he'd pay the ransom—a small amount by his standards—and be done with it. That morning Kestrel proved her right. If things went as planned, in a couple of days Ronnie and Alex would have a million dollars and her mother would be out of Jerrold House.

— • —

Pike was frustrated when he found nothing about Newman on the Internet so he walked up to the eleventh floor where the research traders worked. Other workers called the research traders "gossips" because they scoured countless social media sites and even visited stores and schools to see what was selling, what was hot, what adults and children were buying and wearing and reading and cooking.

On the basis of what they learned, they suggested investments. They were like gamblers. With someone else's money.

Pike caught his breath when he got to the eleventh floor. He wandered around the large room, empty because it was lunch hour. There were no walls, no offices where people worked in private. This was the 21st century and workers were happier and more productive sharing their spaces, even their bathrooms. Pike didn't buy that bullshit for a minute, but it's how businesses were run now, playschools for wannabe billionaires.

Only one man sat at a desk staring at his computer screen. He was older than most of Boundary's research traders, maybe forty. Pike walked over and said hi.

Surprised, the man looked up. "Hey."

"Sorry to bother you."

"No problem. I was praying someone would save me from any more of this bullshit."

The man, John Bradley, knew who Pike was. Everyone at Boundary did. Pike and Bradley made small talk about the Boundary softball team and its loss to Citibank last season. Pike asked Bradley if he knew which desk Martin Newman worked at.

Bradley thought for a moment. "I don't think I do."

Pike asked if he could access Newman's Boundary file on Bradley's computer.

"Be my guest," Bradley said and Pike brought Newman's face up on the screen.

"This is him," Pike said.

Bradley looked at Newman, his expression still blank.

"Everybody says he's a quiet guy," Pike said. "And that he walks with a limp."

Bradley thought for a moment before saying, "Oh yeah, him. Martin Newman. That's what you said his name was, right? I remember him." Bradley went on. "I think Marty was only here for a short time before they sent him somewhere else."

Two minutes ago the man didn't know who he was and now Martin was Marty. They were buddies.

"What about him?" Bradley asked. Pike said nothing, but Bradley read something in Pike's silence and grinned. "Marty's getting promoted, isn't he? And you're vetting him, right?"

Pike shrugged noncommittally. Other workers were coming back from lunch and starting to fill the floor.

Bradley smiled. "Good for Marty. He deserves it."

"Thanks for your help," Pike said.

"No problem. And say hi to Marty for me if you see him."

Pike said he would and started to walk away when Bradley called to him.

"Hey," Bradley said, "you hear anything about the Salient deal?"

"Nobody tells me anything," Pike said.

On the elevator Pike wondered again if Newman himself might be behind the scheme. From what he'd read of Newman's file it seemed uncharacteristic, but maybe the death of his wife had caused the man to snap and do something crazy. Maybe that's why he used a voice modulator. So no one would recognize his voice. Martin Newman's voice.

— • —

Ronnie returned to Boundary with Kestrel's new suit. He wasn't there so she hung it in his closet. Natalie Jenkins was waiting at the elevator when Ronnie came out of Kestrel's office. She walked quickly to Natalie and asked in a whisper so neither Heidi or Shelby could hear, "Did you hear anything about Mr. Newman?"

Natalie grabbed Ronnie tightly by the wrist. "Come with me," she said and pulled Ronnie into a small room next to Kestrel's office. It was called the Sanctuary Room. There were no charts, no television, no computers here. It was designed to get you away from all things business and, to make sure of that, the designer of the space had installed a device that blocked Internet service.

Natalie switched on the espresso machine and dropped a capsule into it. "You want a coffee?"

"No thank you, Ms. Jenkins."

"Call me Natalie. We ladies have to stick together." Ronnie was the only other woman in Kestrel's small circle and Natalie would often corner her for "girl talk"—her expression, not Ronnie's. These conversations, more monologue than dialogue, usually entailed Natalie sharing her concerns about being a forty-something year old single mother.

But that wasn't her concern today. She pressed the button to start the coffee brewing. "I'm worried, Ronnie. I know this morning we agreed that we should keep this thing between ourselves. But I'm not so sure anymore."

Ronnie didn't like hearing Natalie say this. "What do you mean?"

"If we don't tell anyone and something happens to Mr. Newman aren't we liable? Not you, of course, because you don't count. But me, I'm a partner. Couldn't I be held responsible for whatever happens to the poor man?"

"But they said nothing would happen."

Natalie tore open several packets of sweetener and sprinkled them into her coffee. "I can't go to jail. What would happen to Courtney? Who would take care of her? She couldn't live with my parents. That'd be worse than – what do they call it? – the system. I'm thinking that we should report this."

Ronnie had to get this idea out of the woman's head. "You won't go to jail and Courtney won't be put in the system, Natalie. You're only following Mr. Kestrel's orders, so you're not liable. He is."

Ronnie had no idea if this was legally true, but it sounded correct and she was a good enough actor to sell it. So Natalie jumped on the possibility. "You're right. I'm not liable, am I?"

"Not at all," said Ronnie. "And you can't blame Mr. Kestrel, either, because the Salient deal is probably gonna be a lot of money for everyone. You included. Millions. And millions," she said, steering Natalie away from her momentary altruism and toward her more natural greed. "Think how much better Courtney's life will be with all the money you'll get if Salient buys us. Buys you."

Natalie downed her espresso. "It goes against my inclinations, but you're right. Not telling anyone is probably the smartest thing we can do right now."

"And the safest thing for Mr. Newman, too."

"Undoubtedly."

"Why don't we see how tomorrow morning's call goes and take it from there?"

"You're so smart, Veronica."

Ronnie smiled her thanks. I can even tie my own shoes and flush the toilet myself, she thought.

Natalie handed her empty espresso cup to Ronnie before leaving the room.

Ronnie looked out the window at the street below. The protesters were gone. Had she persuaded Natalie not to say anything to the police? But what if Natalie changed her mind after she got home? Spending time with her child might make her more sympathetic to Newman's plight.

And what about Walter Shaw? He'd been the strongest advocate of telling the police. But that might have been an act. Walter knew that Kestrel would do whatever Kestrel wanted to. So maybe Walter had only voiced his concerns to cover his own ass in case anything bad happened to Newman. "I told them to go to the authorities," Walter could honestly tell the authorities. "I begged Kestrel to report this. So don't blame me."

Pike knocked on the glass door of the room before he opened it. "Can I come in?"

"Of course," Ronnie said. "Do you want a coffee?"

Pike shook his head. "Are you okay?"

"You mean about the…thing this morning?" She avoided using the word "kidnapping" to drive home how much it upset her. "I'm worried about Mr. Newman."

"You shouldn't be too worried."

"Did you find something out?" Ronnie said.

"Not really."

What did he mean by "not really"?

Pike looked toward the small room's door to make sure no one was listening. "I did some investigating," he said.

"His Boundary file, right?" she asked, hoping that was the extent of it.

"That and a bit more."

Ronnie swore to herself. Pike had done exactly what Alex had told them not to do. But what did she expect? The guy was a cop. Ronnie didn't need to manufacture any false concern when she said, "They said if anyone did that, they'd hurt Mr. Newman. They might kill him."

"They won't kill him."

"How do you know?"

"Because they need him to be alive to get any money."

"That's true." Ronnie nodded like she hadn't thought of this before, that this was all too much for her, a simple actor, to deal with. "So what did you find out?"

"I went through some video files."

"And?"

"I think I saw him in the lobby."

"What do you mean 'you think'?"

"I never got a clear view of him," Pike said.

Of course you didn't get a clear view of him, Ronnie thought, because there was no one for you to get a clear view of. Alex had created an artificial Boundary ID number for Newman and made sure the records indicated that he'd logged in two or three days a week for the last few months. But unless someone pretended to be Newman entering the building there'd be no one for Pike to see. Maybe it was good that Pike thought that he'd seen Newman. It'd prove to him that there actually was a Martin Newman. Even so, she had to persuade him to stop investigating the nonexistent man.

"But he didn't have a limp like Jenkins and Shaw said," Pike said.

"No?"

"Didn't you say he had a limp?"

"Did I? I don't remember." She didn't. Was Pike trying to confuse her?

"I figured that might've been from a climbing accident."

"What climbing?"

"On his Boundary file he says he's a rock climber."

"I was tempted to look at his file, but it would depress me," Ronnie said.

She figured that Alex had added the part about Newman being a climber, the same way he'd added the stuff about him being a widower. But what else had Alex added that she hadn't seen yet? Whatever it was, they couldn't change anything now that Newman had been kidnapped and Pike and the Boundary people had seen his file.

Ronnie was genuinely anxious when she said, "I've got to tell you, Mr. Pike, I know you're a cop and everything, but the caller said that if they found out that anyone was investigating Mr. Newman they'd hurt him."

"They didn't catch me."

"How do you know that?" She rubbed her hands together. "These computer people are really clever. Remember the ransomware attack two years ago? We were helpless. They knew everything we did. We had to hire outside people to come in and save us. That's why we can't trust them." Her eyes blinked with tears. "So promise me you won't do any more investigating of Mr. Newman. Please."

"I won't."

Did that mean he wouldn't do any more investigating or that he wouldn't promise not to?

"The best thing that can happen," she said, "is that Kestrel and the caller agree about the payoff tomorrow morning. Then we get Mr. Newman back as soon as possible."

Pike's phone rang. "That's the boss now," he said and smiled at Ronnie. "Get some rest tonight. Like you said, everything will work out tomorrow."

When he left the room Ronnie realized how quickly she was breathing. She crossed to the small sink in the room and splashed her face with cold water.

— • —

Pike sat in Kestrel's black Escalade in front of the Boundary building. Had he told Ronnie too much about his looking into Newman's records? What he said had upset her. So he decided not to say anything else to her about any investigations he might make.

Kestrel approached the car. He never wanted Pike to get out and open the door for him. He said that it made him look elitist. But before Kestrel even got to the car, a reporter from Bloomberg news came out of nowhere with a man behind her holding a small camera. She stuck her mike in Kestrel's face. Pike opened his own door to get out, but Kestrel held up his hand to him as if to say he had it under control and he answered the reporter's question. She asked a second question and a third. Kestrel finally said, "That's all today, Lucy," and he got into the front passenger seat of the car where he always sat.

Kestrel turned to Pike as they pulled away from the curb. "So what do you think?" he asked.

"About the kidnapping?"

"What else would I be asking about?"

"We should wait until tomorrow's call and see what happens," Pike said.

"That's it? You're a cop. You must've come up with a million possibilities."

Kestrel was right, but Pike wasn't about to admit it. Nor was he going to tell Kestrel that, against both the caller's and Kestrel's orders, he'd looked up all he could find about Martin Newman in both Boundary's records and on the Internet and that he'd even questioned one of Newman's coworkers.

"Do you think he's involved?" Kestrel said.

"Who, sir?"

"Newman. You must've considered that. It might be a scam and not a kidnapping at all. He could be doing it himself or with other people who work here."

Pike was impressed that Kestrel had come up with this possibility. But he was a businessman. From what Pike had seen, there wasn't much difference between how businessmen and criminals thought. "I considered that, sir."

"And?"

"From what I can see about Mr. Newman in his Boundary file I think it would be uncharacteristic of him."

"It could be someone at Salient," Kestrel said, "hoping to undo the deal. Or someone who wants to lower our price. What if Newman was working with people at Salient? They might be paying him a percentage."

"I hadn't thought of that."

"Or it could be someone who just wants to fuck me."

That would be a long list of people, Pike thought.

"We'll see how he reacts to my counter offer tomorrow morning," Kestrel said.

"There's something else you should do."

"What's that?"

"When they call tomorrow morning," Pike said, "you should tell them you want to talk with him."

"With Newman?"

"For starters you want proof that he's still alive before you pay anything, don't you?" Pike was being overly dramatic on purpose.

"Of course."

"Then tell them you want to talk to Newman."

"I should've thought of that myself."

Pike said that it would also give them a good idea if Newman were behind the scam because Pike doubted that he'd be a good enough actor to play a convincing victim. "I've seen more than my fair share of criminals in interrogation rooms, sir, and I can promise you that they're all terrible actors."

They pulled up in front of Kestrel's building. The doorman hurried to open Kestrel's door for him.

"I'll know if Newman's lying, " Kestrel said. "Because if there's one thing I know, it's people."

Kestrel disappeared into the building and Pike pulled back into the traffic.

— • —

On the subway going home, Ronnie considered that maybe she and Alex should end the kidnapping. It was a real crime, not a game or theater improv, and as bad as her mother's situation was now, what would happen to her if Ronnie were thrown in jail? Natalie's attitude worried her. And Pike's admission that he'd investigated Newman frightened her even more. Maybe he'd already found things that he hadn't told Ronnie about.

Alex would be upset if she said they should call it off, but he always did what she asked him to do. He was a kind man, a boy really, and Ronnie was smarter than he was. She'd always been smarter than the men she'd dated, but Alex was the only one who admitted that. She and Alex jokingly called her previous lovers Ronnie's "overcoat men," guys like Kestrel that you see in expensive camel hair or woolen navy overcoats. Those men don't listen. They talk. They don't walk. They stride. "Boom boom boom," Alex would say imitating them. Why had Ronnie dated men like that? Why had she married one?

Her marriage lasted all of nine months. In that time her husband, a prominent theater producer, cheated on her with at least three actresses. After him, Ronnie figured that every man was going to cheat on you one way or another and so that was the truth she lived by. Until she met Alex. He was different. She trusted that whether it was after the tenth time they fucked or the hundredth, Alex wouldn't be planning to run off with his nineteen year old costar or the barista at Starbucks. Did she love Alex? What is love anyway? Alex was a good person and she liked who she was when she was with him. That was enough for her.

When she got pregnant Alex played a big part in her decision to have the baby. He came from a large family and he loved the idea of having a kid with Ronnie. He bought all kinds of books about raising children, from the many *New York Times* bestsellers to one by a biologist who claimed that modern parents were ruining their children's health by keeping them too clean. "We're going to feed our kid dirt. Organic dirt," Alex proclaimed in a scene about expectant parents that they wrote for Jubilee together. Alex collected games and clothes, used and new, and he made sure Ronnie's diet was perfect. He took her to her doctors' appointments and he came up with countless names for their child from Agamemnon to Zanzibar. She figured that he'd be as much a big brother to the child as he'd be its father, but what was wrong with that? She never loved Alex more than at this time.

When she miscarried Alex was as devastated as she was, maybe more. But he kept her from getting too depressed. He convinced her that they'd have a child another time. His simple optimism, so easily mocked by others, was what got her through all that.

Ronnie entered their tiny apartment that had a kitchen only one person could comfortably stand in and a bedroom barely big enough for a double bed and a chest of drawers. There was a small bathroom with a shower and no tub. The décor was made up of found and borrowed furniture and a few pieces they'd bought. Mid-Century Ikea, they called it.

The most noticeable thing in the apartment was the dummy that sat in the center of the living room on a simple wooden chair. This was Martin Newman, a full sized mannequin that wore a dark business suit, a white shirt and striped tie. On its feet were black leather shoes and on its too-fat head sat a pair of glasses like the ones Cary Grant wears in *Bringing Up Baby*. The dummy's expression was somewhere between amusement and surprise. Like child actors and animals on film, it displayed whatever emotion the viewer gave it.

Alex got up from his computer when Ronnie came in. He went over to the dummy and hugged it. "It's alive!" he yelled, à la Dr. Frankenstein.

Ronnie pointed to his laptop. "What were you writing?"

"Some Newman stuff."

"Not in his Boundary file."

"Course not. I didn't even look at that because I know we can't change any of it now. This is his private diary, the one I write just for myself. He's freaking out about being kidnapped." Alex was excited by the new material, but Ronnie's silence concerned him. "What's the matter?"

"People are looking into him," she said pointing to the dummy.

"Who is?"

"Pike for one."

"How do you know?"

"He told me he looked through video files of the lobby and matched them up with the records that you put in of Newman entering and leaving."

"Shit."

"You didn't walk into Boundary pretending to be Newman, did you?" she asked.

"Why would I?"

"Pike thinks he saw him in the lobby."

"Then he saw someone else. I told you how messed up those Boundary files are. They're never aligned with the digital records. You said Pike was an idiot when it came to electronic stuff."

"You changed things in Newman's Boundary file, too."

"Like what?" Alex said.

"You said he was married and that his wife died."

"Did I?"

"And that he was a rock climber and that he lived at The Maxwell."

Alex thought for a moment. "Maybe I did. I don't remember. I changed a lot of stuff. We both did. So what? That's the point. We're creating him."

Ronnie knelt in front of Alex. "What if we've gone too far?"

"What do you mean?"

"We're not criminals, Alex. I never even got a jaywalking ticket. All we'd have to do is delete Newman's files and it's over."

"You're getting stage fright."

"Kidnapping's a federal crime."

"It's not kidnapping if no one's been kidnapped."

"We're extorting a million dollars."

"No one will be able to trace us, Ronnie. I made sure of that."

"It was one thing when Kestrel and the rest of us were in the office listening to you and your demands, but once people were by themselves they changed. What if Walter Shaw's calling the cops right now?"

"Not at the risk of losing his money from the Salient deal, he isn't."

Alex was probably right, but Ronnie pressed her point. "You don't know these people like I do. And if we get caught then it's Kestrel who wins. People like Kestrel always win. People like us always lose."

"Not this time," Alex said.

Ronnie's phone rang. It was Nadine Patrick, a Jamaican orderly at Jerrold House, and one of the few staff members who treated Ronnie's mother well.

"Your mother, she very agitated tonight," Nadine said. "They threatening to take her downstairs." That meant the security ward. "You want I should give her some Haldol?"

"Half a pill, that's all," Ronnie said, "and I'll be there as soon as I can. Thanks, Nadine."

"I do what I can 'til you get here, darling."

Ronnie hung up. "I gotta go see my mom," she said to Alex and left.

— • —

The cab driver had never driven to that part of Queens so Ronnie had to give him directions. Because it was late and the traffic was light they made good time.

Ronnie was an only child. Her mother met Ronnie's father Robert, who was also an English transplant, after a Broadway performance of *Good Evening,* the Peter Cook and Dudley Moore review. Robert and Carlotta sat several rows apart, but they both laughed at many of the same things that none of the Americans in the audience did. When the show ended Robert Hewitt looked for and found the woman who'd laughed so hard at the same bits he did and, in the process, he found the woman he'd marry.

Robert Hewitt hated his accounting job with Capital Brands and the only thing he looked forward to was spending time with his wife and daughter. He adored the comedy of his homeland, so Ronnie and her father would watch *Monty Python* and *Beyond the Fringe* sketches on VHS tapes for hours. Robert laughed like a madman when Ronnie did her own version of the one-legged Tarzan scene. But the "don't mention the war" scene from *Fawlty Towers* was her father's and her favorite. Whenever the word "war" was mentioned— by Carlotta or a newscaster on TV or even by an unsuspecting diner at a nearby restaurant table—both Robert and Ronnie would jump to their feet and proclaim, "Don't mention the war!" The irony that her father in his gray business suit and with his small moustache looked exactly like a Monty Python character didn't escape Ronnie.

— • —

When Ronnie got to Jerrold House, Nadine Patrick was with her mother, holding her hand. Carlotta shared a room with three other women.

"I'm here now, Mum," Ronnie said, using the British term for Mom that her mother liked.

"Don't let that man hit me," Carlotta said.

"What man?" Ronnie asked, looking around the room. There was no man in it.

"She talking about one of the orderlies," Nadine said in a low voice.

"One of them hit her?"

"Sometimes they gotta be rough," Nadine said. She didn't want to implicate any of her coworkers out of fear of what the man might do to her if he found out that she did.

"Don't let him hit me," Carlotta said again just as one of the orderlies, a tall white man with a shock of bright red hair, walked past the room staring at Ronnie and Carlotta through the windowed wall.

"I give her the Haldol like you told me," Nadine said. Carlotta reminded Nadine of the British families her parents worked for in Jamaica. "They was rich and fancy," she once told Ronnie. "And they wear white all the time like they was some kind of birds. I always want to be fancy like that. But look at me now."

"I think you're fancy, Nadine," Ronnie said.

"Child, you such a liar," Nadine said and they both laughed. Nadine was a good woman.

Dora, the woman in the bed closest to the wall, began to mumble. But her voice quickly grew louder and soon she was yelling, unleashing a fury that seemed far too big for her shrunken size.

"I'm here," Dora screamed. "I'm here. Look at me. DON'T YOU FORGET ME. LOOK AT ME." No actor could recreate the intensity of this tiny woman's voice or her rage as she shrieked proof of her existence to anyone near enough to hear. "LOOK AT ME, YOU MOTHERFUCKERS. LOOK AT ME."

"What's happening?" Carlotta asked Ronnie.

"Dora's having a bad dream, Mum," Ronnie said as two orderlies came in the room, quickly sedated Dora with an injection and left.

"You said I wouldn't have to stay here," Carlotta said.

"You won't." Ronnie squeezed her mother's hand. "I promise."

Her mother fell asleep and Ronnie took a taxi back to Brooklyn. A segment of the Bloomberg show played on the small screen on the back of the driver's seat. In it Kestrel was heading to his car in front of the Boundary building when the reporter asked him about the Salient deal. "They'd be lucky to get us," was the last thing Kestrel said to her. Ronnie was surprised. It was unlike him to say something like that.

When she got home Alex was relieved by how recommitted to the scheme Ronnie was again. They went over the plans.

"And when you talk to Kestrel in the morning," she told him, "you should say you found out that someone was investigating Newman. Don't say Pike, but tell them you know someone did what you told them not to and it was the last chance you'll give them. It'll scare them from doing any more investigating. I'll write it all down for you in the morning before I leave."

TUESDAY

It was drizzling slightly. Pike leaned against the gray wall of the Boundary building. He took a drag of his Marlboro as he lit the Newport of the young woman looking at the photo of Martin Newman he'd just handed her. Pike coughed. He hadn't smoked a cigarette in almost twenty years.

He'd asked two other Boundary employees earlier that morning if they knew Martin Newman. Neither of them, a man who looked about forty-five and a much younger woman who said she was once a cheerleader for the softball team, remembered him. "But I didn't follow the team last year," she said.

"Martin Newman?" the Newport woman asked Pike looking at his photo. "That's this guy's name? I don't know him. What did he do? Steal some pencils? He looks like everybody else around here," she said and handed the photo back to Pike.

"Are you sure?" Pike said.

The woman took a deep drag and said, "Lemme see that again." She grabbed Newman's photo back. "Maybe I do remember him," she said. Then she nodded. "Yeah, I do."

"What do you remember?"

She shrugged. "He's the same as the rest: a pig in a suit. You're cute, you have a rack, they treat you just fine. You don't and you're just another bitch getting them coffee."

"It never changes, does it?" Pike said.

"It doesn't," the woman said and dropped her cigarette onto the sidewalk. She didn't bother stepping on it. "You're not gonna tell anybody what I said, are you?"

Pike shook his head with a conspiratorial smile and walked away holding Newman's photo.

Alone in the elevator, Pike looked at Newman's photo. Who was he? A sweet, hard-working compatriot or a rude, sexist asshole? That some people had no memory of him and that others had differing memories didn't surprise him. On the witness stand one person would testify the defendant was a saint. Two minutes later another would say he was the devil.

— • —

Ronnie waited with the others for Alex's call in Kestrel's office. Kestrel had asked Pike if anyone had called security to report that Newman hadn't come home last night. Pike said no one had and Kestrel was relieved to hear this.

"Do you know what you're gonna say to this guy?" Natalie asked him.

"I know exactly what I'm gonna say." Kestrel looked at the wall of clocks. "This prick was supposed to call me at ten. No wonder he's a kidnapper. I'd never hire his ass."

Ronnie planned it so that each time Alex was scheduled to call Kestrel he'd do it at least a few minutes later than he said he would. This would upset Kestrel and she hoped it'd throw him off his game a little.

When the phone finally rang, everyone froze. Kestrel leaned over his desk and waited a moment before punching the speaker button. "Barry Kestrel here."

But the speaker's voice was not that of someone using a voice modulator. It was a man's voice and it said, "You answering your own phones now, Barry?"

"Who's this?" Kestrel asked.

"Tom Bowden. Remember me?"

Kestrel mumbled, "Shit," under his breath and Natalie and Walter looked at one another. Tom Bowden had a seat on the Salient board. Ronnie had dealt with him many times. He was young and full of himself, but he claimed there was a good chance he'd end up holding the swing vote on the board regarding Salient's bid to take over Boundary. If that were true, he might be the person who'd determine how rich three of the people in the room would be by week's end.

"It saves us money," Kestrel said.

"As your potential buyer, I like hearing that, Barry."

"Potential buyer?" Kestrel said.

"Look, bro, you know I'm on your side, but I'm having a tough enough time selling you to the other assholes here as it is. The last thing I need is you on Bloomberg shooting your fucking mouth off about how lucky we'd be to get you."

"She cornered me. I had to say something."

"Say something else. Don't make waves. Don't make ripples, for fuck's sake. Find a rock, crawl under it and stay there until this deal is done. You hear me?"

Kestrel bristled at being spoken to like this, but if he wanted Salient's money these were rules and he'd broken them. "Loud and clear, Tom."

"I hope so," Bowden said. "Ciao."

Kestrel punched the button ending the call. " 'Ciao.' He talks like a homo."

Ronnie was glad that Tom Bowden called and reminded them all how important it was not to make waves now. She couldn't have written what he said better herself.

"You all heard him," Kestrel said to the others. "We get this bullshit out of the way ASAP."

The phone rang again and Kestrel hit the speaker button. "Barry Kestrel here."

"Good morning, Mr. Kestrel," Alex said through his modulator, "we're eager to hear your decision."

"I spoke to my associates," Kestrel said without looking at Natalie and Walter, "and we can offer you five hundred thousand."

Walter and Natalie were shocked when Kestrel said this. "We agreed to one million," Walter said.

"What are you doing, Barry?" Natalie asked.

"Shut up," Kestrel said to both of them.

Ronnie wasn't surprised. She told Alex that Kestrel would try to lowball him. They'd prepared for it. Now Kestrel would negotiate.

"You can't be serious," Alex said.

"Two million is too much for us," Kestrel said.

"It's lunch money to you."

When Alex said this, Pike turned and looked at Ronnie. When she saw Pike looking at her she rolled her eyes at him as if to say she hoped this would all be over soon.

"It's the most we can get you in cash without raising suspicions," Kestrel said. "You don't want the police involved, do you?"

"It's you who don't want the police involved, Mr. Kestrel."

Ronnie worried that Alex's kidnapper was starting to sound like a parody of a villain you'd hear in a movie. But, even so, his delivery seemed to be working because Kestrel's expression tightened.

"I can make one million work," Kestrel said.

"That might work for you, but not for us."

Kestrel didn't budge. "That's our final offer. Take it or leave it."

After a pause Alex said, "I'll talk it over with my people and I'll let you know tomorrow morning what we decide. But there's something else we have to discuss."

"What?"

"One of you went against my directive and looked into Mr. Newman's records."

"How do you know that?" Kestrel said.

"It doesn't matter how we know. What matters is that we do."

"Who was it?" Kestrel asked the caller as he looked from face to face in the room.

"Find that out for yourself. This was your first slip. We'll forgive you this time, but you have to assure me it won't happen again."

"It won't," Kestrel said.

"For Mr. Newman's sake it had better not."

Ronnie turned to Pike who looked quickly away from her. He was clearly anxious at nearly being outed for his investigating Newman.

"We'll call you the same time tomorrow morning," Alex said.

Ronnie was relieved. Alex had done everything she asked him to. Tomorrow Alex would tell Kestrel they'd accept his offer of one million dollars.

But then Kestrel said, "There's one more thing."

Not expecting this, Alex paused. "What?"

Kestrel looked at Pike before he said, "Before I give you anything I want to talk to Newman."

"We can arrange that," Alex said.

Kestrel's request didn't faze Alex because Ronnie and Alex figured that Kestrel would probably ask to speak with Newman. And since Alex used the voice modulator for the kidnapper character he could come up with another voice for Newman. He had a gift for accents and a few weeks earlier he and Ronnie went through a string of them that he might use. They hadn't yet decided on one, but they'd choose Newman's accent when she got home.

"But here's the thing," Kestrel said. "I don't just want to talk to Newman. I want to Skype with him."

This threw Alex. He was silent.

Hearing Kestrel say this threw Ronnie, too. How could they let him Skype with Newman? The man didn't exist. And everyone knew Alex. Shit. What now? Why didn't they foresee this?

"Why?" Alex asked. He sounded like an actor who'd forgotten his line in the middle of a scene and prayed that someone would toss him a cue.

"Why do you think? So I know it's him. So I know he's alive. I want to talk to him. Face to face. I'm not gonna give you a million bucks for a dead body, am I?"

This changed everything. Even through the caller's modulator, Kestrel could tell that he'd thrown the kidnapper off his game. He'd become the predator and Alex his prey. "Or maybe Newman's dead already," Kestrel said, "and we're talking bullshit. Is that what's happening here?"

Alex was silent.

"Is that what's happening?" Kestrel asked again, louder.

"Say something, baby," Ronnie thought.

"Mr. Newman is not dead," Alex said.

"Then make it so I can talk to him face to face before we discuss anything else."

"Fine," said Alex and even through the voice modulator his eagerness to get off the line was obvious.

"Have a nice day," Kestrel said to Alex and, feeling powerful, added, "Call me on time tomorrow." Kestrel pounded the button on the phone, ending the call. He turned to Pike. "The Skype idea changed the game."

"It did," Pike said.

Natalie shook her head. "I can't believe you did that."

"Asked to Skype with the guy?"

"Tried to lowball him with five hundred thousand."

While Kestrel and Natalie argued about how much he'd offered the caller, Ronnie thought about the problems that a Skype call with Newman presented. She quickly went through the actors they knew who'd make a believable Newman. There were a couple that might work, one in particular. But what would they tell him about the role he'd be playing? That it was some kind of YouTube performance? Why not? People make ridiculous videos all the time. Cats sang Verdi. Pigs cooked pasta. The actor they chose would never hear anything else about it because it would never go public. That was the whole point of it. So it might work.

Kestrel's voice took Ronnie out of her thoughts. "Make sure the Skype bullshit is set up."

"I will, sir," she said.

Natalie was still upset about Kestrel's lowball offer to the kidnapper and said so.

"I wanted to see what he was made of," Kestrel said to Natalie. "And I found out. He's a weakling. I should've offered him fifty thou to start. And another thing—which one of you investigated Newman?" Kestrel looked around the room. "Was it you?" he asked Walter.

"Of course not."

Kestrel looked at Natalie. "You?"

"It wasn't me, Barry."

He looked at Ronnie and said dismissively, "I know it wasn't you." He turned to Pike. "Then it must've been you."

Pike shook his head. "I only looked at his Boundary file like the caller said I could."

In the pause that followed Ronnie said, "Maybe no one investigated Newman."

Kestrel turned to her. "What do you mean?"

"Maybe the guy was lying."

"Why would he do that?"

"To make us argue among ourselves like we're doing now. It would weaken us."

Kestrel begrudgingly said, "You might be right. But listen to me when I say this: from now on no one looks into this guy's shit, you got that?"

Ronnie looked at Pike whose ass she just saved. He would owe her.

Kestrel turned to Walter. "How long would it take you to get a million cash ready?"

"Not long."

"What if they don't accept a million?" Natalie asked.

"They'll accept it," Kestrel said.

"What makes you so sure?"

"Because I know people, that's why," Kestrel said.

Walter shook his head. "I don't like it, Barry."

"Neither do I," said Pike.

"That's because you're a wuss," Kestrel said to Walter. "And you," he said to Pike, "you're a cop, so catching the bad guy is in your DNA. But you work for me now and I'm telling you to let it go. We save this guy's ass and we wash the whole thing away with a million cash. Everyone's safe. Everyone's happy. Everyone's rich. Tomorrow this whole thing will be over."

— • —

On her way back to her desk Ronnie read a text from Alex. *We need a rewrite.*

We'll go over the dialogue when I get home, Ronnie texted him back.

But how would they figure their way around the Skype call? So many things could go wrong. She looked up to see Pike standing over her desk.

"Hey, Detective."

Pike smiled. "Thanks."

She knew he was referring to how she'd taken the heat off him by saying that the caller might have been lying about finding that someone had investigated Newman. "No problem," she said. But she wanted to hear what Pike thought about Skyping with Newman. Was it his idea? Or was it Kestrel's?

"You want to get some lunch?" she asked Pike.

"I gotta take the man home." Pike walked away from Ronnie. He was holding his copy of *The Picture of Dorian Gray.*

"You still like the book, Mr. Pike?" Shelby asked him.

"I do."

"It's scary, isn't it?"

"In its way," Pike said.

Kestrel exited his office, saying nothing to anyone. Pike joined him on the elevator and, as door closed on the two men, Pike stared at Ronnie.

— • —

Jubilee's theatre had ninety-nine seats, the number they were allowed by Actor's Equity. The more controversial their material, the more publicity they got. Protestors sometimes picketed them and when that happened the cast and crew would share coffee and donuts with them on the street in front of the theater. Ronnie had made the news two weeks before when an interviewer questioned her about "cultural appropriation," which a critic had accused Jubilee of. "All art is appropriation," she said. "If you don't like it, then don't come." They got a lot of publicity—most of it negative—from her answer.

Ronnie stood at the back of the theater watching a sketch called *The Water Ambulance*. It mocked people's absurd need for water, specifically expensive water. The idea for it came when she was having lunch with Pike in the Boundary cafeteria one day and he noted that the bottled water they were drinking cost more than the gasoline for his car did.

"And when did everyone decide that they couldn't live without drinking water all day long?" Ronnie said. It became a running joke between them and for a while whenever they'd see each other at Boundary they'd ask, "Would you like some water?"

So Ronnie wrote a sketch in which Alex played an "emergency hydrationist", a character who combed the New York streets looking for people needing water. His prop was a papier-mâché ambulance he wore over his shoulders. From the prop, he'd pull plastic bottles of expensive water (filled with tap water for the production). He'd yell, "You need hydration!" and spritz actors playing pedestrians with the phony Perrier or Evian, sometimes reaching people in the front row.

Ronnie had named the police character in the sketch Officer Pike. When Pike first saw it he was touched. He told Ronnie that he wished Claire could have seen it.

The scene was working well tonight. Onstage, an actor's body lay on the ground and the actor playing Officer Pike knelt over the body. "This woman is dead," he said.

"Then get her some water!" Alex said, pushing the actor playing Pike aside and spritzing the "dead" body with an expensive water. The "dead" actor jumped immediately to her feet and the audience cheered.

— • —

While the Jubilee sketch took place across town, Pike was in the Boundary offices, deserted apart from the night cleaning staff, a few security people and traders talking to people overseas. Kestrel was on the phone in his office talking to someone in Hong Kong. Pike would drive him home when he finished.

Kestrel's demand to Skype with Newman was a good one. So good that Pike wished he'd thought of it. But when he'd been a cop there were no things like Skype and not a lot of people even had cell phones. Talking to Newman would tell them a lot, both about the kidnappers and Newman himself.

Pike still considered everyone a suspect and since he didn't dare go online again to investigate Newman, he fell back on more traditional detective work. So he sat at Heidi's desk and looked through its drawers. He'd gone through Shelby's desk minutes before. He hadn't expected to find anything in either desk and he didn't.

Pike then walked to Ronnie's desk and sat at it. Unlike the other two women's desks there were no personal photos on it. Pike opened its drawers and looked through them. He didn't want Ronnie to be involved, but there were things he couldn't ignore.

In Kestrel's office that morning the kidnapper had used the phrase "lunch money" to describe the size of the payoff, the same expression Ronnie had used the day before. But a lot of people used that phrase, didn't they? Especially guys on Wall Street trying to sound old school macho. And Ronnie, along with Walter Shaw, had seemed eager to tell the authorities what was going on. But she was a performer. Her concern for Newman's jeopardy could be an act.

And the morning before, when they looked at Newman's Boundary file for the first time, she appeared surprised when it said that Newman was a widower. Did she expect it to say something else? Did she know Newman well enough to be surprised by something he'd written on his file that he hadn't told her about?

Ronnie was the only person Pike had told about his investigating Newman. Sure, it was possible that the kidnappers had really discovered that Pike looked into the Boundary video files. But if Ronnie was involved, she could have told her accomplices what Pike said to her, allowing them to use that information in the morning's call and warn the Boundary people not to investigate Newman any further.

Pike pulled out a flyer from Jubilee from a lower drawer in Ronnie's desk. How would Kestrel react if he found out that his personal assistant wrote the strident anti-Wall Street material that Jubilee performed? And did Ronnie's animosity towards capitalism increase her possibility as a suspect?

Pike found an 8x10 photo of Alex in the same drawer. Pike had never spent any time with the young man apart from shaking his hand a few times after shows, but the kid was always polite. He was younger than Ronnie and didn't look capable of even playing—forget being—a felon.

Pike wanted them to be innocent. But if they were involved, one thing was certain: it'd mean that Newman was involved in it, too, because there was no way Ronnie would be capable of doing anything as violent as kidnapping someone.

Pike was eager to see how the Skype call went in the morning. What would Newman look like? Sound like? What would he say? What would his manner tell Pike?

Maybe Kestrel and the kidnappers would come to an agreement and Newman would come back safe and sound. In that case there'd be no need for Pike to know any more than he did.

— • —

Ronnie waited for Alex outside the theater. It had rained and the streets were wet and shiny. Piles of black garbage bags reflected the lights overhead.

Alex walked up to her. "What do we do about the Skype thing?"

"Not here." Ronnie took him by the hand and they walked down the street together. They stopped in a doorway.

"So what now?" Alex asked.

"It's over."

"You don't think we can find someone to play him?"

"We can't risk bringing another person in."

Alex accepted the inevitable. "We worked so hard."

"Tell me about it."

"Fucking Skype," Alex said.

Ronnie smiled. "I'll skewer it in my next sketch."

"What about your mother?"

"I'll call Miriam Klein at CAA. She wants to submit me to some shows."

"You don't want to do that."

"I have to now."

"Maybe we could find someone who looks like—"

But Ronnie cut him off. "We can't, Alex. It's over. And it's good that it is. Whatever the last few months were, it wasn't us. We have to delete everything about Newman that we can. Tonight. Can you do that?"

Alex nodded. "What will Kestrel and the others do tomorrow?"

"You won't call them and that'll be the end of it. They'll do some investigating and they'll find out that Martin Newman never existed."

"They'll think it was a scam."

"Which it is. Or was," Ronnie said. "And they'll never trace it back to us." She looked at Alex for confirmation of this. "Will they?"

"We're good," said Alex.

They flagged a taxi and were both silent for the ride until they got over the bridge when Alex said, "You're relieved, aren't you?"

She nodded. It felt like someone had taken a boulder off her back. A mountain.

"Me, too," Alex said.

"I got news for you," she stage-whispered to Alex. "We suck as criminals."

"We're like the Marx brothers."

"Worse. We're Laurel and Hardy."

Alex laughed. Ronnie reached over and stroked his cheek. "I'm so lucky that you love me," she said.

Alex grabbed her face in his hands and kissed her hard on the mouth. He held his hand behind her head as he kissed her, something Ronnie loved. The only thing she wanted to do now was fall onto their bed and make love, have sex, fuck, whatever, all night long. She'd be in Kestrel's office in the morning when the scam evaporated somewhere in the cloud.

The cab pulled up in front of their building and Ronnie tossed some cash to the driver who sped off before either one of his fares realized they'd given him more than twice what was on the meter. Alex kissed Ronnie on the back of her neck as she fumbled to open the building's door with her key.

"This is better than make-up sex," she said sticking her key in the lock.

"It's not-committing-a-felony sex," Alex said.

They ran up the three flights of stairs, Ronnie first with Alex grabbing at the tail of her coat. "Stop that, young man," she said haughtily, "you're going to make me fall."

They kissed again at their apartment door. Alex began to unbutton her shirt, causing her to drop her keys.

"Hold on," she said. They shut the door behind themselves and stumbled into the living room. The lights were already on.

They started to rip each other's clothes off. In seconds Ronnie's shirt was on the floor. Alex unfastened her bra and threw it over his shoulder to where the Martin Newman dummy sat. Ronnie hopped on one foot as she kissed Alex and struggled to take her jeans off at the same time. She finally kicked her jeans across the room and Alex slipped his hands into her panties.

She fumbled with his belt. "I hate this belt," she said. Alex stopped kissing her breasts long enough to unbuckle his belt. His pants fell to the floor around his ankles and he kicked them aside. Ronnie felt him pressing hard against her thigh. He took her head in his hands and looked into her eyes. Suddenly his focus shifted to something behind her and he said, "Holy shit."

Ronnie pulled back. "What?" She turned around to see what Alex was looking at.

It was a man and he was sitting where the Martin Newman dummy had been. The real man was the dummy's size and color and he wore a shirt, a sports jacket and a tie, not unlike what the dummy wore. That's why they hadn't noticed him.

"What the fuck?" Alex said, backing away. "Who are you?"

"What are you doing here?" Ronnie asked at the same time.

The man held up his hand. "My apologies," he said. "I should've said something, but you were…distracted…" He grinned sheepishly before looking modestly to the floor. "Tell me when you're comfortable," he said.

Only when the man said this did Ronnie and Alex both realize how naked they were. They grabbed their clothes from the floor and, handing them to each other, quickly put them back on.

Ronnie said, "Who the fuck are you?" She looked at Alex. "Do you know him?"

Alex shook his head. "Do you?"

"Does it sound like I know him?" Ronnie looked over her shoulder at the man as she put her bra back on. It was tangled and she fumbled with it. When she finally got it back on, she turned to the man and said, "Are you a cop?" Before letting him answer, she turned to Alex who was buckling his belt. "Is he a cop?"

"How should I know?" Alex said and then turned to the man himself. "Are you? A cop?"

"I'm not a cop." The man stood up and picked up Ronnie's shirt that had landed on the floor behind him. He held it out to her and she grabbed it from him.

"Did Kestrel send you?" she said. "Or Pike? Shit, it was Pike, wasn't it?"

"No one sent me."

"Maybe he knows you from Boundary," Alex said. "You think he's from Boundary?"

Ronnie looked at the man as she buttoned her shirt. He looked vaguely familiar. But why? Where did she know him from? She stood still. "I know you, don't I?" she said to the man.

"Of course you know me, Veronica."

"Who are you?"

"I'm Martin Newman," the man said.

— • —

In the Escalade, Kestrel turned to Pike. "It was you, wasn't it?"

"What was me, sir?" Pike asked.

"The person who investigated Newman."

"It wasn't."

"I don't believe you," Kestrel said.

Pike was impressed. Maybe Kestrel wasn't wrong when he said he knew people. But who didn't guess right at least some of the time? "It might be what Ms. Hewitt said," Pike said. "No one investigated and they only said that to scare us, to make us doubt one another."

"Or maybe it was her," Kestrel said, unconvinced one way or the other.

Pike changed the subject. "The Skype call was a good idea."

"It was, wasn't it? It put that asshole back on his heels. Or her heels." Kestrel turned to Pike. "You suspect someone, don't you?"

"I suspect everyone," Pike said. "It's how I was trained." It's what life had taught him, too.

"But you think it's someone on the inside, don't you?"

"Do you have enemies, sir?"

"You don't get to be as successful as I am without making enemies." They pulled up in front of Kestrel's building. The doorman rushed out to open the car door, but Kestrel waved him off and the doorman went back to his post under the awning.

"Maybe I should go to the police," Kestrel said.

"That wouldn't be a good idea, sir."

"What changed your mind?"

"We both know there's a possibility that Newman might be involved. But if he's not and he's really been kidnapped then you've waited two days without telling anyone. You've put yourself in a bad position, legally speaking."

Kestrel stared at the street traffic. "I hate that someone's fucking me over like this. Once this deal is done, I'll find them and I'll make them pay. I promise you that." He paused. "What do you think I should say to this Newman guy tomorrow?"

"Let him do the talking. Read him like you do everyone else." Pike knew enough to flatter Kestrel. "If he's really been kidnapped you'll know. He'll be scared. Tell him that you're gonna get him home safe. We'll figure out where to go from there."

"You'd have made a good businessman," Kestrel said and opened the Escalade's door. The doorman rushed to the car and nodded silent greetings to Pike before he shut the car's door and accompanied Kestrel into the building.

— • —

Ronnie stared at the man sitting in their living room. "Who are you?" she asked him for the third time.

"Martin Newman," he said once again.

"There is no Martin Newman," Alex said.

"This is a joke, right?" Ronnie looked at the man. "Are you in the show? You are, aren't you?" She turned to Alex. "Is he in the show? Did you put him up to this?"

"I didn't put him up to anything."

"I'm not in any show," the man said.

"Did you hire him to play Martin on the Skype call?" she asked Alex.

Alex shook his head. "No."

"Because I told you we couldn't do that."

"He didn't hire me," the man said.

"I don't know who the fuck he is," Alex said.

"Hold on," the man said and got up and walked to the computer desk.

"What are you doing?" Alex asked, following him and blocking him.

The man politely held up his hands. "Relax," he said and sat at the monitor. He pulled up a file and pointed to the screen. "Check this out."

Alex pushed the man aside and sat down to see what was on the screen. Alex looked back and forth several times from the screen to the stranger standing next to him. "Holy shit," he said each time. "Holy shit. Holy shit. What the fuck is this?"

"What the fuck is what?" Ronnie said.

"This."

"What?"

"It's him."

"It's who?" Ronnie asked.

"Shit, shit, shit," Alex said over and over as he stared at the screen.

"What am I missing here?" Ronnie said.

"Look for yourself." Alex pointed to the screen. On it was the fictional Boundary file of Martin Newman, the one that Ronnie had pulled up in Kestrel's office that morning. "Is this the photo of Newman you saw in Kestrel's office?" Alex asked her.

Ronnie looked at it. "What if it is?"

"It's him," Alex said, pointing at the man.

Ronnie looked at the face of Martin Newman on the computer screen and then turned to the man standing next to her. They were the same. This is why the man looked so familiar. "How can it be?" she said looking back to the screen. "He's not real." She turned to the man. "You're not real."

"I beg to differ, Veronica," the man said. He posed theatrically, holding his arms open wide. "Thirty-three years old, five foot ten, one hundred and fifty-five pounds—"

"I don't get it," Ronnie said as the man kept talking.

"—dirty brown hair, a scar on my left cheek here from a childhood sledding accident and a tattoo of a question mark on my right arm."

Alex kept reading through Martin Newman's file as the man rolled up his sleeve and displayed the small tattoo. "He changed it," Alex said. "He changed everything."

"Not everything," the man said. "I was cautious at first about making changes because I didn't want to give away what I was doing. Then I realized you each thought the other one was making the changes that I was making. That made it easier for me. It was fun. And it gave me some latitude."

Now Ronnie understood where many of the changes in Martin Newman's file had come from. Alex hadn't made them. This guy did, starting with putting his own photo in the file. They'd originally photoshopped their version of a nondescript man, someone who could easily be the unnoticeable worker they were creating. But this guy was so much like the original picture they created that Ronnie didn't notice when he'd changed it to one of himself. They'd purposefully created someone forgettable. Then they forgot him.

"You changed it so that he's a rock climber," she said to him.

"So I'm a rock climber," the man said.

Alex scrolled through Newman's file. "He changed a lot of other shit, too. He said he's married. This is bullshit."

"I was married," the man said. "My wife died."

Ronnie stood behind Alex at the computer and saw other things on Martin Newman's Boundary file that she'd never seen before.

Alex saw the newly added part of Newman's file that Pike had read. "He added this shit about moving back home and coming back to work at Boundary."

Ronnie didn't care what his file said. She wanted to know what game the guy in front of them was playing.

"You have to admit that Martin Newman is more interesting now," the man said. "And real."

"He's not supposed to be interesting or real," Ronnie said. She stared at him. He wasn't ugly; he wasn't handsome. He was what he was supposed to be: Martin Newman. But not really. He couldn't be. "I know you, don't I? I know who you are," she said.

"Of course you do, Ms. Hewitt. I'm Martin Newman. I've worked for Boundary the last seven years as a research trader. It's all there in my file." He smiled. "We've passed each other many times in the halls and in the cafeteria."

"No, we haven't," she said.

"How can you be so sure?"

"Because you don't fucking exist," Alex said. "That's how."

Ronnie couldn't be sure now. That was the whole point of Newman, wasn't it? That he was invisible, interchangeable. You wouldn't notice him, but you wouldn't miss him, either. "Was it you who Pike saw on the video coming in and out of the building?"

The man shrugged. "Possibly." His tone was patronizing.

Ronnie looked over Alex's shoulder at Newman's file. "This is crazy," she said. "What about your address at The Maxwell? What if someone went there and found out Martin Newman doesn't live there?"

"But I do live there. I rented an apartment at The Maxwell under my name, Martin Newman. I've been there for the last three weeks."

Ronnie stepped back. "You're crazy."

"He has to work at Boundary," Alex said. "That's the only way he could have gotten into the files."

"That's not true, Alex. You got into the files, didn't you?" the man said condescendingly. "Today all houses are glass houses. As someone who works in the field, you should know that I can go anywhere I want without even leaving my chair. I followed your emails, your texts, your phone calls. When I found the character that you guys were creating I was intrigued. It was funny, if a little condescending. I read your personal diary for me, Alex. I even went to a couple of your shows to see if you'd put Martin Newman in any of your sketches like you were planning to do from the start, but you didn't. It was too tempting not to get involved so I went deeper. I liked him. So eventually I decided to become him." He grinned. "It's been fascinating."

The man didn't speak like Ronnie imagined Martin Newman would. He sounded affected and calculating like Claude Raines in *Casablanca*. "How'd you figure out about the kidnapping?" she said.

"I saw the early drafts of your play in which I get kidnapped. It was a funny idea. And surprisingly moving, too. You both wrote a lot about it in your emails for almost a year. About how you were going to spring it on the audience in the theater. Then you stopped writing about it. Suddenly: nothing. So either you decided it was unbelievable or you decided to actually try it."

He was right. They stopped writing about the imaginary kidnapping when they decided to kidnap Newman for real.

"That made me curious," the man said. "I figured something was up. That's when I found the phony bank accounts you created," he said to Alex. "People who do that are trying to hide money. But you're actors, you have no money. Not yet anyway. And I thought that a crime like that was too out of character for you, a little too real for people used to working in make-believe. So I figured you'd forgotten about the kidnapping idea. Until yesterday. I saw that Detective Pike was looking into everything about me. Everywhere. That's when I figured you'd actually done it. You kidnapped me."

What could Ronnie say? The guy had read all the clues correctly.

He went on. "I thought, damn, these people are brilliant. If they get away with it, they've committed the perfect crime: a kidnapping with no victim. You'd be heroes in the hacker world. Then I thought: I'm smarter than they are. No offense, Alex, you're good, but you're like the middle reliever who comes in when the game's already won or lost. Me, I'm the star closer." He grinned at Alex. "I said to myself, I can top what they did. And to prove it, here I am."

"How is what you did better than what we did?" Ronnie asked.

"Because now you have a victim which means you've committed a kidnapping, a felony punishable by life imprisonment."

"We didn't kidnap anybody," Alex said.

"You kidnapped me. How much did you ask for?"

"Two million," Alex said. "And we decided to end the whole thing because Kestrel wants to Skype with us tomorrow—"

Ronnie waved her hand at Alex and said, "Shut up." She looked at the man. "Here's the deal," she said. "Forget it. Forget the whole thing, Mr. Newman or whoever you are. It's finished. Right here. Right now. You're right: we're idiots. You're smarter than we are. Way smarter. You win. What do you want? A drink? Dinner? A little trophy? You want to see my tits again? Take whatever you want. The whole thing's over."

"It's not over," the man said.

"I'm telling you it is." Ronnie pointed to the door. "Take your shit and leave."

The man didn't move. "You can't end it now."

"Why not?"

"Because I don't want you to."

"It doesn't matter what you want."

"But it does, Veronica. Try to end it now and I'll turn you both in."

"For what?"

"You kidnapped me."

"You don't exist," Alex said.

"I have a record of what you did and I can make it so that, at the very least, Kestrel and the cops will find you guilty of attempted extortion."

This shut Ronnie up. "What happens to you?" she said.

"I hit 'delete' and I, Martin Newman, disappear. Unfortunately for you, you can't do that."

"I'll find out who you really are," Alex said.

"Do you really think I'd leave a trail that someone like you could follow, Alex? I made contingencies, too."

"What do you mean?" Ronnie asked.

"If something unfortunate were to happen to me, say I were to meet with an accident, a number of people including Mr. Kestrel and Detective Pike would receive emails with links to damaging information about you and your plans. Martin Newman might be gone, but you'd remain very much the center of their attention."

Ronnie realized that she and Alex were screwed. She turned to Alex. "Why didn't you see this?"

"Why didn't you?"

"I'm not the computer genius in the room. You said you could do it and no one would catch on. I plot the story, I write it and you act it out. Like we do in the shows. That's how it was supposed to work."

The man interrupted. "Don't be so hard on yourselves. You were visionary. Not the stuff you did with the computer, Alex. Any nine-year-old could have done that. Probably better."

"Fuck you," Alex said.

"But your genius was realizing that the computer doesn't just record people. It creates them." He pointed to Alex's laptop. "Whatever that thing says is true. It must be. I, Martin Newman, exist because I'm there." He pointed to his image on the screen. "Now I'm here. Look at me." They did. "Who can prove otherwise?"

"Eventually they'll figure it out," Alex said.

"Not before we get the ransom," the man said.

It finally made sense to Ronnie. "That's why you did it. For the money."

"Not at first, no," the man said. "But now, yes. Tomorrow morning you'll up the ransom demand to three million."

Alex scoffed at this idea. "You can't be serious."

"Kestrel will never go for that much," Ronnie said.

"Probably not. But I'm betting he'll settle for two million and we'll split it."

"This might force them to bring the cops into it," Ronnie said.

"If they do, that's not my problem. Remember, I'm the victim here."

— • —

Ronnie looked out the small window of their bedroom to the dark courtyard below. Pigeons scratched and cooed on a neighbor's air conditioner while Alex sat on the bed, buried in his Mac.

She tried to make sense of what just happened. When Alex left for the show earlier that afternoon, the man in the other room broke into their apartment and waited for them to come home.

Ronnie was furious. Everything had been so close to being over. A few hours before she'd felt like a kid who just got out of school for the summer. With the kidnapping behind her, she could quit Boundary, sign up with an agent and get a writing job for a TV show. She and Alex would have kids and take care of her mother until she died. They were smart. They were talented. This was America. Things worked out for people like them.

Then Martin Newman appeared. It was like a sketch she'd written had come to life. No, it wasn't like that. It was that.

Alex looked up from his computer. "He deleted my diary," he said.

"Your diary?"

"Not my diary. Newman's diary. The one I was writing for his character. I can't find it. He must've got into my system and deleted it or stole it, all of it, everything I wrote."

This frightened Ronnie. The man in the living room wasn't exaggerating. He had access to everything of theirs.

"He probably watched those sex videos we made," Alex said.

"He saw us doing it live right in front of him less than an hour ago so what does that matter?"

How had this guy come across Newman's Boundary file and its link to Ronnie and Alex to begin with? Was he a cybercriminal who stumbled onto it while trying to steal passwords for her credit cards? But why break into hers or Alex's accounts? Like he said, they had no money.

Was it because of her? Did he know Ronnie from before? Had he seen her in a show? Or in one of the stupid commercials she did? Men had crushes on her before. Women, too. Every actress has them. There was one guy during the run of The Seagull who'd wait outside the stage door each night with flowers. He was sweet; he was harmless.

So who was the guy in the other room? He didn't really believe he was Martin Newman, did he? He spoke like he did. But it had to be an act, didn't it? She opened Newman's Boundary file and read it again, hoping she'd find something she could use either to place him, or even better, to use against him.

His file was the same as what she'd read in Kestrel's office that morning and what Pike had told her about later. Newman was a widower, a rock climber and he had an apartment in The Maxwell. He played bass guitar in a band called the Avatars with some friends. Big surprise. What asshole who knows how to play five notes on an electric guitar doesn't form a band at some point in their shitty life? There must be some clue in what he wrote about himself that would tell her who or what he really was.

Alex slammed his Mac shut. "We gotta end this."

"How? You heard him. He won't let us. He's got his hands around our throats."

"Maybe I can get into his computer when he's asleep and figure out who he is."

"Get real, Alex. You think someone like him isn't gonna have a firewall like Fort Knox? You're in a whole other league now. He can do whatever he wants. So we have to play along with him until we figure out who he is." She was putting down Alex's computer skills, but what could she say? Newman, or whoever this guy was, was far more skilled than Alex. He stared at her.

"What?" Ronnie asked.

"You're on his side all of a sudden, aren't you?"

"What do you mean I'm 'on his side'? What are you saying?" Ronnie asked.

"That it's weird how he finds Martin Newman like he did and he suddenly shows up and now you say we should play along with him."

"Are you saying you think me and that guy out there are in on this together?"

"How did he find Newman?"

"You think I'm double-crossing you with that asshole?"

"Look at it from my point of view."

Ronnie was furious. If nothing else, she could always rely on Alex's simple trust in her, but had Newman's appearance changed that? "Is that what you're saying?" she said. "That you think I've been playing you? With that asshole out there?"

Faced with a fury he'd never seen in her before, Alex backtracked. "No, that's not what I'm saying."

"Then what are you saying? Tell me, Alex. Tell me right now."

"I don't know what I'm saying," Alex said and fell back onto the bed like a chastised schoolboy. "What do you expect me to think?" he said, his voice muffled by the pillow.

"I expect loyalty from you, that's what I expect."

"I freaked out."

"In case you forgot, this whole thing was my idea," Ronnie said, not willing to let go of her anger.

"I know it was. It is."

"We couldn't have done any of this without me working on the inside. Nothing. Not to mention that if anything goes wrong, I'm the one most likely to get caught."

"You said we wouldn't get caught," Alex said.

"We won't. Not if we're smart." She'd quieted Alex's suspicions about her, but they still pissed her off. "I'm gonna check this asshole out," she said and walked out of the bedroom.

In the living room Newman worked on his laptop. Ronnie walked past him and went into the kitchen to get a beer.

"I upset Alex," Newman said. Obviously, he'd heard them arguing.

"Actors. Save me," Ronnie opened the beer and drank out of the bottle.

"You're an actor."

His saying that meant he must've seen her the first year at Jubilee when she performed. Or maybe he'd seen her before that in The Seagull or some other Off- or Off-Off-Broadway show. Or in a commercial she did. Was he fixated on her? There were women more beautiful than her, even a couple of others in the plays she did, but you can never figure what will turn a man on.

"Was an actor," she said.

"How come you don't do it anymore?" he said.

"I prefer watching what I write from the audience."

"Why?"

"From on the stage I can't tell how or why my material's working. When I sit in the house I know what's working and what's not. In the house you know when you've lost an audience and you know when you own them." It's not unlike how I can watch this performance of yours right now, she thought, but you're too busy acting it to know if it's working or not. She pointed to his laptop. "What are you writing?"

"My diary."

"Martin Newman's?"

"Who else's?" he answered, as if hers was a stupid question.

"You deleted Alex's version."

"I liberated it. It was artificial. And insulting. My diary is real. And more interesting, too."

"Are you gonna let me see it?"

"If things go well, maybe I will."

"I'd like that," she said, almost flirtatiously. "But tell me something. Are you the person pretending to be Newman who Pike saw walking through the Boundary lobby in the videos?"

"I was Martin Newman walking in and out the building."

His certainty surprised Ronnie. But why should it? People posted imaginary shit on the Internet all the time now. They made up all kinds of lies about themselves on Snapchat and YouTube and other sites. They took countless selfies and videos on their cell phones so they could star in the only movie anyone was ever gonna make about their boring, insipid lives: their own. But how much of that shit did they really believe? And how much did this guy in front of her believe?

"You messed us up coming out of nowhere like that," she said. "The Martin Newman we created was never meant to be real."

"Think of me as his understudy."

"Understudy," she repeated sarcastically. This was enough for now. She didn't want to show too much of herself to this guy. Besides, he was freaking her out. "Sweet dreams, whoever you are," she said and left the room.

— • —

Ronnie shut the bedroom door and sat next to Alex on the bed. "Here's the thing," she said. "We can't let him get us going against each other like before. Look at us. We're already at each other's throats. That's what he wants because if he splits us up he has all the power. We can't let that happen."

Alex lowered his head. "It's my fault."

"That's what I mean. He wants us to blame ourselves, blame each other. But it's not your fault and it's not mine." She pointed to the door. "It's his fault and don't forget it. We're gonna make him regret ever getting involved with us. To do that, you and me, we gotta stick together. That's how we're gonna win this thing."

For the first time in a long time Ronnie would have liked a stronger man than Alex to help her think this through, one of those men she used to date and now made fun of. Even a piece of shit like her ex-husband. Or Kestrel. But she only had Alex and Alex wasn't one of those men.

There was only Newman and he was the puzzle she had to solve.

WEDNESDAY

Pike sat at a table in the Boundary cafeteria with four employees, three women and a man. They were all in their late twenties except for one woman closer to forty. They were research traders like Newman. Pike jokingly complained that he'd lost some money to one of their coworkers, Martin Newman, in a poker game the week before.

"Martin Newman?" asked one of the women, trying to picture him.

"He said he works with you guys," Pike said.

"Is he the cute one?" a second woman asked.

"You tell me," Pike said.

"Adorable," said the man. "And he's got great taste, too."

The older woman spoke up. "He was all over me at the Christmas party."

"Who wasn't?" the man said and she playfully slapped his arm.

"Did you take him home?" Pike asked her. He hoped being blunt would make him sound like a coworker and not Kestrel's man.

"Who doesn't she take home?" the first woman asked.

"She's such a slut," the man said, grinning.

The woman they were talking about pretended to be offended. "Look who's talking," she said to the man and they all laughed, Pike included.

One of the women grabbed Pike by the arm as he left the table. "What can you tell us about the Salient deal?"

"Nothing yet," Pike said.

As he walked away, the man said, "Say hi to Martin for me."

Pike nodded that he would. But did they even know whom Pike had asked them about? Were they confusing Newman with someone else? The Martin Newman who, in his file, said how devastated he was about losing his wife was not a man who'd pick up a coworker at the Christmas party and take her home with him. Or was he?

— • —

The first thing Ronnie did when she got to the office that morning was to start going through the files of every Boundary employee who might have the IT skills Newman did. She did this on her laptop in the cafeteria so no one would see her. By 8:30 she'd gone through at least fifty files. More than a few of the men looked like Martin, but after a while they all began to look the same. The only photo that looked exactly like the man in her apartment was, of course, Martin Newman's. They had no choice but to play along with him until she found out who he really was.

Earlier that morning Ronnie told Newman about the Skype call. "I guess you're lucky I showed up, huh?" he said.

"We'd have figured something out," Alex said.

"Like giving up? That's what you were planning to do before I appeared, wasn't it?"

Alex didn't answer. His anger worried Ronnie. She'd never seen him lose his cool like he did the night before and she didn't like the idea of leaving him and Newman alone in the apartment. But what choice did she have?

Newman would play himself in the Skype call. To prepare for it, they hung a plain white sheet as a backdrop. Ronnie made sure that nothing recognizable could be seen in the background, none of their posters or books or photos. Alex would stay off camera and speak through his modulator if necessary. The last thing Ronnie did before she left was to write down a couple of things that the guy pretending to be Newman should say to Kestrel during the conversation.

"But the most important thing to remember," she said to him, "is that everything that happens has to be a surprise to you because you don't know what's coming." This was the first thing she always told actors she was directing. "To make it real you have to play it as if you haven't read the script." She hoped that by couching her suggestions in acting terms, Alex would think of it as a performance and it would calm him down. She had no idea if Newman could pull the Skype call off.

— • —

Kestrel's phone had rung three times already. Pike, Natalie and Walter waited for him to answer it.

"Do you want me to get it for you, Mr. Kestrel?" Ronnie asked, knowing he'd say no.

Kestrel held up his hand. He punched the speaker button on the fifth ring. All he said was, "Kestrel."

Alex spoke through the modulator. "We've considered your offer, Mr. Kestrel, and we're willing to negotiate."

"What's to negotiate? We agreed on one million."

They hadn't agreed on a million, but this was a tactic Ronnie had heard Kestrel use before. "Put words in your opponent's mouth," Kestrel told her. "Convince them they just said what you want them to say."

Ronnie had prepared Alex for this. "Correction, sir," Alex said. "You proposed one million and we didn't officially respond. That's why we're negotiating."

"I want to speak to Newman."

"We negotiate first," Alex said. "Because if we fail to arrive at a figure then there's no point in your speaking to him, is there?"

Alex sounded confident, but Ronnie was worried what Kestrel would do when he heard the figure Alex was about to propose.

"Okay, what's your counter-offer?"

"Three million," said Alex.

"THREE MILLION?" Kestrel shouted. "WHAT THE FUCK IS THAT? THREE MILLION?"

Natalie motioned to Kestrel. "Barry, don't—" she started to say, but he waved her off.

"I hate to tell you, pal, but that's not negotiating," Kestrel said to Alex.

"It's not?" Alex said.

"Negotiating is when you say two and I say one and then you come back with, I don't know, one five or one six or something like that."

"Well, now I'm saying three," Alex said.

"I wrote the book on negotiating."

"I guess I didn't read that chapter."

"Suck my dick."

Ronnie had never heard Kestrel lose his cool like this before. No one else in the room had either.

"Calm down, Barry," Walter said and Kestrel threw the pen he was holding at Walter who ducked it clumsily.

"One million is the best we can do," Kestrel said.

"I don't believe you."

"Then don't."

"Goodbye, Mr. Kestrel," Alex said. "I'll give your regards to Mr. Newman."

"Wait," Kestrel said and paused. Everyone in the room stared at him. "I want to talk to him."

"Does that mean we're still negotiating?"

"It means I want to Skype with Newman. Otherwise this is all for shit."

"Fair enough," Alex said. "We'll need a few minutes to set it up."

"Do what you have to," said Kestrel. "My girl will arrange it on this side. Call me back at 10:15. On the dot."

Ronnie set up the Skype call as Kestrel turned to the others. "That asshole's crazy if he thinks I'm paying him three million."

"What choice do we have?" Walter asked.

"Not paying him, that's the choice we have."

"We're talking about a man's life," Walter said.

"He's negotiating is all he's doing," Natalie said.

"He'd better be," Kestrel said, "because I'm not giving that scumbag three million dollars."

Kestrel looked at Pike. "What do you think?"

Pike was noncommittal. "Let's hear what Newman has to say first."

Ronnie was nervous as she set up the call. She'd warned Newman that if they asked for too much Kestrel might balk and go to the cops. She'd seen him walk from other deals, bigger deals, only because someone had pissed him off. But if Kestrel did walk then it would be Newman's fault, wouldn't it? Not hers or Alex's fault. Newman had come up with the three million dollar figure and he couldn't blame them for a misjudgment he'd made, could he? Maybe that would give her and Alex a way out of this. But there was still the chance that Kestrel would settle on the two million Newman wanted. He was willing to pay a million yesterday. Two million wasn't that much of a jump. Not for a man like him. It was lunch money.

Ronnie made the Skype connection. "I've got him," she said to the others who crowded around the screen to get a look.

What they saw was Martin Newman sitting on a simple wooden chair, the same chair the dummy had sat in before its human version appeared. He held a cell phone. Behind him hung the white sheet that looked gray on the screen. Nothing else in the apartment was recognizable.

"Hello?" Martin said hesitantly.

"Hey, Marty, Barry Kestrel here. Can you see me?"

"Yes, sir, I can. Can you see me?"

"I sure can, Marty." Kestrel's tone was forced, like the coach of a Little League team that was losing. "How are you doing?"

"Okay, Mr. Kestrel, considering." His eyes blinked a lot. He looked distracted, anxious.

"Call me Barry, Marty. You're gonna be fine. We're gonna work this thing out."

"I want to g-g-go home," Newman said stuttering a little. It was a good touch, Ronnie thought, but she hoped he wouldn't overdo it.

"We all want you to come home, Marty. You're like family to us."

Marty looked to his left. "Whatever you said to them just now really pissed them off."

"There's more than one?" Kestrel asked.

Newman sat up tensely as if he'd said something he shouldn't have. "I can't say." His breath was heavy and rapid. Natalie took Walter's hand and held it. Everyone was gripped by Newman's performance, including Pike who looked like he was buying it, too. Ronnie was impressed.

"We're trying to keep the police out of this, Marty," Kestrel said. "For your safety."

Ronnie had told Newman to be sure to say one line at least once, maybe twice: "You should give them what they want, Mr. Kestrel." And, as if on cue, Newman said it. "Then you should give them what they want."

When she looked away from the screen Ronnie saw that Pike was looking at her. She held up her hand and crossed her fingers to suggest how eager she was to safely settle Newman's fate.

Kestrel hesitated. He didn't like being told what to do even by an innocent man whose fate was in his hands. "Three million's too much for us to hide, Marty. It'll raise all kinds of questions."

"Are you saying I'm not worth three million dollars, Mr. Kestrel?"

"Of course you're worth it, Marty," Kestrel said. "Human life is priceless." After a pause he said, "Within reason."

"What if they become violent?"

"Let me do the negotiating, okay?" Kestrel said. He was starting to get impatient.

"I don't want to die," Newman said staring at the camera, not blinking at all now. Natalie let go of Walter's hand when he said this and she turned away from the screen.

Everyone in the room stared at Kestrel. "No one's gonna die, Marty," he said. "Tell them that one point five million is the best I can do without bringing in the authorities."

"I don't think they'll take that."

"I'm trying to help you here, pal." Kestrel said, clearly annoyed now by Newman and how the call was going. "Offer them that and see what they say."

Martin stood up and walked out of the picture. No one in the office spoke. Martin, the understudy, had played his role well. Ronnie would have felt sympathy for the man if he actually existed. After a moment he stepped back into frame and sat down again. "They'll take two."

"Two million?" Kestrel said.

"You got them down from three, Mr. Kestrel."

Ronnie was impressed when Newman said this. He'd raised the payoff from one million to two million and in the process he'd made it sound like a win for Kestrel. The guy wasn't stupid.

"Give them the two, Barry," Natalie said.

"I agree," Walter said.

"Both of you shut up," Kestrel said. He was caught and he knew it, but he wasn't going to give in too easily.

"Give them the two million, Mr. Kestrel, and this will be over," Martin said.

"I'll see what I can do."

"Please, Mr. Kestrel?"

"I said I'll see what I can do."

"They said they'd give you until tomorrow morning at 10 AM to decide," was the last thing Newman said before the screen went blank. Kestrel punched the button on his phone so hard it nearly fell off the desk.

"That was some fine negotiating, Barry," Natalie said.

"Like you could've done any better."

"He looked scared," Walter said.

Kestrel moved to the window and looked out. The sky was darkening and it would rain soon. He turned to Walter. "If I agree to the two million—and I'm not saying I am—how easy would it be to get?"

"No one would bat an eye," Walter said.

Kestrel turned to Pike. "What would you do?" They all waited to hear what Pike would say.

"I'd give them the two million," Pike said.

Everyone, especially Kestrel, was surprised by how unequivocally Pike said this. Ronnie was relieved, but it surprised her, too. Why was he so willing to cave?

— • —

Kestrel pulled Pike into his sanctuary room and made an espresso for himself. "What did you think of Newman?" he asked and, like most people in power, he didn't wait for Pike to answer. "Me, I was surprised," Kestrel said. "I believed the guy. He was too real to be fake. Right? The way he acted, what he said. The whole thing. In the middle of it all I said to myself this sonofabitch really was kidnapped. Didn't you think so?" He didn't wait for Pike to answer this time either. "I was hoping he'd look totally bullshit and this morning I'd have bet you anything that's what would've happened. If I was sure that Newman was involved I could've threatened his ass and ended it all right then and there." Kestrel paused. "But this is the real deal. I know people and I know this. I've gotta pay 'em, don't I?" Kestrel downed his espresso in a gulp and put his coffee cup in the small steel sink for someone else to clean. He left the room.

— • —

When Ronnie got back to the apartment Alex was arguing with Newman, accusing him of hijacking the negotiations like an extra who'd upstaged the star.

"If it was me," Alex said, "I would've been much better than you."

"I am me," Newman said.

"No, you're not, asshole. I don't know who you are, but you're not you."

Ronnie interrupted them. "What matters is that they believed him."

Newman shrugged. "See?" He turned to Ronnie. "I was good, wasn't I?"

Ronnie thought that he was better than good, but she wasn't going to tell him that, not in front of Alex, anyway. She shrugged. "Don't dress for the Tony's," she said, a dig her ex-husband used whenever a critic had said something positive about her work.

"A good actor doesn't cry," Alex said to Newman. "He tries not to cry so that he gets the audience to cry."

Newman thought about this. "That's true. Thank you for that advice, Alex."

"Fuck you," Alex said.

"Bottom line, the call worked," Ronnie said to Alex. "That's all that matters."

But Alex was angry. "It's crazy that we asked for three million," he said. "We should've stuck with the original plan."

Newman shrugged. "I was just doing what you guys do all the time: improvising."

"Not everything we do is improvised," Ronnie said. "No part of this plan was."

"Until you showed up," Alex said.

"I'll bet you anything the man's gonna give us the two million," Newman said.

"We had him at one for sure," Alex said.

"He had you at one," Newman said.

"Fuck you," Alex said again and grabbed his jacket from the back of a chair.

"You watch," Newman said. "In the morning Kestrel will offer us two million."

Ronnie agreed with Newman, but saying it would sound like she was siding with him. To placate Alex, she said, "Maybe he will. Maybe he won't. We'll have to wait and see." She read a text from Kestrel about an errand he wanted her to run.

"Kestrel wants me to pick something up for him in Soho," she said. "Can I leave you two alone here without killing each other?"

Neither man said anything. Ronnie kissed Alex on the cheek and left.

Alex put on his leather jacket.

"Where are you going?" Newman asked him.

"Rehearsal. We have to do everything like we would in a normal week."

"I saw your show last week," Newman said when Alex was at the door.

Alex turned back to Newman. "Which one?"

"Saturday night. You were good."

Alex shook his head. "I sucked Saturday."

"That's some radical stuff you do. How come you hate this country so much?"

"We don't hate this country," Alex said. "It's scumbags like Kestrel we hate. In the crash when his company bottomed out, everybody lost. Except him of course. People like him are too big to fail. Now he's gonna make a fortune selling his company while most people are out there still scraping by. We don't hate America. We're saving it."

Halfway out the door Alex stopped and turned back to Martin. "You should've seen the Friday show," he said. "I was awesome."

— • —

Pike took a seat in the back row of the Jubilee theater and looked to see if Ronnie was standing where she always did: against the back wall of the house. But tonight she wasn't there.

She told him that she never sat in the audience because she fidgeted too much while watching her own work. She'd mouth the lines of a scene, sometimes even saying them aloud along with the actors. "It drives the people sitting near me crazy," she said.

That morning in Kestrel's office Pike thought he saw her doing that same thing during the Skype call. Twice Newman said, "Then you should give them what they want," and both times Ronnie looked like she was mouthing Newman's words along with him. Was she doing that because, like the scenes for Jubilee, she'd written them for him?

After the call, Pike leaned toward believing that Newman really was a victim, not a perpetrator. Newman had struggled to hold himself together during it, clearly upset, stuttering as he spoke and constantly looking off camera at the other person or persons in the room. He seemed genuinely upset by Kestrel's manner that came across as his being more annoyed about the money than concerned about his employee's welfare. Did this mean that Newman had been kidnapped and that Ronnie wasn't involved?

Still, Pike couldn't get Ronnie's reactions during the call out of his mind and he'd come to the theater to talk to her, hoping to see if she'd say or do anything to make him more or, as he hoped, less suspicious of her. But she wasn't at the theater. That alone was unusual for her.

The first four sketches had already been performed. The next scene was the hydrationist sketch that Pike had seen several times before. The audience laughed when Alex walked onstage wearing the large prop with WATER AMBULANCE written on its side. He pointed to an actor lying on the stage floor and yelled to another actor wearing a policeman's hat, "This person needs hydration, Officer Pike!" Alex shook a bottle of soda water and sprayed the actor lying on the stage with it. Just as when Pike had seen it before, when the actor popped up immediately and shook his head, the audience laughed like they always did.

After the show, Pike waited in the dark across the street and watched the cast and crew meet outside the theater. Pike couldn't hear what any of them said, but he didn't need to. They were congratulating themselves on the night's work. They were all happy. Why shouldn't they be? They were young and everything was possible.

Alex moved away from the other actors to answer his phone.

— • —

Ronnie sat at her desk in the Boundary office looking at the files of employees who could possibly be the man in their apartment. She called Alex after the show. "How'd it go?"

"I missed a couple of cues, but once I got into it I was okay." Ronnie was happy that Alex's work distracted him. He sounded calmer, but the show didn't distract him for long. "You find anything about Newman?" he said.

"Not yet."

"Shit."

"I'm going home now. You should go out with the others."

"Why?" Alex said.

"Because everything has to be as normal as possible. Remember?"

"I don't like you being alone with Newman." Ronnie noted that Alex had finally given in to calling the man Newman.

"I can handle him," Ronnie said. "Get a drink with the cast. It'll be better if you're not here."

"I don't trust him."

"I'll have a better chance of figuring the guy out if I'm alone with him. He's different when it's just me and him."

— • —

Pike sat at the window of his East Village apartment that overlooked First Avenue. He poured himself a shot from a bottle of bourbon that Kestrel had given him for Christmas. As soon as he'd unwrapped the gift he went online and found out that it cost over $900. Knowing that almost ruined it for Pike. Until he drank it. It reminded him how on their wedding night he and Claire spent thirty-five dollars on a bottle of champagne and wondered for weeks what else they might have bought with the money instead.

Earlier that night, Pike stood across the street after the show and watched Alex and the other actors come out of the theater. One of the actors yelled to Alex. "You coming with us to Billy's?"

"I can't tonight," Alex said.

"You need some hydration," one of them said and they all laughed.

"Ronnie needs me back at our place," Alex yelled back. Pike watched him wave goodbye to the others and walk east toward Ninth Avenue. The young man looked very much at ease, not at all like someone who was involved in a kidnapping plot or had anything to worry about. Far from suspecting Alex, Pike envied him.

When he got back home Pike re-read the chapter in the Oscar Wilde novel in which the young actress kills herself because of Dorian Gray's treatment of her. It's after this that Gray begins his transition into a monster. He soon realizes that it's his portrait that reflects these changes in him, not his own face that remains innocent and beautiful.

Ms. Rosen, the teacher, chose Pike to give an oral report on the book in Monday night's class. Most of the class was much younger than Pike and he was eager to show them that a middle-aged ex-cop could understand literature as well as they did. Maybe even better because, after all, this book was a mystery. Ms. Rosen seemed to suggest that's why she'd assigned him the book, referring to him with a smile as "Detective Pike". She was right about him thinking like a cop because no matter how much effort he put into concentrating on Dorian Gray's crimes his thoughts returned to another crime, another kidnapping. Not Dorian Gray's and not Martin Newman's, either.

Monica Florio was fifteen years old in 1994. She'd run away from her East Harlem home at least half a dozen times. It was her mother who reported her missing each time. Never her father. The girl claimed that was because her father had sexually abused her since she was seven. Her mother denied this and blamed the accusation on a teenage girl's wild imagination, fueled by too many hormones and too much pot. Pike didn't know whether to believe the child or not. She'd returned home each time, but so do battered wives. But Pike always leaned toward believing the victim, a tendency his co-officers found frustrating.

The fifth time Monica's mother reported her daughter's disappearance was after someone had called her family and claimed that they'd taken her. They demanded a small ransom for her return. The precinct captain had been involved upstate years before in the Tawana Brawley fiasco so he wanted nothing to do with this. Who would kidnap the daughter of a Puerto Rican butcher anyway? For that amount of money? They might take a kid from Park Avenue, but not one from a hundred and twenty-seventh street. Everyone agreed it was a scam, probably staged by Monica herself so she could use the ransom to run away with her boyfriend, a small-time pot dealer. Pike went along with the others in the department and ignored it.

Three weeks later Monica's body was found alongside the tracks of the Metro-North in the Bronx. Everyone had abandoned the girl and even though Claire told him he shouldn't blame himself, Pike did. He was at the station the night Monica's mother burst in and blamed them for her daughter's death. Monica's father stared at the floor while his wife raged. Pike ordered the officers on duty to keep their hands off the woman and let her scream all she wanted. They'd failed her and it was her right to tell them that in any way she chose. Pike went to Monica's funeral, standing in the back of the church in plainclothes. What moved him most was how small her casket was.

Pike stood up, went into the bedroom, opened the safe in the closet and took his pistol from it. He wouldn't let happen to Martin Newman what had happened to Monica Florio.

— • —

Ronnie had spent much of her day going through countless photos of men hoping to find the one pretending to be Martin Newman. But he was too clever to have left a trail. The only way to get information was from the man himself and to do that she'd need to seduce him. Not sexually, but emotionally, dangling the possibility that sex might come later.

He'd read her emails and seen her writing, so he knew that she wasn't an idiot. She couldn't play the damsel in distress right off, either. It'd be more believable if she kept her distance at first, playing the suspicious tough girl role, like she had the night before. She could slowly warm up to him and go from there.

The first thing she needed to know was whether this guy actually believed he'd become the Martin Newman he hijacked. But the character Ronnie created was a parody, little more than a simpleton. Was this guy so desperate to jettison who he really was that becoming Martin Newman would be a step up? Surely, he'd have used the character Ronnie and Alex created only as a starting point and, from what she read of his version of Newman's file, it seemed that's what he did. He'd made his own Martin Newman more interesting and less pathetic than the one she'd concocted. He was more manly, even if in a clichéd way. And he added things to his file that made him sympathetic, too, like a dead wife.

But was this all part of the con? Did a grifter need to believe who he was impersonating? Method actors like Daniel Day-Lewis will speak and think like their characters 24/7 during a film shoot. And if and when this Newman guy finally got his ransom money would he go back to being the person he really was? Or would he continue to live this version of Martin Newman for the rest of his life? Or maybe he'd live as someone else. With a new name and a new history.

Alex's reaction to Newman last night bothered Ronnie. Looking back at it now, it shouldn't have surprised her that Alex questioned her loyalty. In his place she'd probably have done the same thing, although she wouldn't have blurted it out like Alex did. He often spoke before thinking, like a child. It made him a good actor, but a terrible liar. She hoped that wouldn't come back to haunt them.

His apology for having doubted her was sincere. Alex was nothing if not sincere. She was glad, too, that Newman had heard them arguing. She'd use that to persuade Newman that she had an increasing uncertainty about Alex and that there was a growing distance between them.

Walking from the Bedford Street station, Ronnie stopped at a Thai place to pick up some takeout. Newman said in his file that Thai food was his favorite and there was nothing in the apartment to eat. She guessed that he wouldn't order anything in if he were there alone. The deliveryman could be a witness, a chance Newman wouldn't take. Her bringing food to him might soften him up. He looked like a man who liked to eat. Had he lost weight to become Martin Newman?

Newman stood up when she came in with the food. "You surprised me," he said.

"I'm supposed to knock now to get into my own apartment?"

"It's just that I wasn't expecting—"

She was glad that she'd rattled him, his ultra-cool façade evaporating. She put the food on the kitchen counter. "I got us something to eat. You like Thai, right?"

"You saw that in my file."

"There's a good place on the corner."

With his next question Martin slipped back into the pseudo-debonair tone he'd used the night before. "What was Kestrel's reaction to the call?"

"Nothing. Yet." Ronnie flipped open the tops of the cardboard food containers and took some plates from the cupboard.

"He's kind of slow, isn't he?" Newman said.

"Kestrel?"

"Alex."

"Fuck you," she said matter-of-factly.

"Don't get me wrong," Newman said. "I can see why you like him. He's cute, like a puppy you rescue from the pound."

"A puppy who's gonna make you a shitload of money."

"Is that your way of saying Kestrel's giving us the two million?"

She didn't want to tell Newman that she thought Kestrel might give in to his demands. So all she said was, "I gotta warn you, when Kestrel thinks someone's pushing him, he pushes back. Hard."

"I'll take my chances."

"You'll have to, won't you?" Ronnie handed him a fork and a napkin and she put the food on the table. The Martin Newman dummy sat on the floor now, leaning against the wall like a punished child. Ronnie took a six pack out of the refrigerator. "You want a beer?"

Martin hesitated for a second before he said yes, making her think that maybe he wasn't a drinker. That would be another change from the Martin Newman she'd created, a man who found solace in booze. It was the character's alcoholism that would cause him to walk onto the Jubilee stage and begin his own monologue, mistakenly thinking he'd walked into an AA meeting. Ronnie planned that sketch to be Martin Newman's comic introduction to the world, but this asshole in the other room had introduced himself in his own way the night before.

They sat down at the table. Newman put his napkin on his lap and waited to start eating until Ronnie sat down. Someone had taught the guy manners. Was he a rich kid? Working for Kestrel she dealt with way too many trust fund brats. Ronnie stared at Newman in silence as he chewed with his mouth closed—another telling sign—and swallowed.

"What?" Newman asked.

"I know you."

"I'm a research trader at Boundary."

"I don't mean Newman. I mean you. Who are you? We're partners in this now. You can tell me." This was her first shot at playing the gritty dame. Don't waste my time, buster. Tell me the plot of this story you and me are stuck in and do it fast.

But Newman didn't take the bait. "Who is anyone?" he said.

Annoyed by his deflection, Ronnie said, "People are what they do. At least that's what Sartre said." She wanted him to know she was literate. Even if they don't give a shit about a subject, men hate when a woman knows more about it than they do.

"So according to the Existentialists that makes you a kidnapper," Newman said, proving that he was at least as literate as she was. Touché.

"I didn't kidnap anyone," Ronnie said.

"You kidnapped me."

"You're not real," she said.

"The web says I am. Kestrel and the others think I am. Check out my history."

"Your Boundary file, you mean? That's not a history, sweetheart, that's a wish list. Graduated Princeton Summa Cum Laude. Rock climber. Fly fisherman—"

"I didn't write the fisherman thing. That was Alex's idea."

Newman was right. It was. But Ronnie said, "The only things missing are your Olympic gold medals in high diving and your Nobel Prize in economics. Do you really hate who you are so much?"

"What matters is who I am now."

"Sorry to be the one to tell you, but you're the same loser you always were." This was harsh and she regretted saying it as soon as she did. To mitigate it, she said, "We all are."

"I'm not. No one has to be. Not you. Not me. Not anymore."

"That's bullshit."

"People change all the time. They can change anything about themselves that they want to. People change their sex now the way they used to change their socks. Last week a psychiatrist said that people could change their race."

"Don't tell that to Pike," Ronnie said.

"We all come from the same lady in Africa."

"But not from the one in Mississippi."

"I can become whoever I want to be."

Ronnie got the answer she thought she might get. This guy desperately wanted to be someone, anyone, other than himself. A lot of people did. But they accept what they are or at least learn how to live with it. Not this guy. He believed he was the character he'd created. His desperation was so obvious that she almost felt sorry for him. She continued. "You weren't really married, either, were you?"

"Three years."

"To a supermodel, right?"

Newman stopped eating and looked up at her. "My wife died."

"How?"

"A cerebral hemorrhage."

"Is that right?" she asked dismissively. "What was her name?"

"Sophia."

Ronnie rolled her eyes. "What else would it be?"

"She was perfect."

"Perfect?" Ronnie laughed. "That proves she wasn't real."

"Sophia was very real."

For the first time he sounded passionate. Maybe he wasn't lying about his wife. That might be a way into him. So Ronnie changed her tack. "What would Sophia think about you doing all of this?"

"If she was here I wouldn't be doing it."

"Tell me about her."

Newman got up, brought his plate to the kitchen and rinsed it in the sink. "I don't want Sophia involved in this. She wouldn't understand," he said as if she were still alive. As if she were ever alive.

"Then why are you doing it?"

"The money," he said.

"Is that all?"

Newman looked at Ronnie for a moment before he said, "Maybe." He took her plate from the table and brought it into the kitchen where he rinsed it. "What's your motive?" he asked.

Ronnie shrugged. "Same as you. Money." She got up and walked into the kitchen and stood next to him at the sink. She let her shoulder rub against his before stepping away.

Newman wiped the table with a dishrag he'd dampened, something Alex would never have done. "What about revenge?" he said.

"Revenge for what?"

"For your father," Newman said. "He was a plaintiff in the Capital Brands buyout suit, wasn't he?"

This guy had done his research. "A lot of people were."

"Star Accessibility refused to pay his life insurance because they claimed he committed suicide."

How much did this guy know about her? "Think whatever you want," Ronnie said. "I only want the money."

"It had to be something emotional for you to mastermind a kidnapping."

"It's not a kidnapping," she said.

"You say potato."

Ronnie's cell rang. She was happy for the interruption because Newman had pissed her off. He was harder to figure out than she thought he'd be. She didn't recognize the caller's number, but figured it was one of the burners Alex bought to use for the kidnapping.

She answered her cell. She was right; it was Alex. "It's me," he said.

"Hold on, sir," Ronnie said into her phone. "It's Kestrel," she lied to Newman and moved into the other room so he couldn't hear her. "Are you with the guys?" she asked.

"No."

"Where are you?"

"I'm at Newman's place."

"What place?"

"The Maxwell."

"What the fuck, Alex?" She stepped into the hallway, closing the apartment door behind her. She could hear the traffic from the street in the background on Alex's phone. She hoped that meant he hadn't gone into the building yet and she could talk him out of doing that. "What are you doing there?"

"You're working with Newman at home so I figured I'd come here and maybe find something that'll help tell us who he is."

"Does he have an apartment there?"

"5C."

"How are you gonna get into the building?"

"I'm already in."

"How?"

"He left his keys in his jacket pocket."

This was no spur of the moment move. Alex had planned this without telling her. "Where are you now?" she said.

"The mail room in the lobby."

"Did anyone say anything to you?"

"The guard at the desk didn't even look up when I came in. Newman's name is on the box for 5C."

"What if somebody sees you?"

"Nobody sees anybody at a place like this."

He was right, but going there was still a mistake, a big one. "You've got to leave, Alex. Right now."

"I'll call you when I get into the apartment," he said.

"Alex, wait—" but he'd already hung up. Ronnie paced in the hallway. Alex's going there was not a good sign. He was acting stupidly now, emotionally and on his own. But what could she do? He was already there. She sat on the landing's top step and waited for him to call her back. After what seemed like forever, her phone rang. "Where are you now?" she said.

"In his apartment."

"Did anyone see you?"

"Newman's been here."

"He told us that. You didn't have to go there to figure that out."

"Maybe I'll find something that'll tell us who he really is." She could hear him moving through the apartment. "I'm in the living room now," he said. "It's full of books and magazines and shit."

She heard him drop a book on a table. "Do the magazines have address labels on them?" she asked.

"They do."

"What's the name on them?"

"Martin Newman. They're addressed to him here."

The guy pretending to be Newman had subscribed to magazines in Newman's name at The Maxwell. He'd thought of everything.

"I'm in the bedroom," Alex said. "He's got clothes in here. I'm going through his pockets. They're empty."

Ronnie said nothing to Alex about how stupid, how dangerous it was for him to be there. She didn't want to upset him while he was there.

"I'm in the kitchen now." She heard Alex open and shut the flimsy tin cabinets. "There's nothing. Dirty dishes. A packet of paper napkins. Shit like that."

"What about in the refrigerator?"

"A couple of containers of Chinese food and what's left of a pizza. That's all."

"You should get out of there now."

"I'm gonna check out the bathroom first."

Pike stood outside The Maxwell Apartments. He was here against Kestrel's orders so he had to be careful not to call attention to himself. If he could get into Newman's apartment—and that was still a question—he'd check it out. That's all. Maybe he'd find out that the Skype call came from Newman's apartment here where Newman was living safely, having faked his abduction. Maybe the apartment would be empty.

A hundred years ago The Maxwell was a boarding house for single women who came to the city alone. Now it was a collection of apartments that anyone could rent for a week, a month, or longer. There were a few large suites on the top floor, but most were one bedrooms or studios for people in the city for a short stay.

The Maxwell didn't have a doorman, so Pike stood at the entrance as if he were waiting for someone to come out, pretending to be talking on his cell. Two young women came out of the building together. Pike said into his cell, "I'll go back upstairs and get it, okay?" He turned and headed to front door before it closed again, shrugging at one of the young women as if to say, "You know how it goes." She smiled and held the door open for him. No way was an upscale young white woman going to refuse to let a well-dressed, middle-aged Black man into the building.

The young Black guard at the desk stared at his phone. Pike continued his imaginary phone conversation as he passed the guard. "Relax. I'm getting it," he said into his phone. The guard looked up briefly and Pike nodded at him. He punched the elevator button several times as if in a hurry. Seeing that the car was on the seventh floor he took the stairs. The stairwell echoed Pike's steps as he walked up them. The sound reminded him of high school.

He figured that it wouldn't be difficult to abduct someone from a place like The Maxwell. It wasn't like an apartment building where the tenants knew one another. A lot of people in places like this look the other way because they don't want to be seen. Or see. Given what he saw of Newman on the Skype call, he doubted if he'd put up any resistance to someone taking him.

Pike was breathing heavily by the time he got to the fifth floor. He put on a pair of latex gloves while still in the stairwell and then he pushed open the heavy door and walked into the hallway that was thickly carpeted. Prints of famous paintings hung on its walls. He could hear music from one apartment and people arguing in another. He walked toward Apartment C, Martin Newman's home for the last eighteen months. The door to Apartment B opened and a couple walked out. Pike put his hands into his pockets to hide his gloved hands as he passed them. The man was in his forties and wore a dark suit. The woman was much younger and dressed more casually. They looked like a father taking his daughter to a party. They ignored Pike as they walked to the elevator.

"It's just the usual stuff," Alex said to Ronnie. He was in the bathroom now and she could hear him rummaging in the medicine cabinet. "Toothpaste, deodorant, shit like that."

"Get out now."

"There's something here."

"What?"

"On the floor behind the toilet. I'll get it." Ronnie waited while Alex retrieved it. "It's filthy back here." After a few seconds Alex said, "I got it."

"What is it?"

"A pill bottle."

"Anything in it?"

"It's empty."

"Is it Newman's?"

"Most of the label's been scraped off, but they didn't get all of it. It's from a drug store on Second. It looks like it's been sitting back here for a while."

"Take it with you and get out now," Ronnie said.

Then she heard him whisper, "Shit."

"What?"

"Someone's at the door."

Pike stood at the door to 5C. He was relieved that the building hadn't gone tech yet and that there were only two old-fashioned locks on the door. The one closer to the handle was a simple tumbler lock he should be able to open with a curtain pick. The top lock was a Segal deadbolt that would be impossible to open if it were locked, but he wouldn't know if it was locked until he'd opened the bottom one first. He took a curtain pick out of his pocket, slipped it into the bottom lock and moved it back and forth. He was frustrated when it didn't open immediately. He used to be so good at opening locks that his partners always let him do it and even took bets on how long it would take. It had been a long time since he last tried doing this. But after a few more jiggles with the pick, the lock turned, proving he hadn't lost his touch after all. The deadbolt on top was unlocked so Pike opened the door and walked into the apartment.

"You have to get out," Ronnie said to Alex.

"There's only the one door to this place." Alex went silent for a moment. "Shit. The person's in the apartment now. I gotta hide."

"Where?" she said, but Alex didn't answer. Ronnie heard the sound of the shower curtain's rings scratching along a metal rod before Alex hung up.

Ronnie wondered who'd come into the apartment. It was too late to be the cleaning staff. Was it someone breaking in? Or after the call that morning, did Kestrel say to himself, "Fuck it" and tell Pike or someone else to go to the Maxwell and find out whatever they could about Newman? Or it could be Pike doing this on his own the same way he went through Boundary's video files. If Alex were caught in Newman's apartment they were fucked. She and Alex would be, anyway. Newman not so much.

Pike shut the door behind himself. He stood in the same spot where Alex had stood only minutes before. The small apartment was the same as every other one in the building, filled with heavy furniture, its sofa and two chairs upholstered in a dark brown fabric to hide stains. The thick gray curtains were open and much wider than the small window they covered. The view looked to the backs of other buildings and fire escapes. No one came to The Maxwell for its ambience.

Normally Pike would have looked for clues that told him what the person who lived here was like. But any urge to investigate the apartment was quickly overwhelmed by something else he felt: sadness.

What he saw in front of him were ghosts of the people who'd stayed there. Many would've been businessmen who resented that their visit didn't warrant a stay at a more expensive hotel like The Plaza or somewhere hip downtown in Soho. Other tenants used the apartment to meet their lovers. And then there were the men who'd recently gotten divorced or thrown out of their homes and were forced to sit here and consider their sins and wonder where they were going next because, God knew, they sure as hell weren't going to stay in this place a minute longer than they had to.

Pike couldn't bear being in their apartment after Claire died. So he left and rented a room in The Delancey, a transient hotel in the East Village. He had the money for a nicer place, but he felt like he didn't deserve it and The Delancey matched his mood. He shared a bathroom with a musician and his girlfriend, both heroin addicts, and a drag performer named Gossamer who had a cat. As wretched as The Delancey was, it got him away from Claire's ghost which was everywhere in their apartment. Had Martin Newman come here for the same reason? Was this a place to hide from the emptiness he felt in his home after his wife died?

Pike saw the magazines on the sofa. Their labels were addressed to Newman here at the Maxwell. Most were about computers and video games. There were a couple of books, too. One was a graphic novel and the other was a self-help book that told the reader how they could become the person they always wanted to be.

Pike picked up the remote and turned the TV on to see what channel Newman had last been watching. It was PBS. Suze Ormand was talking about retirement investments. The audience, mostly middle-aged couples, looked at one another and nodded like pet birds.

He left the TV on and walked into the kitchen, full of the usual signs left by a man living alone: dirty dishes in the sink and half-eaten takeout food in the refrigerator. It looked as if no one had eaten anything over the last couple of days, the amount of time that the kidnappers claimed to have had Newman.

Pike walked into the bedroom. In its small closet were the usual things you see thirty-year-old men wearing. An Orioles baseball cap hung from a hook, no surprise since Newman had grown up in Baltimore.

He walked into the small bathroom. The light had been left on and nothing he could see in there told him anything special about Newman. The man was a normal guy, nothing more, apart from the fact that someone had kidnapped him and was asking three million dollars for his safe return.

Pike looked at his own reflection in the mirror over the sink. He was no Dorian Gray, that was for damn sure. He looked old. He hoped it was the lights in the bathroom. A neighbor flushed their toilet. There was always the moment in movies when the cop yanks the shower curtain open and exposes the criminal. Or the body. Or nothing. Pike didn't do that. Instead, he turned off the bathroom light and walked back into the living room and sat in one of the large brown chairs.

While Suze Ormand rattled on, Pike picked up the graphic novel. This was another thing that Claire had turned him on to. They weren't just the comic books he'd grown up with. Some were considered literature now. There was a course at the New School about graphic novels that he wanted to take.

Ronnie got a text from Alex on her phone. *He's in the living room.*
She answered with a question. *Is it Pike?*
I think so.
"Shit," Ronnie said aloud and texted: *Get out of there.* When Alex didn't answer she added: *Or stay until he leaves.*
What if he doesn't leave?
Ronnie had no answer for this.
Alex texted: *There's a fire escape in the bedroom.*
After he texted this to Ronnie, Alex slowly made his way from the bathroom into the bedroom. On the TV in the living room some woman was speaking loudly, practically yelling, and Alex hoped her voice would cover any noise he might make.

Pike heard the noise Alex made. He dropped the graphic novel and took his pistol out of its shoulder holster. He went into the kitchen and then into the bathroom where the shower curtain had been pulled open. Had someone been hiding there? Would he have exposed who it was if he'd just yanked the shower curtain open?

He heard the sound of a window screeching open. He tried going into the bedroom, but the door was locked. It was only a simple turn lock in a cheap door so, with couple of hard kicks, Pike splintered the door, entered the room and ran to the window that was open. He leaned out of it and saw the back of someone climbing down the shaky metal fire escape several floors below. The person was wearing a hoodie pulled over their head, making it impossible to tell if it were a man or a woman. Wasn't Alex wearing a hoodie like this when he saw him in the street after the show?

"Stop!" Pike yelled, but the person kept going down the fire escape. Pike didn't even know why he'd yelled that. Whoever it was wasn't going to stop and there was no way Pike was going to squeeze through the narrow window opening and chase him down the fire escape. He thought about running down to the lobby, but the fire escape led to the alley, not the street, and he'd lose time trying to find his way into the alley. The intruder would be gone long before Pike got there. Besides, doing all that would call attention to apartment 5C, the tenant in it, and himself, and that was the last thing he wanted to do.

Pike holstered his pistol and walked quickly through the apartment, looking at it with new eyes. Someone had been in it the whole time he was here. Were they really hiding in the shower? God, his detective instincts sucked now. He shut the TV off and put the books and magazines back on the sofa where he'd found them. He turned off the lights, walked out and shut the door behind him. No one was in the hallway to see him. He took off his gloves as he walked down the stairs and into the lobby where the guard was still on his phone, unaware of anything happening around him.

Ronnie waited for Alex's call on the apartment landing. If she didn't hear from him in the next few minutes, would that mean he'd been caught by whoever was in the apartment? She waited; it was all she could do. Call me, Alex, she said to herself. Call me, Alex. Call me. Please. Call me.

Finally, her cell rang.

"I got out down the fire escape," Alex said.

"Did he see you?"

"Maybe the back of me."

"Did he recognize you?"

"I don't think so." Alex was breathing heavily.

"Come back now." Ronnie hung up and walked back into the apartment.

Martin looked at her. "Was that Kestrel calling about the payoff?"

"He's not gonna talk about that to me. That was about some people in London I have to buy gifts for," she said. "I've gotta do that now."
She went into the bedroom and shut the door.

Pike went home and poured himself a shot of Kestrel's bourbon. He drank it standing up, poured a second shot and sat down with it. Pike thought that the person he saw climbing down the Maxwell fire escape was Alex Ryan. He hadn't seen his face and he remembered hearing Alex tell his castmates that he couldn't have a drink with them because he had to go home to help Ronnie. But the man he saw was Alex's size and he was wearing a dark hoodie like the one he remembered Alex wearing outside the theater. But didn't everyone under forty wear hoodies these days?

A part of Pike didn't want it to be Alex that he saw. If it was, then it meant that Ronnie was involved, too. Would that be a surprise? A disappointment maybe, but not a surprise.

Ronnie's involvement would mean that Newman was in on it, too, because people like Ronnie aren't violent. Everyone's capable of doing surprising things, but Pike was certain that violence was not in Ronnie's playbook.

There was another possibility. Maybe there were real kidnappers, professionals who were holding Ronnie and Alex hostage along with Newman, threatening her and Alex unless they helped them carry out their plan. From the first time the kidnapper called, Ronnie was uncharacteristically nervous and tongue-tied in both Pike's office and Kestrel's. Was she reacting or was she acting?

His instincts as a cop told him he should go to Kestrel and tell him what he saw at The Maxwell. But if he were following his instincts he'd have reported the kidnapping to the FBI Monday morning after the first call. But he didn't, not on Monday, not in the two days since and he knew that he wouldn't tonight, either.

Pike decided to find Ronnie in the morning and tell her what he suspected. But what would he do if she admitted being behind the scheme? Would he turn her in to Kestrel? If he did, Kestrel wouldn't pay the ransom and he'd make sure none of this was ever made public. The Salient deal would go through, but after the deal went through Kestrel would get his revenge on Ronnie and Alex. It would be brutal.

He decided to do nothing. After all, in spite of all his suspicions, Pike didn't really know anything.

— • —

Ronnie came out of the bedroom when she heard Alex enter the apartment. "Where have you been?" she asked, acting for Newman's sake as if she hadn't spoken to Alex on his cell while he was at The Maxwell.

Alex figured out what she was doing. "I was at The Maxwell."

Hearing this upset Newman. "Why would you do that?" he asked.

"Because I wanted to."

This was the first time Ronnie had seen Newman angry. His cavalier criminal act disappeared. "What – what if someone saw you?"

Alex ignored Newman's question and pointed at him. "This asshole is living there," he said to Ronnie

"I told you I was. How'd you get in?"

Alex pulled Newman's keys out of his pocket and dangled them. "You should be more careful," he said, and tossed the keys to Newman who tried to catch them, but fumbled and dropped them onto the floor.

"Nice catch," Alex said.

Ronnie was upset that Alex had gone to the Maxwell, but she couldn't rebuke him, not in front of Newman. "Did anyone see you?" she asked.

"Someone came into the apartment when I was there."

"Shit," Ronnie said as if she didn't already know this.

"Who?" Newman asked, upset.

"I'm not sure."

"Was it Pike?"

"Maybe," Alex said.

This upset Newman even more. "Did he see you?"

"It's a tiny apartment."

"Did he recognize you?" Ronnie said.

"No."

"How can you be sure?" Newman asked.

"Because I snuck out the fire escape and by the time he got the bedroom door open and looked out the window I was gone."

"I don't like this. I don't like it at all," Newman said. He was sounding like the anxious character that he'd played that morning on the Skype call.

"What was Pike doing there anyway?" Alex asked Ronnie.

"Didn't Kestrel tell him not to investigate?" Newman said before she could answer.

"He's a cop," Ronnie said. "It's what he does. Or maybe Kestrel changed his mind and told him to check the place out. I don't know. Pike already admitted that he asked other people at Boundary about you." She said "you" instead of "Newman" so that Newman would think she was beginning to see him as the person he wanted her to believe he was.

Alex went into the kitchen and took a beer out of the refrigerator. "Are you sure he didn't recognize you?" Ronnie asked him again.

"Who can be sure of anything now?" Alex took a swig and sat on the sofa.

"We'll find out tomorrow if he did or not," Newman said. And he was right. All they could do now was wait and see.

But Alex wouldn't let it go. He waved his beer bottle at Newman. "Why'd you get the place there three months ago anyway? You didn't know we were gonna kidnap Newman. We didn't even know it three months ago. Sure, you saw him in the Boundary files and in our notes about the character we were creating for Jubilee, but you didn't know anything about the kidnapping being real. You couldn't because it wasn't real then."

Ronnie had wanted to ask Newman the same questions all along, but more seductively, not brandished like Alex's accusations. Still, Alex's question was a good one. If Newman got the apartment three months ago, long before they'd ever considered doing the kidnapping for real, did it mean that whoever this guy was wanted to live an imaginary character's life? To become Martin Newman? Was he insane?

Before Newman could answer Alex's questions, Alex said, "Maybe all this is a sign."

"Of what?" Ronnie asked.

"That we should pack the whole thing in."

"Why would we do that?" Newman asked Alex.

"Because Pike was there tonight. It was crazy for you to get that place."

"By living there I give your story validity, Alex," Newman said.

"We don't need your fucking validity," Alex said and moved toward Newman threateningly.

Newman moved quickly away from Alex, and Ronnie stepped in front of Alex and put her hands on his shoulders. "Calm down," she said.

"You watch," Alex said pointing his bottle at Newman. "This guy, whoever he is, is gonna fuck us over."

"I'm the only thing keeping this all together. And keeping you both out of jail." Newman was more confrontational now that Ronnie was standing between them.

Alex waved Neman off, took another drink of his beer and looked at Ronnie. "What did Kestrel say about the money?"

"He'll decide in the morning."

"It's too much," Alex said and pointed to Newman. "I told him that but, no, he had to keep upping the number. Two million. Three million. Why didn't you ask for fifty million?"

Newman only said, "He'll give us the two million."

"So what then? We split it three ways?" Alex said.

"Two ways," Newman said. "Half for you, half for me."

"Fuck that," Alex said, "and fuck you too." Again, Alex made a move toward Newman, but Ronnie grabbed Alex by the arm and pulled him away. Alex was strong for his size and he was fueled by a rage that she'd never seen in him before.

"Stop it, Alex. All we were going to get was one million anyway."

"I don't like this," Alex said looking back and forth from Ronnie to Newman. "None of it."

This was the first time Ronnie had sided with Newman and she was afraid that Alex might believe what he'd accused her of the night before: that she and Newman were in on this together. Alex finished his beer, slammed the bottle on the kitchen counter and walked to the door.

"Where are you going?" Ronnie asked him.

"Out."

"Out where?"

"Out there."

Ronnie followed him into the hallway. "Wait."

He stopped halfway down the flight of stairs. "We need something to protect ourselves."

"From what?"

Alex pointed up to the apartment's open door. "From him. I'm not letting that asshole fuck this up."

Ronnie followed him down the stairs to the next landing. "I can handle him."

"How?"

"Go somewhere and calm down."

"I'm gonna get something to protect us."

"What?"

Alex stopped midflight. "A gun."

"What are you talking about, a gun?"

"I don't trust him."

"We don't have to trust him, Alex. We can use him."

"You use him all you want. Me, I'm getting a gun."

In the building's entryway Ronnie grabbed his arm. "We agreed that there'd be no violence."

"We also said that there'd be no victim and guess what?" Alex said. "He's sitting upstairs in our apartment right now." He yanked his arm away from her and opened the front door of the building.

"Where are you gonna get a gun?"

"Seriously?" Alex asked with an expression Ronnie didn't remember seeing on his face before. "This is America," he said and he walked down the stoop.

"Alex, stop," Ronnie said, but he didn't and he disappeared around the corner. She was tempted to run after him. But maybe it was better to let him go and wear his frustrations off. Who would sell him a gun anyway? He looked like a high school kid.

Ronnie walked back upstairs and into the apartment, happy that Newman had heard them arguing again. She could use that.

"Where's he going?" Newman asked.

"Who knows?" No way was she going to tell him that Alex went out looking for a gun.

"He's irrational," Newman said.

How rational are you, you digital Peter Pan?, Ronnie thought. Instead she said, "What do you expect? He's an actor. In college he played Tony in *West Side Story* and now he thinks he's a gangster. Most actors ever had a real gun pointed at them they'd shit themselves. None of it's real." She sat down. "Like when my father died," she said. "He's lying there dead, his last breath barely out of his mouth and what do I do? I reach over to close his eyes because that's what everybody in the movies does." She wasn't lying about having done this and the emotion in her voice was real. "But you know what? It doesn't work like that. Dead people's eyes don't slide shut because the director says they should. They stay open so you have to push them closed and even then they don't close all the way. Of course on the big screen Meryl or Denzel wave their hands over a dead person's face and their eyes shut like magic. So there I am, a fifteen-year-old girl, standing over my dead father's body thinking I fucked up because my father's eyes didn't close like they do in the movies. It's all bullshit." She hated using her father's death as a tool to get closer to Newman, but it worked.

"I'm sorry about your father."

Ronnie waved off his sympathy.

"I still can't figure out why you and Alex are a couple", Newman said.

The bluntness of what he said surprised her. "Why is anyone a couple?" she asked. She wondered this every time she saw any two people together.

"He's not smart enough for you."

"No one's smart enough for me. Oh, wait, I forgot. The guy should always be smarter than the girl. That's enlightened."

"I didn't mean it like that."

She knew he didn't, but she said that to keep him off balance. Next she threw him a line by saying, "I don't know. Maybe you're right. Maybe Alex isn't smart enough to do any of this without screwing it up. Maybe I'm not." Then she looked at Newman. "You're the only one around here who knows what he's doing."

He looked surprised when she said this, but he recovered quickly. "I'm no different from you."

"Are you kidding? Look at yourself. You figured us out. You're totally together. I've been watching you." Was this too obvious? His reaction to what she'd just said told her that it wasn't. What compliment is ever too much for someone? Especially a man. Ronnie kept going. "Me, I'm a wreck. I never did anything like this before. I was always the good girl. Never in trouble. I laugh at Alex for thinking that acting is real, but look at me. I'm no better. I'm gonna oversee a big time Wall Street kidnapping and make a ton of money. But I'm full of shit." She sat down and held her face in her hands, like she was on the verge of tears. "Maybe Alex is right. Maybe we should call the whole thing off now."

Martin's answer proved that she'd hit her target. "No," he said, "we finish it."

She looked up at him. "See? Listen to yourself. 'We finish it.' You're certain. Like ice."

"It's who I am."

Jesus, thought Ronnie, did he really just say that? "It's who I am?" His pompous certainty made her want to laugh. If this were a play about the Martin Newman character she couldn't have written any-thing more absurd or fitting for him to say. This idiot believed he was the Martin Newman he'd created and what she was saying to him now confirmed that to him. He was so fucked up.

"You're right about Alex," she said, hoping to pull Newman in more. "He scares me. He's like a kid. He could do something that screws this whole thing up."

Ronnie wasn't lying when she said this. Alex had changed over the last couple of days. He'd stupidly gone to Newman's apartment at The Maxwell where he might've been caught or at least recognized. He came home ready to fight with Newman. Now he was out on the street trying to buy a gun. "We've gotta keep him under control."

"How?" Newman asked.

She looked at Newman as if she were interested in him in more than a practical way. The look lasted for only a second, but it doesn't take any longer than that. Men are the same as any audience. Always leave them wanting more.

"I need your help, Martin," she said, using his first name on pur-pose. "Will you help me?"

He nodded. "That's why I'm here."

"I thought you were only here for the money."

"Mostly."

She looked at him in a way that said she understood what he was implying about the two of them. "I can keep Alex from doing anything else stupid," she said, "but the one thing I do know is that I can't finish this without you." She stared at him. The guy was proba-bly getting a hard-on.

"What?" he asked.

"You and me, we met before, didn't we?" she said. "There's some-thing about you that's memorable." This was her biggest lie yet. The whole point of Martin Newman was that he wasn't memorable. "Who are you?" she said.

"I'm Martin Newman."

"It's just you and me here now. You can tell me who you really are."

He smiled. "I'm Martin Newman."

This guy was stronger—and stranger—than she thought, but she didn't give up. "What can I do to you now? We're in this together. We're partners, you and me. Or maybe you already have a partner. Is that it? Do you? Have a partner?"

He answered as if her question had insulted him. "I don't need a partner."

"You're doing this all by yourself?"

Newman quickly recovered his pomposity. "All by myself."

"That's what I thought," Ronnie said. This guy was a piece of work.

"And you think Kestrel's gonna give us the two million, don't you?" he said.

Her cell rang before she could respond. It was Alex. She answered and spoke before he could say anything. "Where are you?" she asked.

He told her. She hung up and said to Newman, "I gotta go calm Alex down and keep him from doing something stupid." Before she left the apartment she smiled at Newman in a way that he could read as her being torn, confused by both her old feelings for Alex and her new ones for him.

— • —

Alex was waiting for Ronnie at a Starbucks. She sat down at his table and asked him, "You didn't get a gun, did you?"

He shook his head. There was an empty espresso cup on the table and the way Alex jiggled his feet and tapped his fingers suggested that he'd had at least one more before that one. "Do you want to frisk me?" he asked.

"Don't be stupid."

Alex played with the small cup. "I can't be around that guy. He does something to me."

"That's what he wants, so you can't give in to him. If we play him right, we'll have no problems."

"You learn anything new about him?"

"The good thing about people like him is that they're easy to manipulate. I'm getting on his side, warming up to him. He thinks he's changing my allegiance from you to him."

"Is he?"

"Don't be ridiculous. It's you and me. Like it always was. Like it always will be."

"When this is all done," Alex said, "we should get out of here and get a new place. Or maybe even go to LA like we were talking about."

"We can't do that, Alex, at least not for a while." It wasn't the first time she had to remind him that they couldn't spend any of the money for a long time after they got it. If they got it.

"I'm not talking anywhere huge. A million bucks doesn't get you hardly anything in New York, but just someplace newer, something nicer." Alex held up his phone. It was his own, not one of the burners he got for the con. "Look." On the phone was a photo of an apartment. "See this place?" he said. "No one would know if we moved there."

"We're not doing that."

"Check it out."

Ronnie turned away from his phone. "I'm not even gonna look at it."

"I went there today."

"Why would you do that?"

"It's got like a garden in the back."

"Did anyone see you there?"

"Only the real estate agent."

"Jesus Christ, Alex, you talked to a real estate agent? Did you give them your name?"

Alex shrugged. "I guess."

"You guess?" Ronnie said. "You give a real estate agent your name it's like they tattoo it on their arm. How many times do I have to tell you we can't spend any of the money?"

"This place isn't that much."

"It doesn't matter how much it is."

"What about your mother?"

"No one's gonna know if we move her. For you and me, it's different. Kestrel will be looking at everything we do. Everyone will."

"Newman gets to spend his money."

"That's his call, not ours. Once he deletes himself he'll be untraceable."

"What if he still wants you after he gets his money?"

That was a good question, one Ronnie didn't have an answer for yet. "I'll deal with that when the time comes," she said. "But you've gotta promise me you won't spend any of it, not for a while."

"Not even for a ring or something else for you?"

Alex was sweet but, given the situation, dangerously so. "Nothing. Not for at least a year."

"Six months."

Ronnie figured she'd compromise to calm Alex down. Or at least make it look that way now. "Okay," she said, taking his hand. "Six months. Maybe we can get a new apartment then." This was a lie, but she gave him a smile to convince him otherwise. "You watch," she said. "Six months will go by in no time."

Feeling that he'd won, Alex smiled and said, "Deal."

Ronnie had just worked Alex the same way Kestrel worked people he wanted to take advantage of. But what else could she do?

Out of his pocket, Alex took the plastic pill bottle he found in The Maxwell and put it on the table. "This is what I found."

Ronnie picked it up. A part of the label was still attached. She could read several digits of the prescription number and the address of the pharmacy on Second Avenue that had filled it.

"If it's his, it could be what we need," she said and put the small plastic container into her pocket. "I'll take it to this drug store tomorrow and see what I can find out." She took Alex's hand and squeezed it. "It's great that you got it."

Alex smiled. "It was good that I went there, right?"

"Absolutely," she said, still thinking that his going there was crazy. But she needed to keep him happy and there was no point in badgering him about it now.

"Six months," Ronnie said, "and then you and me, we can live it up."

By the time they got back to the apartment Newman had fallen asleep on the sofa. He lay on his stomach. His mouth was open and he snored lightly like a child, looking unbothered by anything happening around him.

Alex stood over Newman and stared at him. Ronnie took his hand. "Come in here and fuck me and I don't care if he hears it. I want him to hear it," she said and pulled him into the bedroom. She hoped that sex with Alex would calm him down and remind them both what everything was like before any of this happened and what it would continue to be like if it all went well.

THURSDAY

The pharmacy where the prescription had been filled was one of the few independent ones remaining in the city. Ronnie walked to the rear of the store where the raised counter was a leftover from the time when the fatherly druggist would look down on his customer from a professorial, but concerned, height.

Ronnie pretended to be looking for something in the cold medicine section as she watched the pharmacist, a woman in her fifties, hand a prescription to an elderly woman. A man about thirty years old assisted the pharmacist, taking orders from her. There was an odd dynamic between them. Was she his boss? His mother? Both?

Ronnie approached the raised counter and held the pill bottle up so the pharmacist could see it. "Is there any way I can find out who this belongs to?"

The woman took the bottle from Ronnie with a surprising roughness and examined it. "It's not yours?"

"No, ma'am, it's not. That's why I asked if—"

The woman shook her head. "I can't refill it or give you any information about it."

"But you did fill it once, right?"

"That's our name and address on the bottle." She didn't end her line with "you idiot", but her tone implied it.

"Could you at least tell me when it was filled?" If Ronnie knew it had been filled sometime over the last few weeks that meant it might be Newman's. If it had been lying on the bathroom floor any longer then it'd be no help.

"I can't tell you that, either," the pharmacist said.

But her assistant looked over. "We only starting using those new bottles about three months ago," he said.

The woman turned sharply to him. "We're not allowed to give any information to anyone other than the person it was prescribed to." She turned back to Ronnie. "That's the law."

Ronnie nodded. "Of course," she said. "I understand. Thank you anyway." The news that the prescription had been filled within the last three months gave Ronnie hope. She asked the pharmacist's assistant, "Is there a coffee shop near here?" That was like asking if there was a bus in the city.

"There's a Starbucks across the street," the man said, pointing at it through the pharmacy's front window. Of course he could have been pointing in any direction and he would've been right.

"I guess I'll go over there now," Ronnie said, smiling at him. "I need my caffeine fix."

In the Starbucks Ronnie devised a new plan for how the pay-off would be delivered. Alex and she had already worked it out, but Newman's appearance changed everything. At one point they'd considered using Bitcoins, but their value was too volatile. Instead, they settled on establishing bank accounts under false names where they'd tell Kestrel to send the ransom money. The guy who ran Nerd Nation, where Alex worked, had spent eighteen month in prison for hacking and now worked as a consultant for the feds and some banks. Alex told him he was writing a play about a crime like that and needed details to make it real. His boss happily showed Alex how easy it was to hide accounts. Alex had convinced Ronnie the plan was foolproof, but since Newman's arrival she'd begun to doubt Alex's knowledge and his ability to pull any of this off. She had to make sure Newman didn't disappear with the money himself. Of course if he was in love with her he wouldn't, but she wasn't going to give him the chance.

It looked like the young pharmacist wasn't going to come see if she'd gone to the Starbucks. Ronnie would have to go back to the store later when the older woman wasn't there and try again with someone else who worked there. But as she was about to leave, she saw the young guy from the drug store standing at the door looking around the room. She smiled and waved to him. When he came over to her table she asked him to sit down.

His name was Bobby Lieberman and Ronnie asked him about his job, where he went to college and what someone has to study to become a pharmacist. She was fascinated by everything he said. It turned out the older woman was Bobby's stepmother. She'd met his late father when she was a customer being treated for irritable bowel syndrome. "What a way to meet someone," Ronnie said and they both laughed. Bobby was flattered by Ronnie's interest in him. It wasn't different from how she'd worked Newman the night before, except that this time she felt bad about what she was doing.

"I'm not trying to refill somebody else's prescription so I can get drugs."

"My stepmother has to be careful," Bobby said. "You'd be amazed how people try to trick us into giving them stuff."

"I wouldn't be surprised by anything an addict does," Ronnie said. "It's my brother. He's been trying to get clean for five years, but I never know." She took the pill bottle from her pocket and put it on the table. "I found this in his stuff yesterday and I wanted to know what it was for."

Bobby picked up the small container and saw that part of the label had been scraped off.

As he examined it, Ronnie said, "I don't even know if it's Tony's— that's my brother. It was in his coat pocket, but it could be someone else's, somebody who's getting stuff for him. Or maybe he took it from someone so they wouldn't use anymore. Someone he's sponsoring." Ronnie was trying not to cry. Like Alex had told Newman, it's more powerful when the actor does all they can not to cry. "I want to believe him, Bobby, I really do, and I want to help him," she said as she put her hand on Bobby's. "But first I have to know if he's using again."

Bobby looked at Ronnie's hand on top of his and then at the partial label on the pill bottle. "I'll check it out for you," he said. "It might have enough numbers still on it for that."

"Would you do that?"

"You can't tell my stepmother or even come into the store again for a few days." He put his other hand on top of Ronnie's, making for him what she guessed was probably the most romantic gesture of his life.

"Of course not," Ronnie said, removing her hand from under his to wipe her eyes. She gave him the number of a burner she'd bought in a liquor store that morning. "Promise you'll call me as soon as you find anything out?"

The expression on Bobby's face looked a lot like Newman's the night before when Ronnie told him that she couldn't continue the scam without his help.

"I'll call you as soon as I know anything." Bobby stood up. "I gotta get back."

Ronnie hugged him. "You're an angel. Maybe we could go out to a movie or something sometime."

"I'd like that," Bobby said and he walked out of the store. On the street he stopped and looked back at her quickly through the shop's window as if to convince himself that Ronnie was there and what had just happened really did happen.

She hated leading the guy on like that, but what choice did she have? Whatever Bobby found out about the pill bottle might be exactly what she needed.

— • —

Pike got to Boundary early because he needed to talk to Ronnie about the kidnapping. He hoped that her answers would tell him whether she was involved or not. But when he got there she wasn't at her desk. He went to his own office for an hour before going to Kestrel's office where the other three were waiting for the kidnapper's call. Ronnie still hadn't shown up. From what Natalie and Walter were asking Kestrel, it was obvious that he hadn't told them if he'd decided to pay the two million dollar ransom for Newman or not.

Ronnie finally came into the office carrying a Bloomingdale's bag, a gift for one of Kestrel's clients.

Pike nodded at her. "Morning."

"Hey," Ronnie answered him, smiling, and put the brown shopping bag on the floor next to Kestrel's desk. She didn't look as if she was worried that Pike had discovered anything the night before. So maybe he was wrong. Maybe it wasn't Alex he saw at The Maxwell. Maybe he'd gone home to Ronnie like he told his friends he was going to do.

The caller was late again. "Where the hell is this guy?" Kestrel said.

"Maybe something's happened," Shaw said.

"The first thing this scumbag should do with his money is buy himself a watch."

The phone rang, but Kestrel waited. He answered it on the fourth ring. "This is Barry Kestrel."

It was not the modulated voice of the kidnapper. It was Martin Newman. "Hey, Mr. Kestrel, it's Martin." He quickly added "Newman" as if any other Martin might be calling now.

Kestrel looked to Pike before saying, "Hey, Marty. How's it going?"

Pike thought the kidnappers were smart to use Martin. It surprised Kestrel, forcing him to speak directly to the man who was going to bear the result of whatever decision he made in the next few minutes.

"These guys—I mean these people—are waiting to hear your decision about the money," Newman said. "So am I." His voice quavered. He sounded even more nervous than he did the day before.

Everyone waited for Kestrel's decision. How would the kidnappers—and Newman himself—react if it were less than the two million they demanded?

After a pause, Kestrel spoke. "We'll give them the two million."

If a room could sigh, this one did. Natalie walked to the window and Walter sat down. Ronnie let out a deep breath and smiled at Pike as if to say, "Thank God it's over." Pike saw relief in her face. But relief for what? Relief that Newman was going to be safe? Or relief that Kestrel had agreed to give her and her cohorts the full two million?

"That's very kind of you, Mr. Kestrel," Newman said.

"What do they want me to do next?" Kestrel asked him.

"They'll email you instructions for the delivery."

"When?"

"Later this morning."

"Tell them I want to get this thing over with. ASAP."

"I can't wait 'til I get out of here, Mr. Kestrel."

"Yeah, us too," Kestrel said and he leaned over his desk and ended the call. No one said anything until Kestrel looked up from his desk as if he was surprised to see the others still there. "I'll let you know when I get their email."

Natalie and Walter left. Pike planned to follow Ronnie and talk to her. But Kestrel grabbed his arm and said, "I need you to take me uptown."

— • —

"Cash?" Alex said. "You want the payoff delivered in cash?"

Alex and Newman both reacted differently to Ronnie's revised plan for the payoff. Alex was upset; Newman unsure.

Ronnie handed Alex a piece of paper. "I wrote everything down."

Alex grabbed the page and waved it without even looking at it. "You can't be serious."

"I worked it all out."

Newman reached for the piece of paper Alex held. "Let me see."

But Alex held onto it. "Fuck off."

"Give it to him," Ronnie said and Alex tossed it in Newman's direction and it fluttered to the floor. Newman picked it up and read it.

Alex paced the small room. "Walking through New York with a bag full of money? That's bullshit."

"That's how we're doing it," Ronnie said.

"I set up a dozen bank accounts in phony names," Alex said.

"And you created a fictional Martin Newman who didn't exist," Ronnie said and pointed to Newman. "Would you like me to introduce you to him?" Alex could say nothing to that. But she had to be careful how she reacted to Alex's anger. She wanted to give Newman hope that she and Alex were continuing to drift further apart over this, but not so much that Alex believed it. "We're doing it in cash," Ronnie said.

"It's bush league," Alex said.

"It is risky," Newman said.

"See?" Alex pointed to Newman. "Even this douchebag thinks so."

"You know another reason why we're doing it this way?" Ronnie said.

"Why?" asked Alex.

Ronnie pointed to Newman. "*Because* of him. This guy knows computer shit a lot better than you. We do it on the computer and guess what happens? The money—our portion of it anyway—disappears. And where does it end up?" She pointed to Newman, hoping he understood why she was making him out to be the villain. "In his pocket, not ours."

"I wouldn't do that," Newman said.

Ronnie scoffed. "Right. We do this in cash. Cash I can hold in my hands and count out on this table when we get it back here: one for you and one for us. That's the only way I know it's gonna happen right."

Alex grinned when Ronnie showed this distrust of Newman. At the same time Newman looked happy that she'd told Alex that things were going to go her way and not his. Ronnie was juggling everything like crazy, but she hadn't dropped any of the balls. Not yet.

"She has a point," Newman said. "Doing it on the computer is dangerous. I could probably clean up our trail, but you can never be certain. There's always someone out there looking for stuff like this. Cash is cleaner. More old school, but that might be a good thing especially since we have someone on the inside telling us what they're going to do."

"And we're going to ask for it in Euros," Ronnie said.

"How come?" Alex asked.

"Because the biggest American bill is a hundred dollars," she said, "and the biggest Euro is five hundred and worth almost a thousand dollars. That way the two million will fit into one backpack. And the Euros will confuse them. They'll probably think we're Russians or something. Kestrel hates the Russians even more than he hates the Chinese. The more confused he is, the better."

Alex finally bought what she was telling him. "Okay."

Ronnie was relieved that he saw it her way. She could still work him when she needed to. She looked at Newman. "What about you?"

"I'm good."

Ronnie continued. "The payoff is outlined on those two pages."

This time Alex looked at the pages. "It's complicated."

"It has to be," Ronnie said. "Like I said before: we have to act as if we have no idea what they're going to do. We have to make it look like we think they might try to do something to catch us during the payoff—like send someone after us. We know they're not gonna do that, but we can't act like we know that. It's like what I told you before the Skype call. We have to behave like we haven't read the script."

Ronnie looked at Newman. "You understand what that means?"

Newman nodded. "Of course."

"I'm going back to the office now." She handed Alex a page. "E-mail Kestrel these instructions in five minutes. It's the first part of the payoff plan."

Newman looked at the plan. "Who are we telling them we want to deliver the money?"

— • —

"Me?" Ronnie said, looking quickly from Kestrel to Pike and the others in the office and shaking her head. "Oh, no, sorry. Not me. No way. I'm not delivering any money to anybody."

The email to Kestrel made it clear that they wanted Kestrel's assistant to deliver the ransom. Pike watched Ronnie closely. If she were involved it would make sense that the kidnappers demand that she carry the money. She'd make off with the money more easily that way.

"No way, no how," Ronnie said, restating her refusal.

"Shut up and listen for a second." Kestrel read the printout aloud. "Tomorrow morning your assistant will take the cash to NYU's Washington Square campus."

Pike knew that both Ronnie and her boyfriend went to NYU. They'd know the area well.

Kestrel looked at Ronnie. "They specifically want you to do it."

"I don't give a shit what they want," she said.

Kestrel ignored Ronnie and kept reading. "When she gets there she will go to the Heidinger Business School building where she will find a notice on the first floor message board with the word Newman written on it. On the back of that message she will find further instructions to follow." Kestrel looked up. "It's smart," he said, showing the printed instructions to Pike. "They don't give any more information than they have to."

"It's clever, too, that they want the money in Euros," Walter said.

"Is anybody listening to me?" Ronnie said. "I'm not taking any money to anyone anywhere."

"Of course you're not," Natalie said.

Ronnie turned to her and said, "Thank you, Ms. Jenkins."

Ronnie's reaction seemed over the top to Pike, but the others in the room were buying it. Walter came to her defense. "You realize that we're liable if anything happens to Ms. Hewitt," he said to Kestrel.

"Nothing's going to happen to her," Kestrel said.

"Because I'm not doing it, that's why."

"You don't and I'll fire your ass."

"You can't fire someone for not delivering a ransom, Barry," Natalie said.

"Why not?"

"For one thing it's not part of her job description."

"She works for me. I decide what her job description is."

"HR would launch an investigation," Walter said.

"Fuck HR," Kestrel said. "They're not going to know about any of this." He turned to Ronnie and said, "That's what wrong with you Millennials. You're spoiled. Should I call up your mommy and daddy and ask them what they think about your doing this? Maybe they can tell you how special you are and give you a gold star if you do it right."

"Don't insult her," Natalie said.

Kestrel sensed that he was alone on this. So he used his fallback method of persuasion. Money. "I'll make it worth your while."

"There's not enough money in the world to make me do it," Ronnie said and turned to Pike. "Tell him it's too dangerous."

Before Pike could say anything, Kestrel turned to him. "What do you say, Detective?"

Pike looked at Ronnie. "It's up to Ms. Hewitt if she wants to do it."

"Do you think she'd be safe?" Natalie asked.

In any other case Pike would have said no, that Ronnie shouldn't get involved in the payoff. But by now he thought there was a better than even chance that she was involved in the scheme. And even if she wasn't involved, the kidnappers wouldn't do anything to harm her. They weren't killers. Whoever they were, they were small-time. All they wanted was the cash.

"As long as she stays in public places and does exactly what they ask her to," Pike said. Ronnie looked surprised by his answer.

"Why wouldn't she do that?" Kestrel said.

"Because I'm not doing it, that's why," Ronnie said.

Kestrel softened his tone. "I know we're asking you to do a lot here, Veronica, so why don't you take a few minutes to think about it?"

But before anyone could say anything else Heidi opened the door and stuck her head into the room. Everyone quickly shut up.

Off their awkward stares, Heidi said, "I'm sorry for interrupting like this, Mr. Kestrel, but Ms. Hewitt wasn't answering her line and everybody's waiting for you downstairs."

Five minutes later Ronnie and the others were in the second floor cafeteria with fifty or sixty other Boundary employees at Shelby's baby shower. Middle-of-the-road champagne was served in plastic glasses and the employees helped themselves to *samosas, pakoras* and other appetizers from a nearby Indian restaurant. Corny pop songs about family and love played over the loudspeaker from a track that had been recorded years ago and was dragged out for every event that Boundary threw, from wedding showers to memorials. The songs were invariably ironic or inappropriate and often both.

Ronnie stood on one side of the room and looked at Pike. If he had recognized Alex at The Maxwell his reactions to her today gave nothing away.

Shelby balanced herself on a table top and opened her gifts. She took a blue infant's suit from inside one box and held it up for everyone to see. The women "ooh'ed" and "ahh'ed". The men smiled.

"Is this the cutest thing you ever saw?" Shelby said. "Thank you, Heidi. I love you."

Shelby opened another card and read aloud, "You were a great help to me over the last year. Best wishes to you and your baby. Barry Kestrel." Shelby took a check out of the envelope and, did a broad double-take. "Good Lord," she said and, using her Southern Belle act, fanned herself with the check as she batted her eyelashes. Everyone laughed. "Thank you so much, Mr. Kestrel," Shelby said. The employees applauded. Kestrel waved briefly to both Shelby and the crowd.

As Shelby grabbed and opened another package Kestrel walked to Ronnie and stood next to her. Pike watched them both from across the room. "The summer I was sixteen," Kestrel said, "I got a job delivering liquor for a store on Madison. I'd bring tiny bottles of vodka to fancy East Side apartments where the wives of men who'd gone to work that morning would spend the day drinking what I brought them. The bottles were small enough so that the women could finish them by the evening and they were always vodka so their breaths didn't smell. I took a flask of cheap vodka to the same woman every day in a huge apartment on Park and 83rd. Her husband was a big player on Wall Street and one day I asked her what he'd studied to become so successful. She told me, 'My husband says business school is a waste of time. The only thing you need to know to be successful is people.'" Kestrel paused as they watched two men place a huge box on the table in front of Shelby. "People," Kestrel said. "You know people and you don't need to know anything else."

Ronnie tensed. Was this Kestrel's way of saying he suspected something about her? "Is that right?" she asked.

"You've been my assistant for what, Ms. Hewitt? Two years now?"

"Almost three."

"That long?" While Shelby cut the ribbon on the package, Kestrel said to Ronnie, "You know everything about me, don't you?"

"That's what you pay me for, sir."

"But I don't know that much about you, though, do I?"

"There's not much to know," Ronnie said while applauding with the others the latest of Shelby's gifts—a stroller from Natalie Jenkins.

"I doubt that," Kestrel said. Was he trying to get at something?

Shelby read another card. "You're like a little sister to me. Love, Ronnie." Shelby opened the box and took a light blue, woolen blanket out of it. "Thank you, Ronnie, it's so beautiful," she said, rubbing the blanket against her cheek. "You're like a big sister to me, too." Shelby blew Ronnie a kiss that she returned. Ronnie had charged the blanket to Kestrel's account.

"Why do you think they want you to deliver the money?" Kestrel said.

Ronnie shrugged. "Maybe because it's not my money I'll give it up more easily than you would."

"Damn right," Kestrel said.

"Then maybe you should deliver it."

"They insist that it's you."

"Phew," said Ronnie. "That was close, huh?"

Kestrel grinned at Ronnie and watched Shelby open another gift. Teasing Kestrel like this was ballsy, but it would show him how determined she was not to deliver the money.

"A man's life lies in your hands, Veronica."

"Don't say it like that," she said, looking away as if the thought of this upset her.

"What are you going to do about it?"

Ronnie paused. "I have to think about it."

"For how long?"

"I'll let you know later tonight."

"Mr. Newman's counting on you," Kestrel said and walked across the room. She was relieved. He'd given no indication that he suspected her.

— • —

Pike drove to the Jubilee theater in his black 1998 Lincoln Town Car. He waited on the street, leaning against the parked car's door. It had gotten cold and he could see his breath in the night air.

He'd spent the afternoon rehearsing the different ways he'd ask Ronnie if she'd decided to deliver the money. From how she reacted he hoped he'd learn if she and Alex were involved. But as soon as he'd decided on one way to start the conversation he'd change his mind and think of another. Standing there in the cold night air, he decided they were all bad ideas. He'd go home and see what happened the next day. But before he could do that, Ronnie and Alex came through the stage door together, walking toward the street.

They stopped when they saw him standing there and every clever thing Pike had rehearsed saying to them disappeared. He looked at Ronnie and simply said, "I know."

Ronnie said nothing.

Alex said, "Shit."

A few minutes later Pike sat opposite them at a small table in the back of a nearly empty bar. Ronnie stared at Pike with a hard look he'd never seen in her before. Alex sat silently in a sulk, his arms folded on his chest.

Ronnie spoke first. "When did you know I was in on it?"

"Pretty early," Pike said. This wasn't true, but you want a suspect to think you know more than you actually do.

"What gave me away?"

"Little things."

"How little?"

"Does it matter?"

"I want to know."

This surprised Pike. What did she care? She wasn't planning on doing something like this again, was she? Or maybe she was. "You overplayed your concern for Newman." Would saying this insult an actress? It didn't seem to.

"What else?"

"When Newman was talking on the Skype call," Pike said, "you moved your lips when he spoke like you sometimes do when you're watching the actors say the lines you write for them."

"Shit," Ronnie said, half smiling at giving herself away so stupidly. "Does Kestrel suspect me?"

"No more than he suspects anybody else."

"What about Natalie? Or Walter?"

"Don't worry about them."

This conversation told Pike that there weren't any experienced criminals forcing Ronnie and Alex to help them with the kidnapping. It was just the two of them. And most likely Newman, too.

"And even if Kestrel did suspect you," Pike said, "he still wouldn't want to rock the boat now and mess up the Salient deal. He wants this all to disappear as quickly as possible. That's what you were counting on, isn't it?"

Ronnie nodded.

"Their precious deal," was the first thing Alex said.

Ronnie ignored Alex and looked at Pike. "So what do you want?"

This was the question Pike had been asking himself for the last two days. What did he want? He gave the simplest answer he could.

"I want to help you."

"Why?" Alex said.

Pike hesitated. He didn't know the answer to this question. But before he even tried to answer it, Ronnie said, "What if we don't want your help?"

The tone of her question angered him. He was here to help them get out of the situation they were in. Instead, they seemed annoyed at him for wanting to do that. These two kids were committing a serious crime—kidnapping or at least extortion. Pike was sticking his neck out, trying to help them and here they were acting like gangsters.

He was surprised by how angry Ronnie's ingratitude made him. But he told himself not to overreact. The girl was in way over her head. She was scared and he shouldn't take what she said personally. But he couldn't help it. She made him feel foolish. Her reaction also told Pike something else. It told him she knew that he wouldn't turn them in. And she was right. He wouldn't. Was it that obvious?

"What do you want?" Alex said.

Pike told himself to be cool. "I said that I want to help you."

"Bullshit," Alex said. "You want the same thing everybody else does."

"What's that?"

"Money," Alex said.

Pike thought, okay, you want me to play tough, kid? I can do that. I'll say what you expect me to say. If that's the only thing that will make you happy, then fine. Still, he was surprised when he heard the next words coming out of his mouth. "I want a hundred thousand dollars."

Ronnie and Alex looked at one another. That Pike wanted money didn't seem to bother them, but something did. Was it how much he asked for? Was a hundred grand too much? Too little? Should he have asked for more? How surprised would they be if they knew he'd originally come here not to ask them for any money at all, but simply to help them get out of this mess they'd got themselves into?

"What if we get caught and tell the cops that you squeezed us?" Alex said.

Now the kid was annoying Pike. "I'm a decorated retired NYPD detective working for the Wall Street CEO who you're conning. The two of you are a personal assistant and an out-of-work actor. Who are they gonna believe?" This came out harsher than Pike intended, but it was true. If these two were going to sit here playing the tough guys in this little play of theirs they'd better get used to hearing shit like that.

"Then why bother to make a deal like this with us at all?" Ronnie said. "Why not wait until we get the money and then take it all from us then?"

"That wouldn't be right," Pike said.

Alex smirked. "And this is?"

The kid's attitude caused Pike to question why he was bothering to help them at all. But he couldn't back down now. He didn't want to. "I know how these things work," he said. "You don't. You're amateurs. You've already made a ton of mistakes. Kestrel isn't stupid. He could figure it out. And even if he doesn't, you can't trust him. You don't know what he might do. You need me."

"You haven't asked us about Newman," Ronnie said. "Aren't you worried about him?"

"You won't hurt him." He didn't say that he knew that Newman was in on the scheme, too. That was a conversation for another time. "And right now you have a bigger problem."

"Like what?" Ronnie said.

"Kestrel told me that he doesn't like that they asked you to deliver the money." This was a lie, but he said it to make what he was about to suggest easier to sell to them.

"That's why I refused to do it this afternoon," Ronnie said. "I was gonna go to his place now to tell him that I changed my mind. That I'd deliver the payoff in the morning for the sake of Newman's safety."

"You need to do more than that," Pike said.

"Like what?" Ronnie asked.

"You need to talk to Kestrel in his language."

"What language is that?" Alex said.

"Money," Pike said. "This is what you'll do. I'll drive you to Kestrel's now. You'll tell him you'll deliver the payoff in the morning, but only on one condition: that he pays you a hundred thousand dollars. That way you'll be telling him that the only money you're gonna see out of all this is what he pays you for the delivery and that you're not getting any of the ransom money."

Ronnie agreed that this was a good idea. She wished that she thought of it herself. But Pike had made his point. They needed him.

— • —

Ronnie said nothing to Alex or Pike before leaving the car and heading around the corner to Kestrel's condo. She hoped Alex would be smart enough to keep his mouth shut and not say anything to Pike about Newman being a fictional character. Or at least that Newman had started out that way.

She wasn't surprised that Pike figured out she was involved. She was annoyed at herself for not recognizing his suspicions earlier. Oddly enough, his involvement made her feel safer. Like Pike said, he knew how these things worked and his collaboration might turn out to be a good thing even if it did cost them a hundred grand. If things did work out then that hundred thousand would come from Kestrel's payment to her for delivering the ransom. So no loss. The only thing she didn't understand was why Pike hadn't asked them for a bigger cut. Did he plan on taking more later?

She said hi to Kestrel's doorman. "Evening, Ms. Hewitt. You're working late tonight, aren't you?"

"As always."

She took the elevator to Kestrel's private floor and stood outside his door prepping what she'd say to him. She was nervous the way she used to be before stepping on stage and her hands shook a little. But she'd use this to convince Kestrel that she was genuinely upset by the idea of delivering the ransom. She rang the bell and heard foot-steps approach the door.

As soon as Kestrel opened the door she spoke at once, blurting out why she was here, trying to make it sound like something she'd been practicing to say to him. "Okay, I'll do it. You're right, Mr. Kestrel. Mr. Newman's safety, his life, lies in my hands. So I'll do what they ask. What you ask. I don't want to do it, but I will. I'll deliver the money tomorrow morning. But only on one condition." She paused for a moment and took a deep breath to show him how difficult this next line was for her to say. "I want one hundred thousand dollars."

Kestrel waited a moment before he grinned. "Sorry, sweetie, but you're too late."

Ronnie froze. What did he mean? Had he decided not to pay the ransom after all? Had he called the police? Did someone find out that Newman was a fraud? Only when he opened the door a little more, did Ronnie see the answer. Shelby stood in Kestrel's condo looking like she might go into labor any minute.

"Hey, Ronnie," Shelby said with a small wave of her hand.

Kestrel pointed to Shelby. "She's doing it for fifteen."

This was the last thing Ronnie expected. Her thoughts raced. How did Shelby know about the kidnapping? Did Kestrel tell her? And Ronnie couldn't let her deliver the payoff. It would fuck every-thing up. She wanted to run out and ask Pike what she should do, but she was here by herself and everything depended on what she said and did now. The first thing she needed to know was whose idea was it that Shelby deliver the money. If it was Kestrel's idea then that would give Ronnie something to work with. "Did you force her to do it?" she asked him.

Kestrel turned to Shelby. "Did I?"

Shelby shook her head no.

"Be honest with me," Ronnie said to her, "did he threaten you if you didn't do it? Because if he did then—"

"She came to me," Kestrel said.

Shelby nodded. "I did. I need the money with Sammy coming."

Since it was Shelby's idea, Ronnie couldn't accuse Kestrel of putting her in harm's way. "How'd you find out about it?" Ronnie asked her.

Shelby looked down to the floor, ashamed. "I was listening in on his private line."

"I could fire her for that alone," Kestrel said.

"I'm sorry for doing that, Mr. Kestrel."

"What about Heidi?" Ronnie asked Shelby. "Does she know?"

Shelby shook her head. "Only me."

That was a relief. Ronnie looked at Kestrel. "The kidnappers told you they wanted me to do it."

"They said they wanted 'my assistant' to do it. Shelby's my assistant, too."

"He's right. I am," she said.

"She's your executive assistant's assistant."

"They aren't gonna give a shit about anybody's title or who gives them their money as long as they get it," Kestrel said.

Ronnie played her last card. "You can't do it," she said to Shelby and turned to Kestrel. "She can't do it."

"Why not?"

"She's pregnant."

"Aren't you being a little sexist?" Kestrel said.

Shelby interrupted them. "I need the money, Ronnie."

"She's a struggling single mother with an absentee father," Kestrel said. "An all-too-familiar tale in our culture today."

"Then Shelby and I will do it together."

"Wouldn't that upset the kidnappers?" Kestrel asked.

"Fuck the kidnappers," Ronnie said, "tell them if they want their money this is how they're gonna get it." She appealed to Kestrel's ego. "You want to show them how strong you are, don't you? Think about it. Shelby doesn't know the city like I do. And if something happens to her—your twenty-four-year-old pregnant executive assistant's assistant—making a secret kidnapping payoff for you—you'll be crucified." Ronnie didn't ask him, "What will happen to the Salient deal then?" because she didn't need to.

What she'd said worked. Kestrel backed down. All he said was, "Shit."

Next Ronnie did what Pike suggested: speak in Kestrel's language and make sure he thought that this was the only money that she was going to see from the kidnapping. "Make it a hundred thousand for the two of us," she said.

Shelby held up her hands. "Ronnie, I don't think—"

"Shut up and let me do this," Ronnie said to her and turned back to Kestrel. "That's our offer. One hundred thousand."

"I'll give you twenty-five. After it's done."

"Fifty," Ronnie said. "Twenty-five each."

Kestrel looked as if he was eager to bargain her down more, but he decided not to bother. "Twenty-five each," he said.

"Deal."

"You're a good negotiator, Ms. Hewitt."

"I learned from the best," Ronnie said, flattering him again.

Kestrel smiled. "I'll see you ladies in the morning."

— • —

Pike waited in his car, holding his copy of *The Picture of Dorian Gray* under the car's dim map light. His book report was due Monday night, but reading it now was impossible. He could see Alex in the rear view mirror leaning against the car's trunk. The kid was probably going over what had happened since he and Ronnie started the whole plan. What went right, what went wrong. Who or what would jump out of the bushes and surprise them next.

Pike was involved in it now and he wasn't sure how he got here. Earlier in the bar Ronnie had made it clear that she didn't want him to talk her out of her scheme. She and Alex had all but told him to go fuck himself. Pissed off by that, he'd overreacted and asked them for the money. But in the end it's what they expected him to do and, far from upsetting them, his demand for money seemed to calm them.

His original goal was to persuade them to drop the whole con and help them get out of this mess. But why did he want to do that? If Ronnie asked him that, what could he say? Because you've read a lot of books that I like talking to you about? Because your father died when you were a kid like mine did? Because you bite your lower lip when you smile like my dead wife did? Those things would sound like a cheap come-on. That's not why he wanted to help her. Or was it? Was he sitting here because he was attracted to her? Because of a man's stupid, never-ending need to impress a pretty woman? Because he thought that there might actually be a way she could love him? It couldn't be that, could it?

Whatever the reason, something made him want to protect her. Now he'd be involved until the scam ended and do whatever he could to help Ronnie not get caught. When it was over he wouldn't take any of the money. Not a penny of it. Not because taking it would make him guilty, but because not taking it would prove to Ronnie why he'd gotten involved in the first place. That he was a good man with good intentions.

Alex opened the door and got back in. "It's cold out there."

"I'll turn the motor on and warm it up in here," Pike said.

"Don't bother." Alex was playing it cool. Pike saw this in most of the suspects he'd collared, especially the young ones. "What are you reading?"

Pike held up the paperback.

"We had to do a scene from that in acting class," Alex said. "You like it?"

"I do," Pike said.

"I love horror stories. *Frankenstein, Dracula, Jekyll and Hyde,* shit like that. I always wanted to do a stage version of *Jekyll and Hyde.*"

"I think everybody has this book wrong," Pike said about the Wilde novel.

"What do you mean?"

"I don't think it's a horror story."

"Then what is it?"

"It's a riddle." This was what Pike planned to say to the class on Monday. He could try it out on Alex here to see how it sounded.

"It's a horror story about a painting that changes into a monster while the guy doesn't," Alex said.

"You're right," Pike said and looked out the window at the passing traffic. Pike's take on the book might be ridiculous and, even if it weren't, there was no way someone Alex's age would understand what Pike thought Oscar Wilde was really saying.

— • —

Ronnie wasn't listening when Kestrel's doorman said something sweet to Shelby about her pregnancy. All she could think about was how close this sorority girl came to fucking everything up.

Ronnie saw Pike's Lincoln parked down the street when she and Shelby turned the corner. Why'd they park so close? Ronnie grabbed Shelby by the shoulder and turned her around so she couldn't see Pike's car. "What were you thinking?"

Shelby was crying. "I need the money for Sammy."

"You should've talked to me first. Kestrel's a bad guy. He uses people. He might've got you to deliver the money and not paid you a penny. That's how he works."

Shelby looked at Ronnie, concerned. "You think he might not pay us?"

"He'll pay us now."

"Don't be mad at me."

"I'm not," Ronnie said. And she wasn't. The poor girl was pregnant and alone. Shelby showing up out of the blue and offering to deliver the ransom might turn out to be an advantage. It might distract Kestrel from wondering why the kidnappers had asked Ronnie to deliver it in the first place. Now Ronnie would have to change some of the payoff's details. She'd have to lose Shelby somewhere along the way, but that wouldn't be hard. The girl was naïve enough to believe anything Ronnie told her.

"We're gonna be all right tomorrow, aren't we?" Shelby asked.

"Those guys won't do anything to us."

"How do you know?"

Because I'm one of them, you stupid Scarlett O'Hara wannabe, Ronnie thought. But she said, "Because all they care about is the money."

"You're probably right."

"We'll be fine as long as you don't go into labor in the middle of it."

They both laughed at this and Shelby hugged Ronnie. "Thank you for understanding," she said. "I gotta get home. I'm so tired." She turned toward the subway stop on the corner, but Ronnie grabbed her shoulder.

"Wait," Ronnie said and flagged a cab heading their way. Ronnie handed Shelby three twenties. "This is Kestrel's, not mine," she said and kissed her on the cheek.

Shelby climbed into the cab butt-first, pulling her legs up behind her. At this point even the simplest movement was a challenge for her. Ronnie shut the door behind her. As the cab drove off, Shelby waved at Ronnie through its back window.

When she got back to the car, Ronnie told Pike and Alex what happened in Kestrel's condo. Pike was typically stoic. Alex was pissed off.

"I told them you should be the one who delivers the money," he said.

"You said Kestrel's assistant. She's his assistant, too. We should've foreseen that."

Alex pounded the car's dashboard. "Shit."

"Relax," Pike said. "This is a good thing. Your asking for money to deliver the payoff and then Shelby looking like she beat you to it and forcing you to beg for the chance do it with her is perfect. It takes the focus off you."

Pike was smart. He thought like Ronnie did. "I have to get home and make some changes to the payoff plan," she said.

Pike started his car. "I'll drop you off."

Ronnie opened the Lincoln's back door. "We'll take a cab." She and Alex got out, shut the door and Ronnie waved at a taxi.

— • —

Alex stormed into the apartment ahead of Ronnie. He took off his coat and threw it onto the sofa.

"What happened?" Newman asked.

"Shit happened, that's what happened," Alex said before going into the kitchen and getting a beer out of the refrigerator.

Ronnie told Newman about the night's events with both Pike and Shelby. And Kestrel, too.

Newman was concerned. "I don't understand. Why doesn't Pike just turn you in?"

Alex slammed his beer on the counter. "Why does anyone do anything? Money, that's why. Fuck it," he said, "it's too complicated now. First you—" he pointed at Newman—"get a piece of the money, most of it, then Pike gets a piece and now this other bitch is mixed up in it, too. Me and Ronnie, we can't even spend it," he said, "but you and Pike can and now that Southern dispshit can, too. But not us, no. There are too many people in this now. The whole thing's gonna blow up in our faces."

"Shelby's not getting any of the payoff," Ronnie said, trying to calm Alex down. "All she's getting is the fifty from Kestrel that she and I are splitting for the delivery."

"Do you trust her to stay quiet?" Newman asked Ronnie.

"I do. And like Pike said, she'll take some of the focus off of us. Off me."

"What if she figures it out?" Alex said.

"She's not smart enough to do that."

"She was smart enough to worm her way into everything."

"That didn't take brains," Ronnie said. "That was luck."

"Shelby doesn't bother me, but Alex could be right about Pike," Newman said. "I don't trust him."

"See?" Alex said, pointing at Newman. "Mystery man here finally says something smart."

Ronnie sat down. "All he wants is a hundred grand."

"But that's the thing," Newman said. "Why does he want so little? What's he doing this for?"

"He's doing it because he likes me," she said. "He always has."

"You mean like he's in love with you?" Newman asked.

"He's always wanted to fuck her," Alex said. "It's obvious."

Ronnie shook her head. "He's protective of me. Like an older brother."

"An older brother who wants to fuck you and steal from us," Alex said.

"All he wants is a hundred thousand."

"That's what he says now," Alex said. "But what happens when he's standing here with two million in cash staring him in the face?"

"He's not getting anywhere near the money," Ronnie said. "I'll make sure of that."

Alex wasn't persuaded. He paced the small room. He repeated his worries about all the people involved in the scheme now and waved his hands like he wanted it all to go away. Ronnie had never seen him this upset. "There are too many moving parts now," he said, "too much that can go wrong."

"So what are you saying?" Ronnie asked him.

"I'm saying we should walk."

"Fine then," Ronnie said to Alex. "You walk if you want to. I'll finish the job without you."

"How?"

"I'll do it with Martin," Ronnie said.

Alex stopped pacing. "That's not his name."

She ignored Alex and looked at Newman. "You'll do it with me, won't you?"

"Of course."

"That's all I need to hear." Ronnie was certain now that she owned Newman.

"Are you crazy?" Alex said to her. "You can't trust this asshole."

"If you walk I'll have to, won't I?"

"The money's as much mine as it is anyone's," Alex said.

"It is if you stick with the program."

"Fuck this," Alex said and grabbed his coat and walked out of the apartment.

This time Ronnie didn't go after him. Alex leaving now was perfect timing. It'd give Ronnie a chance to cement her relationship with Newman, or what he thought was their relationship. She stood at the door listening to Alex's fading steps on the stairs. When she came back into the apartment Newman said, "Why didn't you let him walk? If he drops out, then you and I will have all the money except for Pike's one hundred grand."

"We need him on board," she said.

"Why?"

"Because we need him to be guilty. Same as with Pike. Once someone takes the money, they can't hold their innocence over us. If Alex isn't involved then we'd be at his mercy."

Martin was impressed by what she said. "You know how people think, don't you?"

"You're the craftsman. You know all this tech bullshit. Me, I'm the storyteller. I know people," Ronnie said, echoing Kestrel's tired mantra. "It's what I do." Telling this to Newman was like a snake showing its fangs to its victim, but Newman was too distracted by what he thought was Ronnie's attraction to him to see those fangs.

"I have to keep playing Alex," she said. But she had to be careful not to make her transition from Alex to Martin, as false as it was, look too easy. What kind of woman turns on her boyfriend and walks off with a man she met a couple of days before—a man who's stolen his identity and wormed his way into her life? Still, it's what men do. They take a woman from another man and they're shocked when she dumps them for the next guy.

For the next hour, Ronnie acted as if she were torn. She hoped that the guilt she admitted feeling for leaving Alex would endear her to Newman even more. "Look at me," she told Newman, "I'm not so tough. I'm a wreck for God's sake. And you, Martin, you're the only one who can help me. You can save me."

Men love thinking that they're saving people. And she wondered how many women might actually fall for Newman. He wasn't good looking, not like Alex, but he wasn't ugly either. He was nondescript. But he had manners and he was smart. And he'd played the distraught kidnapping victim so well on the Skype call that he squeezed an extra million dollars out of Kestrel. He might be nuts, but who on any dating site isn't? A lot of women might even see the lengths Newman had gone to to win Ronnie as a sign of true love. He was a Harlequin romance hero who used a laptop instead of a saber.

She went into the kitchen to make coffee and saw that Alex had texted her *It's your mother* three times in the last half hour. Ronnie hadn't answered her phone while working Newman, so the staff at Jerrold House had called Alex's number, the back-up number Ronnie had given them in case of an emergency.

Alex's next text said *I'm at Whitney's.* That was a diner in Queens not far from Jerrold House where he and Ronnie sometimes hung out when visiting her mother. Ronnie grabbed her coat.

"What's the matter?" Newman asked. "Is it Pike? Is it Kestrel? Did something happen? What?" His face looked like a little boy's might after being told there was no Santa Claus.

"No." She walked to the door.

"What then? Tell me."

Jesus, one minute this guy's John Wayne, the next he's Woody Allen. Still, she reached out and softly stroked his cheek. "I'll tell you when I get back," she said. "Don't worry. Everything will work out."

— • —

A thunderstorm was drenching the streets when Ronnie got to Whitney's Diner. Alex and her mother were sitting in a window booth. Ronnie hurried inside and took Carlotta's hand. "Mum, you can't go out by yourself in the middle of the night."

"I was getting the Sunday paper," Carlotta said, showing no surprise at seeing her daughter there. Her mother was in a rare verbal, if not entirely coherent, state.

"Where's Nadine?" Ronnie asked Alex.

The tall Jamaican orderly came out of the bathroom just then and walked to their booth. She laughed as she told Ronnie how her mother had stolen various pieces of clothing from other patients. "Once she gets herself all dressed up in this outfit she's wearing," Nadine said, "she walks down the hallway and saunters out the front door into this damn rainstorm like Moses crossing the Red Sea."

"Who found her?" Ronnie said.

"Jimmy did," Nadine said and pointed to diner's front door. Jimmy, the orderly that Ronnie had seen the other night, the man she believed had hit her mother and looked at Ronnie so threateningly, walked to the table holding a yellow sweater. He smiled warmly at Carlotta. "Here, you go, doll, I keep this in my car for all you runaway girls." He draped the large sweater carefully over Carlotta's shoulders and told Ronnie how he'd been on his way home from his shift when he saw Carlotta on the street.

"Please inform my daughter that I'm perfectly capable of entertaining myself, James," Carlotta said.

"You entertain us all, Carlotta," Jimmy said. His voice was high and cheery. "She's a magician, your mother is," he said to Ronnie. "We call her Houdini." Jimmy crouched in front of Carlotta and she touched his cheek not unlike the way Ronnie had touched Newman's cheek just before leaving to come here. But her mother's gesture was real. Jimmy pointed to Carlotta's outfit. "Look at what she decked herself out in. She's fabulous," he said in an exaggeratedly campy way. They all laughed, even Carlotta who said, "Don't be disrespectful to your elders, young man."

Ronnie was ashamed by what she'd thought about Jimmy when she saw him Monday night at Jerrold House. She'd cast him as some kind of monster. But he was nothing like that and it upset her how badly she'd misread him. Was this true about the others in her life? Had she misread Kestrel? Or Pike? Shelby? Newman? Alex? Or, worse, herself? She'd always prided herself on studying and knowing people's characters. It was what she was good at. But looking at Jimmy now she wondered if maybe she wasn't as good at it as she thought.

— • —

Kestrel looked out his co-op window at the traffic on the street below. He'd called Pike to his place to ask him what he thought about letting both girls deliver the money. Pike already knew this, but he pretended to consider it for a moment before he said that it'd probably be fine, maybe even safer with the two ladies doing it together.

"Follow the money," Kestrel said. "Who said that?"

"That was from Watergate, sir."

"Follow the money. It's what I've been doing all my life and I should do it tomorrow." Pike was silent. "What's the matter, Detective? You don't think I should follow my cash?"

What Kestrel said concerned Pike. "If the kidnappers think they're being tracked," Pike said, "they could panic and hurt Newman. Or the ladies. If something like that goes wrong, the authorities will find out that you never told them about the kidnapping and nail you for it."

"I negotiated for the guy, didn't I?"

"That's not how police think," Pike said, "and that's not how the press will see it either. It's not worth the risk. It's only two million dollars." Pike was surprised to hear the words "only two million dollars" come out of his mouth. But he'd been surprised a couple of hours earlier, too, when he heard himself say "one hundred thousand dollars" to Ronnie and Alex. "If you want to make sure this thing ends successfully you should let the two women deliver the money and stay completely out of it."

"I hate being played like this, but you're right. I won't do anything to get in the way of the payoff."

"That's the smart choice, sir," Pike said, relieved. Still, Pike didn't trust him. There was a chance that he'd change his mind and hire a private security firm or someone to follow the money. He might have done that already. Maybe not to stop the payoff or get the cash back, but to learn enough about the kidnappers so that he could identify them, hunt them down after the Salient deal closed, and punish them.

"If it makes you feel better, sir," Pike said, "I can follow them." If Kestrel did hire someone to follow Ronnie and Shelby, then Pike would know and he might be able to help Ronnie escape their surveillance.

"You can do that?" Kestrel said.

"I've done it more times than I can remember."

"And you can do it so neither the two girls or the kidnappers see you?"

"Easily."

— • —

Ronnie used a knife and fork to cut a large piece of pastry on the plate in front of her mother.

"When am I going to see my new home?" Carlotta asked.

"Very soon, Mum." Ronnie said, "You're gonna love it. It's what you deserve." She didn't say "unlike the shithole you've been forced to live in until now." But it's what she thought.

Jimmy and Nadine sat in another booth doing what all employees do: complaining about their schedules, their pay, and making fun of their superiors.

Ronnie needed to talk Alex off his angry ledge. She was relieved to see that he seemed to be over the initial rage that had owned him earlier in the apartment. She took his hand. "You okay?"

He shrugged. "I guess."

"You can't seriously believe that I want anything to do with that asshole."

"I hate that word," Carlotta said without looking up from her pastry.

Ronnie ignored her mother. "I'm playing him," she said to Alex. "He wants me and I have to make him think that I want him, too."

"Do you?"

"I'm not even gonna answer that. But I want him to think that when this is all done, he and I are gonna run off into the sunset together."

"With the money."

"With the money," she said and laughed to show how crazy the idea of that was. "It's the only way I can protect us from him."

"Are you still gonna let him take his million?"

"We have to."

"Why?" Alex's distrust of Newman was still strong.

"We were only planning on getting a million anyway," Ronnie said.

Carlotta interrupted them. "Will my new home have a garden?"

"A big garden, Mum."

"It's beautiful," Alex said to Carlotta.

She stared at Alex. "Who are you?"

"This is Alex, Mum," Ronnie said. "Alex is my boyfriend."

"We're probably going to be moving pretty soon, too," Alex said to Carlotta. He wouldn't let go of his idea of moving somewhere new and moving soon.

"Don't start with that again," Ronnie said. "You don't know Kestrel like I do. After he pays the ransom and the deal goes through he'll sit around counting the Salient money for a few days and then he'll try to find out who took him for the two million. He'll have all the time and money he needs to do that. He'll hire the best detectives and the best computer people. We should pray that Newman deletes our trails like he says he can do. That's another reason I'm playing up to him."

"Newman again," Alex said.

"Promise me you'll follow the plans tomorrow."

"Don't talk to me like I'm stupid." Alex folded his arms and sat back against the booth.

Ronnie reached for his hand, but he didn't let her take it. "I know you're scared, baby," she said.

"I'm not scared."

"Of course you are. You'd be crazy if you weren't. I am. I'm terrified. But we can pull this off. The main thing to remember is that it's not a play. It's real life. So we can't improvise. Neither of us can. If we do, then we give Kestrel an opening. Newman, too. We have to stick to the script we wrote. Can you do that?"

Alex nodded. "But when this is all over, can we at least go somewhere? It doesn't have to be anywhere expensive. A few days somewhere to chill out. Can we do that, you and me?"

Alex was still impatient about spending the money and this worried Ronnie. But rather than argue with him about it anymore, she said, "Okay, we can do that. We'll use the money Kestrel gives me for delivering the ransom and go somewhere nice with it. No one will suspect anything if we do that. But tomorrow you have to stick to the plan."

"I will," Alex said, but Ronnie wondered what he'd do when he saw the cash.

A song started to play over the diner's tinny loudspeakers. It was an oldie from the sixties, one of the cooks' favorites, and since there was hardly anyone in the place the waitress turned the volume up. Carlotta looked up from her pastry and said to Alex. "Remember this song, Robert?"

"He's not Daddy, Mum."

But Carlotta ignored Ronnie. "They played it at our wedding," she said to Alex. "You remember, don't you, Robert?"

Alex smiled. "Of course I do."

"Don't," Ronnie said to Alex. "You'll only confuse her."

But Alex played along with Carlotta. "How could I forget?" He stood up and held out his hand to Carlotta. "Would you care to dance, my dear?"

Carlotta took his hand. "When have you ever known me to turn down an opportunity to dance?"

Ronnie watched Alex help Carlotta to her feet. He took her gently in his arms and they danced with a tentative elegance on the diner's worn black and white linoleum floor. The few customers looked up from their plates and smiled before turning back to their food. Two cooks leaned out from the kitchen and shouted encouragement in Spanish. The waitress grinned. Nadine and Jimmy watched and clapped their hands.

Ronnie was moved watching her mother dancing with a man that she thought was her dead husband. Alex was a good man. He could be boyish and sometimes petulant, and right now dangerous because of that, but he was kind. Wasn't that the most important thing?

Ronnie watched her mother try a fancy dance step that Alex helped her pull off. She was a woman who'd never done anything for herself. She'd never asked for more than what she deserved. And what did that get her other than being screwed by the faceless men who sat behind desks in the tall gray buildings in all the world's downtowns? What she and Alex were going to do for her mother—and all Carlotta's—tomorrow was the right thing.

FRIDAY

Like he did every morning, Pike bought a copy of the *Wall Street Journal* before picking up Kestrel. A story on the paper's front page read: *Boundary – Is Salient Having Second Thoughts?* When Kestrel got in the car he picked up the paper, glanced at its headline and tossed it into the backseat. "We all set?" he asked Pike.

"Everything's in order, sir."

Kestrel stared out the window and said nothing else to Pike during the ride. He seemed uncharacteristically anxious. When they got to Boundary the only thing Kestrel said was, "Let's get this shit over with," before walking out of the car and into the building.

Pike parked the SUV and went to the bank in the lobby. As arranged by Walter Shaw, he met with Carl Schramm, whose sole job at the bank was to deal with Kestrel's personal business needs. The banker handed Pike a plain cardboard box. In it were two million dollars' worth of Euros.

Schramm grinned at the detective. "I'm not even going to ask."

Pike said nothing and, using the private elevator, took the box to Kestrel's office.

Kestrel, Natalie and Walter were waiting in the office for him. So were Ronnie and Shelby.

— • —

By the time Ronnie got to Kestrel's office that morning he'd already told Natalie and Walter that both she and Shelby were going to deliver the payoff together. Neither Natalie nor Walter were happy about Shelby's involvement, but there was nothing they could do about it. And Kestrel gave them no explanation. Quoting Pike who hadn't shown up with the cash yet, he said it'd be safer if the two women did the payoff together. But he said nothing to Natalie or Walter about paying the two women fifty thousand dollars for delivering the money. Why should he? It was his money anyway.

Pike came into the office and put the cardboard box full of cash on Kestrel's desk. Kestrel took a large black backpack from under his desk and put it next to the box with the money. "This backpack is what you're gonna carry the money in," he said to Ronnie and Shelby. Kestrel then opened the cardboard box and began loading the purple-tinted, five hundred note Euros into the backpack. Pike made an attempt to help him, but Kestrel waved him off. So Pike and the others watched in silence as Kestrel loaded the money himself, block by block.

Ronnie tapped her foot nervously but stopped, thinking it might be too much of a cliché. Shelby cracked her knuckles loudly. Pike looked uncomfortable to Ronnie, like he was afraid that he might give something away. Ronnie reminded herself that he was a cop, not an actor. Still, she hoped that he'd remember her direction.

Walter walked over to the two young women. "You can still refuse to do this," he said.

"Who's gonna do it instead?" Kestrel asked Walter, pointing a wad of Euros at him. "You?"

"Yes, me," said Walter. "I could do it."

Kestrel sneered. "In your dreams."

"Would you like me to prove it to you?" Walter said.

"Will you two gentlemen put your dicks back in your pants and get on with this?" Natalie said.

Pike looked at Ronnie and Shelby. "Which one of you is going to wear that?" he asked about the backpack.

"I will," Ronnie said. "It's too heavy for her."

"What about Newman?" Walter asked.

The whole time Kestrel was loading the money no one had even mentioned Martin Newman, the reason for all this.

"They said in their email they'd let him go as soon as they got the money," Kestrel said. "I told them to tell Newman to come straight here to my office. We need to go through everything that happened with him."

"Debrief him," Natalie said.

Kestrel agreed. "We gotta make sure he doesn't tell anyone about any of this until the deal's finalized."

"We should find out if he's all right," Walter said.

Kestrel nodded. "Yeah, that, too."

"Maybe we should plan something for him," Walter said.

"Like what?" Kestrel asked, stuffing another wad of bills into the backpack.

"We could take him out for a meal," Walter said. "He might be hungry."

"He'll need counseling, too," Natalie said. "People who go through something like this suffer from PTSD."

"I don't give a shit what you do as long as we keep this quiet until the deal's closed," Kestrel said. "After that you can take him to Disneyland for all I care." Kestrel finished loading the money. "That's it." Then he said, "Wait," and he took a small plastic box that was on top of his desk.

"What's that?" Walter asked.

"It's a watch," Kestrel said, taking the watch out of its case. "The cheapest Timex I could find at the drugstore down the street from me. Maybe that asshole will learn to tell time from now on."

"Do you really want to risk pissing them off?" Natalie said.

"It's a guy thing. He'll understand. They won't see it until after they get their money anyway, so they won't care." Kestrel forced the watch into the backpack and zipped it closed.

Shelby spoke for the first time. "I shouldn't be worried, should I? I mean we're not actually going to meet these guys, are we?"

"The last thing these people want is for you to see them," Pike said.

"That's true," Ronnie said and looked at Pike for encouragement the way anyone might expect a young woman in her situation to do. But when she did, Pike looked away.

Natalie handed Shelby a large designer handbag. "Here."

"What's that?" Kestrel asked.

"It's a prop," Natalie said and turned to the girls. "You're two girls going shopping for stuff for the new baby. That's all anybody will think when they look at you."

Shelby took the handbag from Natalie. Ronnie picked up the backpack. It was heavy enough that both Pike and Walter had to help put it over her shoulders.

"Can you handle that?" Walter asked Ronnie.

"It's fine." Natalie kissed her on the cheek after Ronnie adjusted the straps and had the pack securely on.

"Be careful," Natalie said. She kissed Shelby, too. "We're here if you need us."

"Jesus, Mom, they're not going to the prom," Kestrel said.

Pike looked at both Ronnie and Shelby. "Remember to do whatever they ask you to do on the note you find," he said. They all expected that the payoff would begin as written in the email that Ronnie, pretending to be the kidnappers, had sent to Kestrel. That email said that Kestrel's assistant should go first to a message board at NYU where she'd find a note with further instructions. "That way you'll both be safe," Pike said.

"Okay," Ronnie said to him and turned to Shelby. "You ready?"

Shelby nodded. Kestrel watched the two women leave his office. "Good luck," was the last thing he said to them.

Kestrel had given Heidi the morning off. In the outer office, Ronnie smiled anxiously at Pike who looked away as she walked to the elevator.

On the elevator with Shelby, Ronnie pushed the ground floor button and the doors closed. Shelby said nothing as the car descended, but Ronnie could see her lips moving. Was she praying?

In her head Ronnie went over the plans that she'd rewritten earlier that morning, taking into account that both Pike and Shelby were now involved in the payoff. All she told Newman was that Alex would return to the apartment later in the morning with the backpack full of cash. They should both wait with the money until she got there. Kestrel would expect her to go to his office first and tell him everything that had happened. She'd do that and, claiming to be anxious and exhausted, she'd go home. With any luck, Alex and Newman wouldn't have killed each other by the time she got back to the apartment. Once she got there the three of them would split up the money like they agreed.

But what would happen after that? Did Newman expect her to run away with him? And how would he react if she told him, as she planned to do, that she was still torn between him and Alex and needed more time to make a decision? She hoped that the two million dollars sitting on the table in front of him, half of which would be his, would be enough to ease any disappointment he might feel hearing her say this. But the guy was a freak, so who knew how he'd react?

When the elevator opened in the lobby Hector greeted them. "Good morning, ladies." He pointed to Ronnie's backpack. "What do you got there? Money?"

Ronnie returned his grin. "I wish."

At the security gate Pete said, "You two ladies playing hooky today?" Shelby answered him the same way Ronnie had answered Hector. "I wish," she said.

The two women walked through the security stile to the revolving door. Ronnie took the backpack off her shoulders and held it in her arms before she entered one of the door's chambers. Shelby sneaked into the same chamber with Ronnie making it a tight fit. With the many workers arriving and pushing hard in the opposite direction, Shelby lost her chance to exit onto the street with Ronnie on the door's first go around. So she ended up in the lobby again where Pete said, "See? We won't let you ladies go." Shelby smiled at Pete and entered the revolving door again.

While Shelby was still in the lobby, Ronnie took a photo of the backpack sitting on the sidewalk. She texted the photo to Alex.

Shelby finally came out of the revolving door. Ronnie said, "Alex is calling me. I should get this. It's like Pike said: we can't act as if anything is out of the ordinary."

Shelby nodded. "Right."

"Hey, Alex," Ronnie said into her cell phone. "I'm busy right now."

"I got the photo," he said.

"Great. I'll call you later. Bye, sweetie," Ronnie said and hung up. She opened the door to one of the cabs that was waiting there and helped Shelby climb in. Ronnie opened the door on the cab's other side and slid inside.

"Washington Square," Ronnie said to the cabbie and through the taxi's back window she looked at several cars parked in front of the Boundary building.

Pike had called her late last night and told her about Kestrel wanting Pike to follow them so she shouldn't be surprised if she saw him along their route. He asked her for more details of the plan, but she said it was better if he didn't know them.

Knowing Kestrel like she did, Ronnie told Pike she wouldn't be surprised if he did hire someone else to tail them. Pike agreed and said he'd already planned to look for a third party on her trail. But Ronnie was relieved when she saw that none of the other cars parked in front of the Boundary building followed them when their cab pulled away from the curb and headed into the traffic.

"What are you looking for?" Shelby asked.

"Nothing," Ronnie said and hoped that Shelby didn't ask questions the whole time.

Ronnie's phone rang again. "It's Alex," she said to Shelby. "He's waiting for a plumber." Into her phone she said, "The guy get there yet?"

"I got a backpack at REI just like yours," Alex said.

"They never come on time," Ronnie said to Alex, loud enough for Shelby to hear her.

"I bought five copies of *The New York Times* and put three into the backpack. I crumpled up the other two copies and stuffed them in so the thing looks really full."

Ronnie had given Alex a couple of hardback books they'd found on the street to put into the case to give it more weight. "Great," she said, "call me when the plumber leaves." Ronnie hung up. She looked at Shelby and shook her head. "Men are hopeless," she said and they both laughed.

— • —

Natalie said that she was too nervous to do any work until she'd gotten news from the girls that the payoff had been delivered and that both they and Newman were safe. Walter agreed with her and so the two of them went to the executive dining room to wait for updates.

Kestrel stayed in his office.

Pike took his pistol out of his locked desk drawer in his office and put it into the shoulder holster under his jacket. He didn't foresee needing it, but when you're following two million dollars in cash around the streets of New York you can't be too safe. He went to the building's garage, got his Lincoln and drove it to a spot across the street from the Boundary building. From there he saw Ronnie helping Shelby into a taxi before Ronnie got in with the backpack. It headed north and Pike followed it at a discreet distance.

— • —

Shelby asked Ronnie what she thought the note they were looking for might tell them to do next. Ronnie put her finger to her lips in a gesture of silence and pointed to the back of the taxi driver indicating that Shelby shouldn't say anything that the driver might hear.

"Right," Shelby said, embarrassed by her carelessness. She grabbed her belly. "Sammy's really moving." Her smile faded. "I hope he's not nervous."

They said nothing more until their taxi left them at Washington Square. Ronnie paid the cabbie and helped Shelby out of the cab. "That's the building we want over there," Ronnie said and they headed to it.

"You went to NYU, didn't you?" Shelby said.

"Four years."

"I wish I went to college. I started, but I dropped out after a year. My father thought college was a waste of time for a girl, especially a pretty one. My mother was upset because she was a Tri-Delta legacy. But what difference does it make how pretty you are if your boyfriend and the father of your child ditches you as soon as you get pregnant?"

Shelby finally shut up when they entered the business school building. It was full of people, mostly students. On the wall was a message board covered with notices of all sizes and colors.

"You start at that end and I'll start at this one." Ronnie said. She knew exactly where the notice with "Newman" written on it was. Alex had posted it on the board earlier that morning, wearing dark glasses and his hoodie so that the security cameras couldn't make him out. Ronnie saw their notice on the board, but she wanted Shelby to find it.

The board was covered in posters for foreign movies and garage bands as well as ads for jobs promising how you could make thousands of dollars while never leaving your bedroom. A student director wanted actors for their movie about suicide. Another was casting a movie about prostitutes. The notice next to it offered free kittens. Another promised the reader they'd be speaking fluent Chinese in less than a month.

Ronnie pretended to search the notices. She said, "Where the fuck is it?" loud enough that Shelby could hear. If Kestrel grilled them later she wanted Shelby to tell him how upset Ronnie was when she couldn't locate the notice at first. But when was Shelby going to find the damn thing? The message had NEWMAN written on it in big red letters. How hard was it to find?

Ronnie looked at the people passing them in the hallway. No one looked out of place. Had Kestrel kept his word to Pike and not sent anyone else to follow them?

Shelby shouted. "Ronnie, is this it?"

Ronnie walked over and ripped an ad for "Newman's Computer Repairs" off the board.

"Good job," Ronnie said and pretended to read the ad, acting as if she found nothing unusual about it until she turned it over. More directions were on its back. She had them written by Newman, not her or Alex, so no one could trace their handwriting.

"What's it say?" Shelby asked.

"That we should go to St. Patrick's."

"The church on Fifth?"

"Not that St. Patrick's. There's one on Mulberry Street. Here. They wrote down the address." Ronnie and Shelby walked out of the building. Ronnie pointed south. "It's that way."

"Is it far?" Shelby asked.

It was far enough that they needed a cab to get there. Ronnie waved to the only one she saw, but it was snagged by a man in a suit before it reached them. Ronnie swore at the guy, hoping it would show Shelby how anxious she was about everything they were doing. The guy ignored her and got into the cab.

"Does it say what they want you to do in the church?" Shelby asked.

Ronnie looked at the back of the notice again. "It only says there's a note taped under the back pew. We'll see what that says when we get there."

"It's like one of those scavenger hunts they used to have every Fourth of July at my parents' club."

Sure, just like that, Ronnie thought. But aloud she said, "Let's hope." While they looked for another taxi, Ronnie checked out the cars on the street to see if she recognized one that might have been parked in front of Boundary when they left. Thankfully, she didn't.

— • —

Ronnie wouldn't have seen Pike's car even if she'd looked in his direction. He was double-parked in the loading zone of a market, surrounded by three trucks. A young traffic cop approached his Lincoln and tapped on its hood. Pike rolled his window down, smiled and held up his Policeman's Benevolent Association card. The patrol lady gave him a friendly salute. "Have a nice day, officer," she said and walked on.

It was then that Pike saw Ronnie and Shelby talking about the notice Ronnie had posted that morning and which they'd just found. Ronnie flagged a cab, but lost it when a man took it instead. They both walked past Pike's car to the corner where they got into another cab that an older woman had just gotten got out of. Had Ronnie seen his Lincoln as she walked past it? It didn't matter. Ronnie knew he was following her and Shelby had never seen his car.

— • —

Ten minutes later their cab pulled up in front of St. Patrick's church on Mulberry Street. "You stay here," Ronnie said to Shelby. "I'll go in with the money."

"Will you be all right?"

"Stay here." Ronnie grabbed the backpack and told the cabbie to wait for her. He questioned her in a mix of Bengali and English, but when she handed him a twenty dollar bill and said, "Wait," he shut up.

It took a moment for Ronnie's eyes to adjust to the darkness inside the church. She sat where she told Alex and Newman she would sit: in the second to last pew on the far left side. A mass was being said on the main altar. Scattered in the other pews were a dozen parishioners, mostly old women who probably came here every morning. Ronnie was reminded of her mother, a Roman Catholic who went to mass every Sunday morning. Unlike most parents, Catholics especially, she never insisted Ronnie come with her. Carlotta loved her faith, but she thought religion, like good food, was wasted on children. So Ronnie and her father, who was a non-practicing Methodist, stayed in their apartment Sunday mornings and watched videocassettes of old TV shows. Their favorite was *The Rocky and Bullwinkle Show* and their favorite characters in that show were Boris and Natasha. In every episode Boris would find himself in a life-threatening position with a boulder on his chest or a landmine under his foot. And when Natasha saw him like this she'd say in a version of a Russian accent, "At leest you're leeving" to which Boris would reply, "Theese ees leeving?" That became Ronnie and her father's catch phrase. Theese ees leeving? They'd say it whenever anything got screwed up. Her father said it when he lost his job, trying to lessen the fear of its impact on them. Ronnie even said it to her father on his bed minutes before he died, hoping that he'd hear it and smile. But he didn't.

Ronnie went to Sunday mass with her mother after her father died. She liked it. It was theater, after all. And early on this Friday morning it wasn't lost on Ronnie that she was sitting in a dark church with two million dollars cash next to her because of her mother.

Ronnie felt under the seat of her pew and found the small index card that Alex had taped there earlier. On it were the instructions that she'd show to Shelby. She also felt the backpack that Alex had left there for her under the pew. She looked across the center aisle and saw a man. Was that Alex? No. He was too old and well dressed. She looked a few pews behind him and saw a younger man in a worn coat and a black wool cap pulled down over his ears. This was Alex, wearing the old overcoat that he'd once worn in a production of *Waiting for Lefty*. Alex rocked back and forth like a junkie in need of a fix. When he turned and looked at Ronnie their eyes met briefly before they each looked quickly away.

Ronnie placed her backpack full of money on the floor. She pushed it under her pew with her foot. Now there were two backpacks there, side by side, one with two million dollars' worth of Euros in it and the other stuffed with newspaper and books.

She had a decision to make, one she'd gone over again and again in the last two days. Did she trust Alex enough to leave the money with him? He'd changed since Newman showed up, convinced that the imposter would steal their money. Would his distrust of Newman cause Alex to do something foolish, something that would jeopardize them all? Even without Newman's role in all this, would Alex have spent the money too soon and called attention to them both?

Ronnie watched the priest on the altar. She thought about how often people put themselves through long, drawn-out processes to decide a choice they have to make. She'd always thought that was self-indulgent bullshit. Most of the time everyone knows what they're going to do from the start.

But this was one of those few times when Ronnie had a real choice to make, yes or no, black or white. She sat in the church listening to the other congregants mumbling their prayers. She closed her eyes and held her head in her hands.

— • —

Pike was parked up the street from the church. His cell rang. It was Kestrel who didn't give Pike a chance to say anything before asking, "Where is it?"

Pike lied. "They're in a cab with it heading north on Fifth."

"You sure?"

"They're right in front of me. But it's gonna be hard to follow them in this traffic."

"Don't worry about it," Kestrel said. "If you lose 'em, you lose 'em. As long as they get the money to these people and we get Newman back safe."

"I'll do my best, sir," Pike said.

Kestrel hung up. Pike was surprised how unlike himself Kestrel sounded. Had he finally accepted that giving into the kidnappers' demands was the best thing for both the safety of his employee and the success of the Salient deal? Pike hoped that was the case.

— • —

Following the priest's evocation to the congregants, the woman in front of Ronnie turned around and extended her hand across the empty pew between them. "Peace be with you," she said when Ronnie took the woman's hand that was cold and hard.

"And with you," Ronnie answered. The woman looked directly into Ronnie's eyes and held her hand longer than Ronnie expected her to. Was there something in her expression that the woman could see? Of course there wasn't. Ronnie was overreacting.

She pulled her hand away from the woman's and looked across the aisle at Alex who rocked rhythmically in his pew, waiting for her to leave so he could take the backpack she left for him, the backpack with the ransom. He turned his head slightly and when he saw that Ronnie was looking at him he smiled like a little boy. It was his most beautiful feature. She reached under the pew, grabbed the backpack and left the church with it.

— • —

Outside the church, Ronnie held her hand over her eyes as they adjusted to the brightness. She walked down the stone steps and got into the waiting taxi.

Seeing that Ronnie still had the backpack, Shelby said, "You didn't leave it in there?"

Ronnie shook her head. "There was a note under the pew. They want me to bring it to a park on 51st Street."

"Why?"

"51st between Second and Third," Ronnie said to the cabbie and he pulled into traffic.

— • —

Pike watched Ronnie exit the church with the backpack. Someone else might have gotten into a cab, dumped Shelby and disappeared with the money. But Ronnie's plans did what she said they would: they made it look like the kidnappers had no idea what Kestrel would do and they hoped to outsmart him and anyone who was following them. Ronnie was clever, hopefully not too clever.

Pike then saw a young man with a woolen hat pulled tightly down over his head exit the church. It was Alex and he carried a backpack identical to Ronnie's. Ronnie must have made the switch in the church while Shelby waited outside. Alex now had the two million dollar backpack.

Alex unlocked his bike chained to a pole in front of the church and pedaled off on it. Pike started his car, but the street was one way so he had to swing around the block to catch up with Alex. Pike sped up the narrow street and, at the corner, Alex's bike pulled in front of both Pike's car and Ronnie's cab at the same time. Both Pike and the cabbie slammed on their brakes. Alex paid no attention to either one and pedaled on.

— • —

As Ronnie's cabbie honked and swore at Alex, she and Pike saw one another. She was relieved that Shelby hadn't seen him. Pike's car made a quick turn and followed Alex on the bike.

"That was close," Shelby said. But she didn't know it was Alex on the bike they'd almost hit.

Ronnie watched Pike's car disappear into the traffic. After heading a few more blocks north, Ronnie tapped on the plastic divider and spoke to the cabbie. "Stop here."

"Here?"

"One of us is getting out."

The cabbie pulled over.

"Who's getting out?" Shelby asked.

"You are."

"Why?"

"Because it's too dangerous for you to go any further."

"What do you mean?"

"This was under the pew in the church." Ronnie showed Shelby an index card on which Newman had written:

ONLY ONE OF YOU WILL TAKE THIS TO THE PARK ON 51ST STREET BETWEEN SECOND AND THIRD AVENUES.

"Only one of us?" Shelby asked. "Does that mean they know there's two of us? That they've been following us the whole time?"

Ronnie nodded. "Probably."

"Oh, my God."

Ronnie looked at the cabbie who was arguing with a dispatcher on his cell phone. He was paying no attention to them, so she opened the backpack.

It was filled with the cash.

Ronnie had chosen to keep the money and not leave it in the church. Now she had to figure out what to do with it. But first she had to get rid of Shelby. The girl wasn't gonna be mistaken for a genius, but she wasn't so stupid that she couldn't put two and two together. Ronnie would tell Shelby she was dumping her for the safety of her and her soon-to-be-born son.

"Take this and go," Ronnie said and grabbed a wad of the Euros, maybe a quarter inch of bills. She held them out to Shelby low behind the back of the driver's seat so he couldn't see them.

Shelby shook her head. "I can't do that to you."

"Look at yourself for God's sake. Go home. Go to a hospital. Go back to Georgia. Have your baby."

"It's not right."

But Ronnie was adamant. "Take it."

Shelby stared at the cash in Ronnie's hand. "What if the kidnappers see that this money is missing from the payoff?"

Jesus, why couldn't this dipshit just take the money and go? "It's not that much. They won't care." Ronnie held out the wad of cash. "Take it. Get out of here."

Shelby looked at the rest of the cash in the open knapsack. "Won't they hurt Newman if we give them less money than what they asked for?"

"No one's gonna hurt anyone."

"Will Kestrel still give me the twenty five thousand?"

"Of course he will. And if your getting out now upsets him, we'll say I threw you out of the cab because you were having contractions or something. He won't even know what that means."

"But I didn't do what I promised him I would."

What was wrong with this girl? "Do you want it or not?" Ronnie asked. "Because if you don't take it right now, I'm not holding myself responsible for whatever might happen to you. Or Sammy."

Shelby took the cash from Ronnie. "Are you taking the rest of it for yourself?" Shelby asked.

"The rest of what?" Ronnie said.

"The money."

"Of course not."

"Are you a part of this, Ronnie?"

"Part of what?"

"The kidnapping."

"No."

"You can tell me."

"There's nothing to tell. Jesus, I'm trying to help you out here." Apparently, Shelby wasn't as stupid as Ronnie thought she was. "If you don't want the money, then give it back to me and we'll put Sammy and Newman and all of us in as much danger as we can." At this point Ronnie's exasperation was genuine.

The look on Shelby's face suggested that she didn't believe Ronnie. But she said, "Okay," and stuffed the wad of Euros into the handbag Natalie had given her in Kestrel's office. There was room in there for it.

"Now get out of here. For Sammy's sake," Ronnie said.

But Shelby didn't move.

"What?" Ronnie asked.

"I need more," Shelby said.

"More what?"

"More money."

"Seriously?" Ronnie asked.

Shelby nodded. The girl's unexpected greed shocked Ronnie. Or maybe it didn't. Everyone else was grabbing what they could get, so why not Scarlett O'Hara? Ronnie reached into the backpack, grabbed more bills and thrust them at Shelby. "Here."

Shelby took the money and stuffed it into her handbag. She still didn't move.

"What?" Ronnie asked.

"More."

Shelby stared at Ronnie like a dog expecting a treat. Ronnie grabbed some more of the Euros and handed them to her. "Here," she said. "Any more and we're gonna put Newman in danger."

"We don't want to endanger Mr. Newman, do we?" Shelby asked with an expression that reflected as much bewilderment as concern. Or maybe it was amusement.

Whatever it was, Shelby stuck this final wad of Euros into her designer bag, opened the cab's door and held onto the door's frame as she pulled herself up and out. Before shutting the door, she leaned into the cab and looked at Ronnie. "Don't do anything you'll regret, Ronnie. You're a good person."

Shelby turned and walked away, leaving it up to Ronnie to lean over and pull the cab's door shut. She watched the pregnant girl walk to the curb and look back at Ronnie a last time. Her expression said a million things and it said nothing. Then Shelby turned and disappeared into the people on the street.

Ronnie was shocked by what had just happened. What did Shelby suspect? How much did she know? Ronnie's only relief was that Shelby could say nothing to Kestrel or anyone else about this. She'd taken the money. She was as guilty as everyone else.

— • —

Pike followed Alex as far west as he could on 43rd Street, but on his bike Alex made it through the traffic much more quickly than Pike, sometimes avoiding it altogether by riding on the sidewalk. There was no way Pike could keep up with him, but the direction Alex was heading told him where he was going, somewhere no one else would be heading this early in the morning, especially not other actors.

When he got to the Jubilee theater ten minutes later, Pike parked his car a few buildings down the street. He put some coins in the meter and walked to the theater. He knew he'd guessed right when he saw Alex's bike leaning against a dumpster in the alley. In his eagerness to get into the theater with the money, Alex had left the stage door unlocked so Pike pushed it open and walked in. Once inside, he locked the door behind himself.

The first thing Pike heard in the theater was Alex yelling. "Shit, shit, shit. You bitch! How could you—do that?" Pike waited until it was silent again before he walked into the wings.

Alex sat on a chair center stage. The large white ambulance prop he wore for the hydration sketch leaned against the wall behind him. The empty backpack was in front of him, surrounded by several books and newspapers strewn across the stage floor.

"Is there a problem?"

Alex jumped to his feet. "What are you doing here?"

"I followed you."

"Why?"

"That was part of the plan. Remember? To make sure you and the money were safe. We're in this together. We're partners."

"We might be in this together, but we're not partners, so get that out of your head right now."

Alex was upset because something had changed and Pike was worried that the kid might do something stupid. He'd seen perps like Alex quickly fall apart when a plan had changed quickly and unexpectedly. They'd start to talk a lot. Invariably, they'd say too much. To too many people. And they'd make bad decisions.

Pike walked slowly to Alex and the books and newspapers scattered across the stage. "Something's changed, hasn't it, Alex?" he said in the calm tone he was trained to use in situations like this.

Alex shook his head. "Why do you say that?"

"Because the money was supposed to be in that backpack, wasn't it?"

Alex stared at the floor for several moments. Finally, he said, "Yeah."

"Where is it?"

Alex got up and crossed the stage. "Something must've happened. Maybe it was Shelby. Maybe that bitch did something."

"Shelby didn't do anything."

"Or Kestrel sent someone to get Ronnie."

"Kestrel didn't send anyone," Pike said and pointed to the empty backpack on the floor. "Ronnie changed her plans when she was in the church. She took the money. And she left you—left us—with this."

Alex kicked at the newspaper on the stage floor. "No," he said, "she'll be here with it."

"I wouldn't count on it."

"How do you know?"

"Because money changes people, Alex, that's how I know. She played us." Pike hated saying this to the kid. He didn't want to believe it himself, but a week ago he wouldn't have believed that Ronnie would be the mastermind of a kidnapping plot, either.

Alex was adamant. "She didn't play me. You'll see. She'll explain everything when she gets here."

"It's messy now," Pike said. "Once a plan starts to come apart like this you can never put it back together again. You think she made a deal with someone else?"

"There's only Newman. And you."

"Maybe he's in with her."

"Newman? No. Not a chance," Alex said, but Pike could tell that the idea of Ronnie and Newman working together had already occurred to him. Thinking about it now made him pace the stage angrily. "No way it's Newman," Alex said. "We'll wait. She'll show up. She always does."

Alex took his cell phone out of his pocket and dialed it.

— • —

Ronnie sat silently in the cab's backseat after Shelby left with her cash. How could she have misread the girl so badly?

The cabbie turned around. "Where you go now, miss?"

"Stay here for a minute," she said.

That morning Ronnie had still been deciding whether to carry out the plan she'd outlined to Alex and Newman or whether she'd take the money herself and decide what to do with it after things quieted down. While sitting in the church, she made the decision to keep the money and leave the dummy backpack under the pew for Alex to take.

Seeing Alex in the church dressed like he was had reminded her how wonderfully childlike he was. But that was a dangerous quality now. Instead of doing what she'd told Alex and Newman, she'd keep the money somewhere safe, making sure that there was no way Alex could spend any of it until the Salient deal was closed. Everyone, flush with cash from the Salient deal, would have forgotten about the Newman kidnapping which they'd know by then was really extortion and not a kidnapping at all. She was doing this for Alex, to keep him safe.

But now that she had the money what would she do with it? She couldn't take it to a bank. And this soon after 9/11 there were no public lockers, were there? Maybe she'd get a room in a hotel and stay with it there until she decided what to do next. At least she could get some sleep. She'd call Alex from the hotel and meet him somewhere. She'd explain to him what she'd done. And why.

But she'd have to go back to Boundary sometime, too, and tell Kestrel and the others that she left the money for the kidnappers in the trunk of a car like their final note had told her to do. She had that note, in Newman's handwriting, in her pocket, ready to give to Kestrel.

And she'd have to meet with Newman somewhere, too, so she could give him his share of the money. If she didn't, he might get revenge on her and Alex by outing them to Kestrel and the authorities like he'd threatened to. But did he seriously think that she planned to run away with him? She'd used all her acting skills to sell him that idea. Maybe she was kidding herself and maybe it was Newman who was playing her. No, she thought, he definitely wants me.

So she'd give Newman his share of the money, the one million dollars in Euros, and tell him that she wanted— she needed—to be alone for a while so she could make a decision about her life and their future together. She'd say it was the only way to be fair to Alex. Newman would buy it as long as she played it right, wouldn't he? He'd bought everything else she told him.

But what about Alex? Would she go back with him? Would they be able to get over this? Did she even want to? She'd figure that out later. Right now she had to decide what to do with the money in the backpack.

Her phone rang. It was Alex.

After letting it ring several beats, she answered. "Alex—"

"Where's the money?"

"I have it," she said. "Hold on." She stuck a couple of twenty dollar bills in the cabbie's money drawer and got out on the street with the backpack.

"Why didn't you leave it at the church like we said?" Alex said.

"I was afraid."

"Of what?"

"That you wouldn't do what we planned. That you'd improvise."

"I'm the one here at the theater. Not you. Who's improvising now?"

"Let's talk this through."

"Did you make a deal with Newman?"

"Don't be stupid."

"I'll kill him if you did."

A part of her was relieved to hear Alex talk like this because his rage justified her decision to keep the money. "I'm going to hold the money until you cool down," she said. "That's all."

"It's my money, too."

"I never said it wasn't. You'll get your share."

"When?"

"When it's safe. When we're both safe."

"I want it now."

"Why?" she said, suddenly furious at him, at everything. "So you can spend it on a new apartment? Or buy yourself a Ferrari? Or a bunch of clothes?" Saying this aloud made her even angrier, the way an actor uses physical movements or their costume and make-up to fuel their character's emotions. Ronnie had been responsible for so much, too much, for so long and it surprised her when she heard her own rage. Passersby looked at her as she yelled into her phone, "I'm tired, Alex. Do you hear me? I'm tired of thinking about you, about Kestrel, about Shelby, about Pike, Newman, the money, my mother, about everyone and everything. I need to be alone. I need to be alone and think about me—ME—for a change." He had to understand what she was saying to him.

But he didn't. He only said, "You don't bring it to the theater now I'll turn you in."

"Don't say that."

"I'll make a deal with Pike. He'll tell the cops that he was setting us up and I was working with him."

"He won't do that, Alex."

"Ask him yourself. He's right here."

Of course Pike was there. He'd followed Alex who was carrying to the theater what both he and Alex thought was the backpack with the money. That was the plan.

"I'll wait here for one hour. After that I'm not responsible for what happens." Alex hung up.

Ronnie looked at the people walking past her. Would any of them ever have guessed what she was trying to decide or what was stuffed into the backpack that sat on the sidewalk next to her?

— • —

Pike was surprised that Ronnie had answered Alex's call. Maybe he was wrong. Maybe she hadn't ditched them and she'd show up at the theater as planned. But he wouldn't bet on it.

"She'll be here," Alex said, pacing the stage and slapping the thick black stage curtain each time he passed it. "You watch."

"Maybe you're right," Pike said, hoping to calm him down.

"No 'maybe' about it. She'll be here."

Alex's emotions were all over the place. After accusing Ronnie on the phone, he was defending her now. "I know her. You don't. You think you do, but you don't. She's confused is all. We'll figure it out when she gets here."

"Maybe we should let her do what she needs to," Pike said. "Let her sit with the money for a while and work it out by herself. She's upset. You know how ladies get. When she's calm we can all sit down and talk. You don't want to make any decisions now. You, me, her, everybody, we're all too hyped up right now."

Alex was torn, furious at being lied to by Ronnie, but wanting—needing—to trust her.

— • —

Martin sat at his computer in Ronnie and Alex's apartment deleting all traces of Martin Newman. Once the ransom was paid, Newman, the victim, would not reappear safe and sound as the kidnappers had promised. Kestrel and the others would worry at first that something had happened to him, even that the kidnappers might have killed him. But after further investigation, Boundary's IT people would tell them that Martin Newman had never existed, that it was all a scam. Martin wished he could see the looks on their faces, Kestrel's especially, when they heard that.

But it wasn't a scam. Not really. Martin Newman had lived and had done things that no one else could have done.

Even so, removing all traces of Martin Newman didn't take long. The only thing left now proving his existence was the diary that Ronnie and Alex had started almost two years before, the one that Martin had hijacked and turned into his own. It outlined Martin's life, his experiences, his goals, his dreams.

He decided to write a final page of it, both a suicide note and an obituary, one that no one other than he would read.

MARTIN NEWMAN'S DIARY

What I have to do now is very hard for me. But I have no choice. In a few minutes I will delete myself. It's as simple as that.

These days people like to say about someone, "He's history". But that'd be the wrong expression to use about me because I'll have no history. Nowhere. How could I? To the world I never existed.

That's the joy—and the sadness—of creating a new identity. You might like that person, you may want to be them, but you have to be realistic. One minute you're there and the next you're not. At least I know that I did exist once and, to prove it, there will soon be two million dollars in cash sitting on the table in front of me.

I'm going to delete myself now. Goodbye Martin.

RIP

Martin stared at the computer screen for a few moments before hitting the delete button. His diary and his existence disappeared.

— • —

Both Pike and Alex turned to the stage door when they heard it open. "Ssshh," Alex said and he took a pistol from his jacket pocket.

Pike was shocked when he saw Alex's gun. "What are you doing with that?"

"Shut up," Alex said and they both stood in silence. Where did the kid get a gun? Was it his? It looked like a Glock, a favorite of gangs. Was it loaded? Did he even know how to shoot it? It didn't matter because the one thing Pike had learned as a cop was that nothing good ever happens once a gun enters the picture.

Pike decided not to take his own gun out of his holster and scare the kid into doing something even more stupid. But he slipped his right hand under his jacket and unlatched the safety band on his shoulder holster that secured his own pistol.

Ronnie carried the backpack with the money in it. She shut the stage door behind her and locked it. From the wings, she said, "Alex? Are you here?"

Hearing no reply, she stepped onto the stage where she saw Alex and Pike standing opposite her. "Alex, I—" she started to say until she saw the gun in Alex's hand that was pointing at her.

"Drop the backpack right there," Alex said.

Ronnie was shocked. What was he doing? Where had he gotten a gun? Did he get it the night he'd threatened to? He told her he hadn't, but he must've lied to her. "What are you doing, Alex? Is that real?"

"It's very real."

"This is crazy. Put it down, baby. Please." She knew that Alex had shot guns before. His father had taken him and his brothers hunting in the Pennsylvania woods for deer and turkey when he was a kid. "Remember what your father told you," Ronnie said. "Never point a gun at anything you don't intend to kill."

"She's right, Alex," Pike said. "Why don't you give it to me?"

Alex turned and pointed his gun at Pike. "Shut up."

Pike stepped back and raised both hands to show that he meant no harm to Alex.

"Let's talk this through," Ronnie said.

"No more talking," Alex said. "I'm tired of talking. Everybody lies."

"I don't," Ronnie said.

"You do." Alex's eyes were filled with tears. He was losing it like a child, a confused child with a gun in his hand.

Ronnie looked at Pike for help, but what could he do? "I made a mistake before in the church, okay?" Ronnie said to Alex. "I was upset. I didn't know who to trust."

"I'm the one who doesn't know who to trust anymore," Alex said.

Ronnie stepped toward him but, when she did, Alex raised his gun again and she froze. "You can trust me, baby," she said. "I'm here now. I got scared about what you might do with the money. What Newman might do when he saw it. That's all. I wanted to keep it until some time went by. Until things calmed down. So we'd both be safe. I never did anything like this before, Alex. I'm not a criminal. All this shit isn't me. I got confused." She looked at Pike again who nodded to her as if to say she was saying the right stuff.

"I did all this for you," Alex said.

"And we're here together now, aren't we? I got the money here for us and we're safe. You want to see it?" She reached into the backpack and pulled out a wad of the Euros.

"Put it back," Alex said and she did.

She pointed to Pike. "We'll give him his cut. Then we'll take the rest home and divide it up. Like we planned. You and me."

"What about Newman?"

"What about him?"

"How do I know you and him aren't in this together?"

"Because we're not."

"First him, then this guy," Alex said, pointing the pistol at Pike again. "I don't know who to believe."

Pike took a step to the side when Alex motioned at him with his pistol.

"Me. You should believe me, baby," Ronnie said, moving towards Alex.

Alex stepped back, his pistol aimed at Ronnie. "Don't come any closer." He was scared and confusing his fear with anger. His eyes were full of tears and his hand shook.

Pike pulled his own pistol from its shoulder holster and held it pointed at the ground. "Put your gun down, Alex. Please."

Alex saw Pike's pistol and said to Ronnie, "See? What did I tell you? He's got a gun."

"He's Kestrel's bodyguard," Ronnie said. "He always carries one." She said to Pike, "Put it away, Detective. Please."

But Pike kept his pistol in his hand, pointing it at the stage floor. "I'm not gonna hurt anyone, Alex," he said. "So do the smart thing and put your gun down."

"I put down my gun and you take the money."

"I don't care about the money," Pike said.

"Then what are you doing here?" Alex asked him.

"I never wanted any of the money."

"Listen to him, Alex," Ronnie said. "We're all on the same side here."

Alex became more unraveled. "You're on his side now?"

"There's no side except ours."

"It was our plan," Alex said. "No one else's."

"It still is."

"Until everyone else got involved. Newman and Shelby and him." Alex turned to Pike and when he aimed his pistol directly at him to make his point Alex's pistol went off mistakenly and fired a single shot in the direction of Pike. But the shot missed Pike who, in turn, instinctively raised his own gun in Alex's direction and fired without thinking.

The hard crack of the two gunshots, one after the other, was deafeningly loud in the small theater. The three of them, Ronnie, Alex and Pike, stood still for a moment, shocked by the sound, and unsure what to do next.

The first of them to move was Alex. He looked down at his chest where a spot of blood appeared on his shirt. He said, "Shit," and dropped to the stage floor.

Ronnie ran and knelt over Alex who was more confused than frightened by what had just happened. "I didn't mean to shoot," he said. "I'm sorry." He breathed heavily as he saw the blood on his shirt. It didn't gush out like it did in the movies. The stain grew slowly. "There's not that much blood, is there?" Alex asked.

"You're gonna be all right. Just stay down," Ronnie said, unbuttoning his shirt. He bled more quickly now, staining the heavy coat he wore. "Lay still, baby. Don't move." She put pressure on his wound with her hands that were being stained with his blood.

Pike stood frozen in place across the stage like one of the props hanging on the wall behind him. "You saw what happened," Pike mumbled. "He fired first. I didn't mean to shoot. It was instinct. I never shot anybody before."

Ronnie paid no attention to what Pike said. She leaned over Alex, trying to stop the bleeding.

"I told Pike that you'd come with the money," Alex said to her. "He said you were gonna cheat me, but I told him you'd never do that."

"You were right, baby. I could never cheat you. That's why I'm here. I got confused. We all did. We're terrible at this. We're like Boris and Natasha."

Alex smiled. "Theese is leeving?" he said, imitating the bumbling cartoon characters. Ronnie hoped this meant he'd be okay, but his voice grew weaker. "Whatever you do, promise me you won't give any of the money back to Kestrel."

"I'd never do that."

"You have to help your mother."

"I will."

"You couldn't have done any of this without me, could you?"

"Not a thing," Ronnie said.

Pike stared at them both without moving. "I never shot anybody before," he said again to no one. Ronnie turned to him.

"Don't just stand there. Call 911," she said.

Pike searched in his pocket for his phone, but he'd left it in his car.

"We're calling 911 now," Ronnie said to Alex. "They'll come get you. When you're better we'll go away somewhere. Just you and me. Like we said we would. We'll take that trip together. Wherever you want to go. I love you so much. You know that. You're my love."

But by the time she'd said all that, Alex was dead. She'd watched her father die and looking at Alex's body she thought the same thing she did when she saw her father's body. Whether you believe that there's a soul or not, something in the body changes when a person dies. It's as sure as night and day, black and white, before and after. Ronnie leaned over and cradled Alex's body. She was both sad and furious, at Pike, at Alex, at Newman, at Kestrel, but mostly at herself. Her grief and rage were inseparable. "Shit, shit, shit," she said over and over as tears fell down her cheeks onto Alex's body.

"Is he dead?" Pike asked, afraid to move any closer.

"What do you think?"

"I thought he was gonna shoot me. I didn't want him to hurt you."

"So you killed him instead," she said and turned back to Alex whose eyes were still open. She leaned over and with her fingers tried to close them. But like she'd told Newman the night before, dead people's eyes don't close easily. "See?" Ronnie shouted angrily to Pike, "It's not like in the movies. They don't close like that. Not at all. Shit."

"He shot at me," Pike mumbled to himself again. "What could I do?"

Ronnie picked up Alex's pistol from the floor and waved it for Pike to see. "It's a blank gun, an actor's prop. He's a child and this was his toy." She aimed the gun at Pike and pulled its trigger several times. Pike flinched each time the prop's firing mechanism clicked harmlessly.

"He said it was real," Pike said.

Ronnie ignored Pike and said, "I should've left with the money and given it to him later like I planned to, but I didn't. No. I had to come back here. And do you know why? Do you?" Pike shook his head. "Because I'm a good person. Shelby told me that in the cab. That's why. Did you know that, Detective? I'm a goddamn saint."

Ronnie leaned over Alex's body and breathed deeply. This was not the time to mourn. She needed to be practical and hard like she was the day her father died and she told herself that nothing was ever going to faze her again. She did it then; she'd do it now. She stood up and stuck Alex's prop pistol into her pocket. She turned to Pike and said, "Kill the house lights."

Pike stood frozen, staring at Alex's body.

"I said kill the lights." Ronnie pointed to a large switch box on the wall. "There."

Pike walked like a zombie to the switch box and shut the house lights off. Only the rehearsal lights, three bare bulbs hanging from the ceiling on wires, remained lit.

Ronnie leaned over Alex's body and took his wallet from his back pocket. She removed the cash and two credit cards and put them in her pocket. She tossed his empty wallet across the stage. "This is what happened," she said to Pike. "He came to the theater to rehearse. Someone followed him in here and robbed him. They shot him. It happens every day, right?"

Pike said nothing.

"Right?" Ronnie asked him again.

Pike nodded. "Right."

Ronnie rounded up the newspaper and the books from the stage floor and stuffed them back into Alex's backpack. She zipped it shut and held it out to Pike. "Take this." Pike took the backpack.

Ronnie looked around the theater to see if there was anything else to do. There wasn't. She walked to Alex's body and leaned over it. She kissed him on the lips. "I'm so sorry, baby." She wiped the tears from her cheeks, took a deep breath and turned to Pike. "Let's get out of here."

Ronnie and Pike went through the stage door and walked past Alex's bike to the street. No one saw them. Even if someone did, it'd be natural for her to have gone to the theater with Alex and left him there to rehearse a new sketch she'd written. It was something they did all the time.

Ronnie walked quickly and Pike, still in a daze, hurried to keep up with her. She told Pike to toss the backpack with the paper and books into a dumpster. He did.

Ronnie planned what to do next. The trick was to think of anything other than the image of Alex lying dead on the theater floor. She wanted someone, she needed someone, a strong man, a strong woman, her father, her mother, an overcoat man, anyone to help her now, to tell her what to do. But what good would that have been? She'd been depending on two people today, both men. Now one was dead and the other had shot him.

Pike took hold of Ronnie's shoulder. "We can do this together."

She pushed his hand away. "What are you talking about?"

"I can help you."

"Do what?"

"I care for you."

"You just killed my boyfriend and now you're hitting on me?"

"No, that's not what I'm doing. I'm saying that I can help you."

"Get that out of your head because it's not gonna happen."

"Of course not," Pike said, stepping away from her. "I'm a foolish man. I got into all this to help you, Ronnie. I never wanted to hurt you. I didn't want any money."

"Then you won't miss it." Ronnie put the backpack with the money over her shoulders. She wiped her face with her hand, smearing some of Alex's blood on her cheek and neck as she did.

"Wait," Pike said as he reached over to wipe the blood off her cheek, but she pushed his hand away and wiped the blood off with her sleeve. She walked away without looking back at Pike.

She heard Pike call, "Ronnie" after her. She stopped and turned to him. "Tell Newman that if Kestrel finds out he was involved he'll hunt him down and do whatever he can to hurt him. Tell him that."

Ronnie stared at Pike. "There is no Newman," she said. "There never was. Alex and I, we made him up. Everything about him."

Pike was silent.

"We created a person on the computer called Martin Newman as fictitious as any character in those books you read. That's who we kidnapped. That's who Alex died for. Someone who never existed."

Pike watched Ronnie turn and walk away, disappearing behind a stack of crates being wheeled into a bodega. What did she mean that Martin Newman had never existed? Pike read the man's Boundary file. He was born in Baltimore. He was thirty-three years old. He was a rock climber. He played second base on the Boundary softball team and his wife had died eighteen months earlier. He'd rented an apartment at The Maxwell. Pike had been to his apartment there. But Pike also recalled how no one at Boundary remembered Martin Newman the same way. Some didn't even remember him at all. Was he a fiction and was that what made Ronnie's creation so easy to believe? That the employees at a place like Boundary had no real identity? Were they all so interchangeable? So forgettable? Is everyone? Whatever the answer to that question, there was no Newman. There never was.

But there was a young man named Alex Ryan who, along with Ronnie, had created Martin Newman. Pike was certain of that because a few minutes ago he'd shot and killed him. He'd watched Ronnie try to close the dead boy's eyes as he lay on the dusty stage floor.

A homeless woman asked Pike for a handout and, still in a daze, he shoved a couple of dollars into the woman's hand. Pike walked quickly to his car where he'd parked it down the street from the theater and got into it. He'd drive back to Boundary and tell Kestrel that he lost the money's trail soon after it left the church. His hands were shaking so much that he had to wait until they were still before he started the car and drove off.

— • —

Still in a daze, Ronnie pushed her way through the maze of tourists, hawkers and deliverymen on Eighth Avenue. Because her backpack was so heavy, it swung from side to side, hitting some of the people she passed, including a short man selling counterfeit watches lined up on a card table. The man spun around, ready to yell at her, but didn't when he saw her. "Yo, lady," he said, "you got like blood and shit on your face."

"I know," Ronnie said as if it were perfectly natural for the blood to be there and ridiculous for the man to have mentioned it. She kept walking. Her short hair wasn't going to hide any blood that might be on her jaw or her neck and she had no idea what anyone else could see. She stopped to look at her reflection in the window of a diner, but she couldn't see anything.

She walked into the diner, a relic of what all New York coffee shops once were—narrow and noisy with a fan that circled slowly overhead like a vulture. Its two waitresses barked orders and insults in English and Spanish and poured the only two kinds of coffee served here: regular from a pot with a brown handle and decaf from one with an orange handle. The sizzle from the eggs and bacon on the griddle drowned out the tinny music playing from a clock radio on a shelf over the counter. Ronnie breathed more easily. This was like the places she used to go with her father. It calmed her.

Two cops, one a Black man, the other a Latina, sat at the corner of the counter. Ronnie turned her head away so they couldn't see whatever blood might be on her face.

Holding her head down, Ronnie squirmed her way to the narrow hallway in the back where there was a single bathroom and another door that opened onto an alley filled with crates on which a few men sat eating and smoking. One smiled at her. She grabbed the handle on the bathroom door, but it was locked. She rubbed her face again with her sleeve and more blood came off on it. She stopped, thinking she might be making it worse and prayed that whoever was in the bathroom would finish soon. She looked at several autographed 8x10 celebrity photos that hung on the wall. One was a famous comedian whose forced smile seemed to be mocking her.

The bathroom door finally opened and a man in a suit came out. In the bathroom now, Ronnie locked the door's small rusted eyehook. She flipped the toilet lid down and sat the heavy backpack on it. She leaned on the sink and looked at herself in the small dirty mirror over it.

Alex's blood was still on her cheek. She grabbed a stiff paper towel from the tin dispenser under a sign that said "Employees Must Wash Their Hands". She wet the towel and wiped her face with it. She rubbed herself clean, but even when all the blood was gone she kept rubbing her face and hands, Lady Macbeth-like, as if trying to take her skin off and her memories with it.

She finally stopped and, breathing heavily, stared at her face in the cracked glass. How did she end up in this grimy little bathroom wiping Alex's blood off her face? Who was this person in the mirror staring back at her?

She'd spent the last three days ridiculing the man who'd transformed himself into the fictional Martin Newman. He believed that he'd jettisoned the loser he was and become someone new and dangerous, someone alluring and fascinating. It was more than laughable. It was absurd. But was what she'd done any better? She'd recast herself, a wannabe playwright and personal assistant, into a criminal mastermind. Worse, she'd persuaded Alex, a simple boy who now lay dead on the grimy floor of a theater, that he could be her accomplice, her co-star in this foolish fantasy she'd concocted.

Her burner rang and she fumbled as she took it from her pocket. She didn't recognize the caller's number, but she answered anyway. "What?"

"This is Bobby," the voice on the other end said.

Who was Bobby?

"Bobby Lieberman, the pharmacist."

"Oh, right," Ronnie said. "Sorry, Bobby. I'm in the middle of something here at work. What's up?"

"I got the information you wanted. From the pill bottle."

"That's great." Ronnie stared at herself in the mirror.

"Maybe we could meet somewhere and I could give it to you."

"Oh, man, I'm getting ready to go out of town for a couple of days. Business stuff. Why don't you give me the information now and I can meet up with you when I get back?" There was a knock on the bathroom door. "Just a second," Ronnie shouted at whoever wanted to get in. "That's my ride to the airport," she said to Bobby. "So what did you find out?"

"The prescription was for a guy called Lance Tolan. For Xanax."

"Thank God," Ronnie said. "That's not my brother."

Lance Tolan. Who was Lance Tolan?

"Xanax is for anxiety," Bobby said. "Stuff like that. You wouldn't believe how many people use it. My mother says they should put it in a dispenser."

Ronnie knew what Xanax was. Who in 21st Century America didn't? "You're my hero, Bobby. I owe you big time."

"Will you let me buy you dinner?"

"No way. I'm buying you dinner."

She could hear the smile in Bobby's voice when he said, "It's a deal."

Whoever was waiting to get in the bathroom knocked again, louder this time.

"I'm almost done," Ronnie said through the door. She said to Bobby, "I'll call you on Wednesday when I get back from my trip."

Ronnie hung up, took a deep breath and put her backpack on. She opened the door. Waiting in the narrow hallway was the Latina police officer. Ronnie tensed. Had somebody heard the gunshot coming from the theater or had the police gotten a call about Alex's body? Maybe they'd seen the blood on Ronnie's face when she came in. But the policewoman only smiled at her and said, "They need another one of these rooms, don't they?"

"They always do," Ronnie said, holding the door open for her.

Ronnie squeezed through the customers with her backpack on and made her way onto the street and got into a cab. She told the cabbie her Brooklyn address and waited for him to ask her how to get there. But he didn't. He knew where it was or at least he started to drive like he knew.

She repeated the name Bobby Lieberman had told her on her burner. Lance Tolan, Lance Tolan, Lance Tolan. She hoped saying his name aloud might help her remember where and how she'd met him. If she'd met him. Lance. Who names their kid Lance anyway? It's what you call a soap opera character. Look, there's Lance with his friends Thud and Burp. That would make a funny sketch for Jubilee, a soap opera reunion, but why was she thinking about that now?

Lance Tolan. Maybe he was just a guy who rented the apartment at The Maxwell before Newman did.

But what difference did it make who Lance Tolan was anyway? Trying to remember him was a distraction, a way for her to forget that Alex was lying dead in the theater. Martin Newman was waiting in the apartment for her to show up with the money. She had to deal with him and his demented dreams. That's what mattered now.

In traffic on the bridge her taxi pulled alongside a bus on the side of which was an ad for a new cell phone. The ad stretched the length of the bus and featured two young men. One was chubby with a scraggly beard and he wore glasses that, nerd-like, sported a bridge held together with packing tape. The ad suggested that, after he got his new cell phone, this loser would turn into the man on the other end of the ad, a much better looking and far cooler guy wearing designer clothes, expensive eyeglasses and smile that said the world was his. Ronnie's taxi and the bus sat side by side. The loser in the ad stared directly at her. If she rolled down her window she could've touched him.

Ronnie remembered who Lance Tolan was.

Eleven months earlier Boundary had gotten a ransomware threat that, if carried out, could have crippled the company. Kestrel wasn't about to give in. A firm called Bright Lights was brought in to help Boundary's overwhelmed IT people respond to it.

It was a Tuesday afternoon, St. Patrick's Day. While the Bright Lights people worked on Boundary's systems, Ronnie arranged a trip to San Francisco for Kestrel. The techies had been jumping all day from Ronnie's to Heidi's to Shelby's desks looking for whatever it was people like them look for. Ronnie had gotten to know two of the guys, Peter and Jason, from earlier visits. A third man was new. He stood over her shoulder while she tried to make Kestrel's hotel reservations.

"You guys c-c-could use stronger p-p-passwords," the new guy said, stuttering every few words. He was overweight and like the man in the ad on the side of the bus, he wore thick glasses and an untrimmed beard that made his face look even fatter. His teeth were a mess, too. If there were a role for an Amish nerd, this guy would have been the first person cast.

Ronnie didn't bother to look up at him. "You're in my light," she said.

He didn't get the hint and stood there looking over Ronnie's back. Shelby tried doing Ronnie a favor by distracting the guy. "Are you new with Bright Lights?" Shelby asked him.

"I'm filling in for C-C-Carl," he said. "He's g-g-got the flu. My name's Lance." He held out his hand and Ronnie shook it over her shoulder without turning to him. The hotel room Kestrel had asked Ronnie to get him, his usual suite, was unavailable and Kestrel would be annoyed.

"I can get into all your p-p-personal files real easy," Lance said. "Want me to show you?"

"No need. My boyfriend's a computer geek." Ronnie mentioned Alex so this guy would figure out two things: that she already had a boyfriend and that said boyfriend was good enough at computers that she didn't need whatever it was this guy was offering her.

But Lance persisted. "You can find things out about people you never knew b-b-before. You can even make a whole new p-p-person out of yourself if you want to."

Ronnie stood up and walked to Kestrel's office. "Thanks, but I got enough trouble being the person I am," she said. She shut the door to Kestrel's office behind her.

The light turned green and the cab left the bus and the two men on its ad behind. Ronnie now knew why she hadn't recognized Lance Tolan as she searched the personnel files of Boundary and Bright Lights. He didn't work there. The day that Lance was at Boundary he'd been filling in for someone at Bright Lights, working off the books. He looked entirely different, too, having lost a huge amount of weight. He'd probably worked with a therapist or someone on his stuttering. Does Xanax help with that? He'd cut his beard, capped his teeth and got contact lenses or had Lasik done. He'd become what he thought Martin Newman should look like.

But it didn't matter to Ronnie who Martin Newman was or what he'd once looked like. He and no one else was the main reason Alex was lying dead on the floor of the theater right now. Not her, not Alex, not Shelby or Pike or Kestrel. She blamed Lance Tolan. No one else.

Ronnie's taxi stopped in front of her brownstone. She paid the driver and got out with the backpack. She walked up the stoop, unlocked the street door and hurried as quickly as she could up the steep, narrow stairs.

She went into the apartment and kicked the door shut behind her. Newman quickly stood up from his computer and stared at her as she slammed the backpack onto the table. It was heavy enough that the table shook under its weight, one tin leg nearly buckling. She stood for a moment, breathing heavily from walking up the stairs with it. She looked around the small room. Everything here said Alex to her. It made her sad; it made her furious. But she wouldn't cry. Not now. Not in front of Newman.

He approached the backpack like it was a bomb about to explode. "Is that the money?"

"No, it's my laundry," she said. "What do you think it is?"

He stepped towards Ronnie, but she moved away from him. Did he think they were going to embrace like lovers? "How did it go?" he said.

"Not good. Not good at all."

Newman's face fell. "What happened?"

Ronnie stared at him for a moment before she said, "Alex is dead."

Newman snorted. "Right."

His reaction pissed her off even more. "He's dead," she said again, staring straight at him.

This time Newman's eyes opened wide. "What do you mean he's dead?"

"What do I mean he's dead? I mean he's not alive anymore. That's what being dead means, asshole."

"I don't believe you," he said.

Ronnie took off her jacket and pointed to the bloodstains all over her shirtsleeve and on her collar. "You see this blood here and on my sleeve? You think it's ketchup? Or stage blood? It's not. It's Alex's blood. You don't believe me, go online, check the news. They've probably found his body by now." She zipped open the backpack. She took the Timex watch out and slammed it on the table. She began taking out wads of the Euros.

"Who k-k-killed him?" Newman asked, his stutter suddenly reappearing. The news that Alex had died changed this guy's persona from the worldly con man he wanted to be to the stammering, sweaty loser he really was. "Who k-k-killed him?" he asked again.

Ronnie looked at him. "You d-d-did, Lance," she said, mocking his stutter and using his real name for the first time. "You k-k-killed him."

Lance didn't move. Ronnie couldn't tell if he was more upset that she blamed him for Alex's death or that she knew who he really was. She didn't give a shit. "That's right, Lance. I know who you are."

"When d-d-did you know?"

"What difference does it make when I knew? I know." She sorted the money into two different piles. "How could I forget those stupid glasses and that beard and your hillbilly teeth? How'd you lose all that weight anyway? Weight Watchers? Did you get your stomach stapled?"

"I ch-ch-changed."

"No, you didn't, not one bit," she said. "Look at yourself. You're sweating, your hands are shaking. Are you having an anxiety attack, Lance? Do you need some Xanax? Is that what it's for?" Lance said nothing. "You know what the funny part about all this is? Do you?" Ronnie asked as she kept dividing the money. "That for all the computer and Internet magic you conjured up and held over our heads, do you know how I found out who you are?" Lance shook his head. "From the label on a pill bottle you left on the bathroom floor of your apartment. A pill bottle. That's about as old school as you can get, isn't it?"

Lance was confused. This wasn't fiction anymore. It was real. He couldn't delete it. And it was happening at its own speed.

The money sat in two separate piles on the table. "Hurry up and put this in your suitcase or whatever," Ronnie said. "We don't have time to waste. It's a whole new game. You're involved in a murder now. We both are." She began putting her portion of the Euros into her backpack. "So take your money and get out of here."

"Alone?"

She grinned at him. "Yes, Lance, alone. You didn't seriously think I was gonna to leave Alex for you, did you?" Martin or Lance or whatever he called himself said nothing. It was obvious that he'd believed that Ronnie was going to ride off into the sunset with him after they got the money. Fuck men, Ronnie thought. Fuck them and their stupid dreams. "You thought I was gonna leave Alex for someone who doesn't even exist?"

"I exist."

"I was working you, Lance. You didn't know that?"

He looked confused. Obviously, he still wanted her, but he couldn't let her think he'd believed her seduction act, not if it really was an act.

"I knew what you were doing," he said. "But, still, I thought maybe—"

"Now you can run off with Sophia."

"She's dead."

"No, she isn't Lance. Sophia's not dead because Sophia was never alive, was she?" Lance looked at the money. "Tell me, Lance. That's the only thing I'm gonna ask about your pathetic imaginary life. Nothing else. I promise. Fuck your garage band, fuck your rock climbing and your degrees. All I want to know is if you were ever married to a beautiful woman called Sophia who died." Lance was silent. "Tell me," Ronnie said. "Were you?"

He looked at the floor. "No."

"Of course not. There was never a Sophia. There never is." Ronnie was more furious that Sophia was a lie than she was at anything else this idiot had told her. She didn't know why, but now wasn't the time to figure that out. "Here's your share," she said. "One million minus what I gave Shelby."

What Ronnie said about Shelby refocused Lance's thoughts. "Why'd you give money to her?"

"Think of it as your penalty for killing my lover."

"Who killed him? P-P-Pike?"

"No, you did, Lance, as sure as if you stood there and fired the gun yourself."

Ronnie put the rest of her money into her backpack. She knocked the Timex watch onto the floor and Lance picked it up. "What's this?" he asked.

"Something Kestrel gave the kidnappers as a joke."

"Why?"

"Because he hates it when people keep him waiting. And I don't like it either, so pack up your shit and get out of here."

Lance held up the watch and looked at it.

"You want the watch, Lance, keep it. Think of it as a parting gift from the game show we've been playing this last week."

Lance tried to open the watch by twisting its casing. When that didn't work he put it on the floor and smashed it with his foot.

"Leave the damn thing alone and pack up your money," Ronnie said.

"It's not a watch."

Ronnie looked up. "What is it?"

"It's a t-t-tracker."

Ronnie looked at what he was holding in his hand. "Shit." But before she could do anything else she heard a voice say, "Freeze!"

She turned to see Barry Kestrel at the apartment door pointing a small pistol at them. In any other situation the sight of Kestrel holding a handgun would've made Ronnie laugh. But an hour before she'd seen what a gun could do and she never wanted to see another one again.

"Jesus Christ," she said to Kestrel. "Put that thing down before you kill somebody."

But he didn't put it down. He kicked the door shut behind himself and he moved closer, his pistol aimed at Ronnie. "Shut up and do exactly what I tell you to."

"You tracked me with the watch," she said.

Before Kestrel could answer her, Lance moved away from Ronnie and toward him. "Thank G-G-God you got here, Mr. Kestrel," he said.

"Don't go there," Ronnie said to Newman.

Kestrel looked at Lance. "Are you okay, Marty? Do you need some water or something?"

"He doesn't need any water and he's not Marty."

"Then who is he and what the fuck is he doing here?"

"He's ripping you off is what he's doing here," Ronnie said.

"She was going to k-k-kill me, Mr. Kestrel."

"That is such bullshit," Ronnie said.

Kestrel looked at Lance. "Are you involved in this scheme, Marty? Tell me. Are you?"

"Of course he is," Ronnie said.

"I asked him," Kestrel said, pointing his pistol at Lance. "Are you, Marty?"

"No, Mr. K-K-Kestrel. They k-k-kidnapped me."

Ronnie pointed to the Euros on the table. "Right. He was helping me stack the money out of the goodness of his heart."

"She's trying to c-c-confuse you, Mr. K-K-Kestrel."

"Don't worry. I know how easily a bitch like her can lie," Kestrel said. He pointed his gun at Ronnie and said, "You thought you played me last night begging for the money to deliver this, didn't you? Is that pregnant dimwit in on this with you, too?"

"No."

"Who knows who to believe now?" Kestrel said. He pointed his pistol at Newman. "Bottom line is: this man is Martin Newman and

I just saved him from you, you treacherous cunt. If I shot you right now they'd give me a medal."

"I'm telling you that he's involved."

"Maybe he is, maybe he isn't, but it doesn't matter." Kestrel said. "All that matters is that I came here to rescue Martin Newman, an employee of mine who, as far as I knew, was in mortal danger."

"You are so stupid," Ronnie said.

"I'm going to look pretty damn smart in the papers tomorrow. Barry Kestrel—the man who put his own life on the line to rescue an employee from a deranged kidnapper." He looked at Lance. "It would've played better if you were a good looking chick, but what can you do?"

"What they're gonna find out tomorrow is that there is no Martin Newman," Ronnie said. "There never was."

"Then who the fuck is that?" Lance tensed and moved some when Kestrel aimed his pistol at him to make his point.

"That's right," Lance said. "Wh-wh-who am I?"

Ronnie was surprised by Lance's efforts to work Kestrel like this. "His name is Lance Tolan."

"Who?"

"Lance Tolan."

Lance shook his head. "I don't know what she's talking about, Mr. K-K-Kestrel. My name is Martin Newman. You want to see my d-d-driver's license?"

"I do," Kestrel said.

"It's a fake," Ronnie said, "like everything else about him. Martin Newman doesn't exist. He never did."

Kestrel looked from Lance to Ronnie and back again. "He's standing right there."

"My partner and I, Alex, we made Martin Newman up. From beginning to end."

"She's t-t-trying to confuse you," Lance said.

"Shut up," Kestrel said to Lance and he turned back to Ronnie. "Keep talking."

"I'll prove it to you," Ronnie said. "Ask him what floor the research traders' offices are on."

"Why should I do that?"

"Because that's where he works, right? Ask him."

Kestrel looked at Lance. "What floor are your offices on?"

Lance shook his head. "She's t-t-trying to c-c-cloud the issue."

"Ask him who the Boundary softball team played in the final last year. You saw his file. He said he played second base."

"Who'd we play in the finals, Marty?" Kestrel said.

"You c-c-can't expect me to answer that. I've been t-t-traumatized."

Now Kestrel was suspicious of Newman.

"One more," Ronnie said to Kestrel. "Ask him what the name of the deal he closed with Jenkins and Shaw was? He's got to know that. Even they knew that."

Lance said nothing while Kestrel stared at him waiting for an answer. Then Lance suddenly kicked the card table with the backpack and money on top of it, sending the cash flying in all directions. He ran past Kestrel and out the apartment's door.

"Stop!" Kestrel yelled and, as he did, he raised his pistol and fired it, not at Lance, but at the ceiling to scare him into stopping. But he'd left the gun's safety on and nothing happened. "Sonofabitch!" Kestrel said when he realized this and he clicked the safety off.

But Ronnie was already running after Lance. On the landing outside the apartment, she saw Mrs. Richfield from 5A struggling to pull her grocery cart up the narrow steps. Newman could never have gotten past her so he must've gone up to the roof. Ronnie headed there and Kestrel followed her.

As they climbed the stairs, Kestrel told Ronnie how he'd followed the tracker to the theater. "Once it got there I knew it was you." Off Ronnie's silence he said, "What? You think I don't know your boyfriend's an actor and you write for that bullshit amateur theater? On my way to the theater I saw that the money had left it and I followed it here."

"All I care about is the asshole on the roof," Ronnie said and on the top floor she pushed open the door to the roof and hurried onto it. Its surface was littered with empty beer cans, cigarette butts and shards of tarpaper. On summer nights Ronnie and Alex would bring food up here and sit on folding chairs under the sky. They did that sometimes in the winter, too, when it snowed.

"Where is he?" Kestrel asked.

Ronnie ran past some rusted garbage cans half filled with rainwater. There was a cage that looked like it had once held pigeons in it. Feathers caught in its wires shook in the wind. No one could hide in it.

Then Ronnie saw Lance trying to climb over the edge of the roof and onto the rusted fire escape. He looked terrified as he carefully put his legs over the edge. He was about to take his first step down the ladder when he heard Kestrel.

"Stop right there," Kestrel said, his pistol aimed at Lance.

Ronnie took Alex's prop pistol from her pocket and pointed it at Lance, too. "You heard him."

Kestrel looked at Ronnie's gun. "What's that?" he asked.

Ronnie ignored Kestrel and ran over to Lance. She grabbed him by the sleeve. He shut his eyes tightly, terrified by the sight of the street far below. She pulled him off the fire escape and he landed hard on the grimy roof. "I thought you were a rock climber," she said.

Sprawled on the tar paper, Lance said, "She's lying, Mr. K-K-Kestrel."

"Then why'd you run?"

"I have PTSD."

"Who doesn't?" Kestrel said.

Lance pointed to Ronnie. "Shoot her or she'll shoot you, Mr. Kestrel."

Kestrel pointed his gun at Ronnie. "Put your gun down."

"It's a prop, for Christ's sake," Ronnie said and she let the plastic pistol fall and clank onto the roof's surface, sounding like the toy it was.

"Talk to me," Kestrel said to her.

"My boyfriend Alex and me, we created a fictional Boundary employee to kidnap." She quickly explained how the timing of his kidnapping was to overlap with the impending Salient deal, forcing Kestrel's hand.

When she finished all Kestrel said was, "That's good."

"That's what we thought until this dweeb figured it out."

"I'm not a d-d-dweeb," Lance said, standing now, wiping the dirt off his pants.

"He was stalking me online—"

"I wasn't st-st-stalking you."

"—and he found the file Alex and I created for the fictional Martin Newman and he worked his way into it so he could become his own version of Newman. He followed everything we were doing online. On Monday when he realized that we were kidnapping Newman he slimed his way into our deal. He threatened to tell you what Alex and I did if we didn't include him and share the ransom with him."

"That's even better," Kestrel said, relaxing his arm and letting his pistol point to the roof's surface.

"Martin Newman never existed," Ronnie said. "That's why he couldn't answer your questions about Boundary."

"I am Martin Newman," Lance said.

Kestrel scoffed and looked at Ronnie. "What's with this guy?"

"He's delusional."

"People can be anyone they want now," Lance said.

Kestrel turned to Ronnie. "Where's your boyfriend?" Ronnie said nothing. "Where is he?" Kestrel asked again.

"He got killed this afternoon."

"Bullshit," Kestrel said.

"Whose blood you think this is?" She pointed to the bloodstains on her shirt.

"I don't believe you."

"Call Pike. Ask him whose blood it is."

Pike's name got Kestrel's attention. "Pike's in this, too?"

Ronnie nodded. "He only got involved at the end," she said. "He figured out what Alex and I were doing and tried to talk us out of it, but we said we were going through with it anyway. He said he'd make sure we didn't screw up and get caught."

"Why?" Kestrel asked Ronnie.

"Because he's in love with me." Why was she even bothering to protect Pike now? But Ronnie continued. "That's when things went wrong. Alex had a blank gun, that phony piece of shit over there," she said, pointing to the prop pistol lying on the roof. "Pike thought it was real and when Alex shot it at him Pike fired his own gun and hit Alex. He died in the theater."

Kestrel mumbled, "Sonofabitch."

"The theater crew will find Alex's body and it'll be on the news anytime now. It probably already is."

"What about Shelby?" Kestrel said.

Ronnie shook her head. "She wasn't in on it. She's a conniving bitch, but she only wanted to deliver the payoff to get some money for herself and her kid."

While Kestrel tried to put all this together, Ronnie had to show him that there was only one way out of this mess. "We're talking a whole other level of shit now," she said. "Do you really want everyone to know you tried to solve a kidnapping you never reported so it wouldn't jeopardize a business deal and in the process you used a pregnant girl to deliver the ransom and, even worse, got someone killed? You'd be held responsible for everything including Alex's death."

Kestrel said nothing.

"Add to that," Ronnie said, "your company got punked by a geek like him."

"I'm not a g-g-geek," Lance said.

Ronnie ignored Lance and said to Kestrel, "This comes out and the Salient deal will disappear. So will a lot of other things. You want to risk what? Four, five hundred million just so you can get back at me?"

Kestrel said nothing.

"I didn't think so," Ronnie said. "So here's what's gonna happen. First you're gonna put the gun down." She waited. "Now."

Kestrel put the pistol into his coat pocket.

"Then Lance here is gonna erase all traces of Martin Newman," Ronnie said.

"I already did."

"And you," she said to Kestrel, "you don't tell anyone about any of this. No one. Not even Jenkins and Shaw. Especially not Jenkins and Shaw. Tell them someone concocted a fake employee and kidnapped him. They'll realize it's true when Newman doesn't show up and no one in IT will be able to find any trace of him. He'll have disappeared along with your ransom. If Jenkins or Shaw ask, tell them I left it somewhere in a dumpster or in the trunk of a parked car, somewhere, anywhere. You'll come up with a good story. It's what you do. They'll buy it. What choice do they have? They want the Salient deal to go through as much as you do. More. It'll all play out fine."

"What about Pike?" Kestrel asked.

"He won't say anything."

"Why not?"

"Because he's guilty."

Kestrel pointed to Lance. "What about him?"

"What about me?" Lance said.

"We give him his million."

Lance was surprised. "R-r-really?"

Kestrel didn't like this idea. "Why would we do that?"

"Because it makes him guilty, too. Guilty people are your best friends. I thought you knew people."

"What about the rest of the money?" Kestrel asked.

"I keep it."

Kestrel shook his head. "We split it fifty-fifty."

"For shit's sake, you've got half a billion dollars to lose."

"I have to get something out of this," Kestrel said.

Ronnie reached into her pocket and pulled out a five dollar bill. "Here," she said and tossed it to Kestrel. But the breeze grabbed it before he could and the bill nestled against the rusted wire of the empty birdcage. Kestrel walked over to the cage, grabbed the five dollar bill and pocketed it.

FRIDAY NIGHT

DIARY ENTRY OF JAKE SUMMERS

My name is Jake. Jake Summers. I was born in Portland, Oregon and I studied economics at Stanford University. My favorite food is Italian. My favorite color is dark green and I'm a San Francisco Giants fan. I like animals, especially dogs, and my favorite breed is the beagle. I was happily married for almost three years, but my wife Julie died when she was hit by a delivery truck on Lexington Avenue in New York City after buying me an anniversary present. It was a heartwrenching experience, but I learned from it and I've recovered. Recently I got a new girlfriend whose name is Veronica—or Ronnie—and once we work things out we'll move in together.

Lance Tolan sat in the large bathtub in the late Martin Newman's apartment at The Maxwell. It was filled with hot water and too many bubbles. On his MacBook Air he read the diary he was writing—that of Jake Summers, the man he would be from now on.

I speak French, too, and I like to cook. Most French people do, even men, especially men. I play tennis very well and I play a musical instrument. Not the guitar like everyone else does, but the clarinet.

Jake Summers—or Lance—looked up when he heard a noise in the other room. "Somebody there?" he said. No one answered. He asked again in a louder voice that he meant to be more threatening, "Who's there?"

"Relax," Shelby said as she walked into the bathroom carrying an empty suitcase and wearing latex gloves. Seeing Lance in the bathtub she said, "And whatever you do, don't get up." Her accent was less Tara than trailer trash, but she was still very pregnant. "Where's the money?"

Lance pointed to a backpack on the bathroom floor. "There."

"What are you doing sitting in a bathtub for anyway? There's a dead man in the story now and here you are acting like nothing's happened."

"Kestrel said he'd bury everything."

"You believe that asshole? Take it from me, shit like this has a way of staying alive and biting you in the ass." She opened Lance's backpack and started taking stacks of the Euros out of it and putting them into her own case.

"Listen to this," Lance said and read more of Jake Summers's diary while she transferred her share of the money.

Shelby had worked scams with her boyfriend for five years. They made a big score at a golf resort in Virginia before coming to New York where middle-aged businessmen easily fell for the pretty, southern damsel's tales of woe. She wrote false records from a business school and became Heidi's assistant at Boundary hoping that the connections there would lead to something bigger, maybe even with Kestrel. They did.

She met Lance when Ronnie did: the day he came to work on the ransomware attack over a year ago. She knew a mark when she saw one and she milked the idiot's obsession with Ronnie, promising him that she'd do everything in her power to get them together. She gave him access to Ronnie's Boundary account and that's all the geek needed to find everything about her, including her Martin Newman creation.

Over the next year while pulling a bunch of smaller scams on some Boundary execs, Shelby watched Lance hijack the Martin Newman files and diaries that Ronnie and Alex wrote for their imaginary character. He became obsessed with them. He believed that he could become the character that the three of them were creating. He even went to the place where Ronnie and Alex said that Newman lived and rented a place there for himself. It was batshit crazy. Who does something like that? Shelby got her answer on the Internet: Lance Tolan, a five year old boy whose alcoholic and abusive father kills his wife, making sure the kid spends the next thirteen years shuttled from one shitty foster family to the next. That's who does something like that. Somewhere along the way the kid discovered the Internet and, deciding he liked that world better than the real one, he disappeared into it.

When Lance first told Shelby about the sketch for Jubilee that Ronnie wrote about kidnapping the imaginary Newman and asking for a ransom, she thought it was a brilliant idea. A kidnapping with no real victim. Shelby wished that she'd thought of it. She should have. But Ronnie would've made a good con. Two women like them would work great together.

Hearing from Lance what Ronnie and Alex were doing, Shelby thought about trying a phony kidnapping herself. Why not? It was just another con. But what imaginary person would she create? And kidnap? Maybe herself. But when? And how? For Ronnie, it was only an idea for one of her plays, but Shelby became obsessed with it. Still, Shelby's boyfriend, Sammy's father, was too stupid to handle anything that complicated. So Shelby kept her eye on everything Ronnie wrote, taking notes. Maybe she'd learn enough to pull something off like that herself one day. But Monday morning when Shelby listened in on Kestrel's private line and found out that Ronnie had actually told Kestrel they'd kidnapped Martin Newman, she saw her chance. She did everything she could to persuade Lance to actually become Newman, the kidnapping victim and her unwitting partner. He hesitated at first until Shelby laid it on.

"You really are Martin Newman, aren't you?" she asked Lance.

"You know that I am."

"Then this is your chance to show Ronnie how much you'll do to be with her. How much you love her. How there's nothing you wouldn't do for her. She'll love you, Martin. I would," she said, making sure to call him Martin. He needed a final push, so she said, "You're the man Ronnie created and now's your chance to come to life. It's what every woman dreams of."

The idiot bought what she said. And here they were.

Shelby finished putting her share of the Euros into her case while Lance, still in the bathtub, worked on his new diary.

"I can't believe you only got one million from that bitch," she said.

"She's not a bitch."

"You should've seen her go all Mother Teresa on me in that taxi. 'Here take this. You need it.' I wish I had a picture of the look on her face when I kept asking her for more money. Priceless. But she worked you like a puppet, didn't she?"

"I worked her."

"Right."

"She and I are gonna get back together."

Shelby laughed. "Whatever you say, Lance."

"I'm not Lance anymore. My name is Jake. Jake Summers. See?" Lance held his laptop over the bubbles so Shelby could see his new diary on its screen. "Read it".

Shelby took it and read aloud from Lance's diary.

"I play tennis very well and I play a musical instrument. Not the guitar like everyone else does, but the clarinet like Woody Allen." She skipped down to the end. *"I drive a Dodge Ram pickup truck. That might seem contradictory for a sophisticated man like me, but*

*the most interesting people are contradictions, aren't they? That's
what my girlfriend Ronnie says."*

Shelby laughed. "This guy's even more of a fairy tale than
Newman was."

"If Newman was such a fairy tale, how'd you get all your money?"

"Like this," Shelby said and she dropped his computer into
the bathwater.

Lance quickly reached for it under all the bubbles. But when
he did, Shelby took a palm-sized Taser from her pocket, jammed it
against the back of Lance's neck and held it there as she Tased him.
He was stunned. Shelby put her palm on the back of his head and
held it under the bathwater. Lance flailed a little at first and, given
that she was pregnant, it wasn't easy, but the effect of the Taser quickly weakened his efforts.

Finally he was still, his head bobbing lifelessly in the sudsy water.
Out of breath, Shelby reached into the water, grabbed his computer,
dried it off and put it into her case.

She looked around the small bathroom and saw an electric hair
dryer on a small table. She plugged it in, turned it on and dropped it
into the bathtub. It made a fizzing sound before it sank unseen under
the bubbles.

She emptied Lance's backpack of its cash and when she'd put it all
in her own case she stood up and looked at herself in the mirror. Not
bad considering. Finding the hair dryer was a piece of luck. The gods
of grift were smiling on her.

She took a short blonde wig out of her coat pocket and, stuffing
her own hair under it, pulled it on.

"Good-bye, Martin. Jake. Lance. Waldo. Whoever you are," Shelby said and walked into the living room. Satisfied that nothing there
would lead anyone to her, she patted her pregnant belly. "What do
you say we go spend some of your momma's money, sweetie-pie?"

Shutting the apartment door behind her, she peeled off her gloves
and dropped them into the garbage chute on her way to the stairs.

In the Maxwell lobby she saw that it was still raining. She had a load of cash on her, but what dipshit cab driver was smart enough to take Euros? There was a bucket full of umbrellas next to the door. Smiling at the guard, she grabbed one and headed to the subway.

— • —

After Kestrel had left her building, Ronnie and Lance divided the money. They were both silent as they did this. Ronnie looked at Lance when he had his share and said, "Get out."

Lance said, "Veronica—"

"Shut up and get out."

Lance did.

Ronnie put her money in the bedroom closet behind a quilt Alex's mother had sent them. She called the director of Ledgewood Gardens and told her that she wanted to purchase a unit for her mother. It was unusual for a resident to move in so quickly, but there was a unit that had recently been "vacated" and the director supposed that it could be arranged. Ronnie would go to Jerrold House in the morning and take her mother out. From there she'd take her to Ledgewood Gardens in a limousine.

What Ronnie wanted to do most now was sleep, but if she'd learned anything over the last five days, it was to be prepared for the unexpected. So first she'd go to Newman's apartment at The Maxwell to make sure they'd left nothing there that would link her or Alex to the place.

— • —

Pike opened *The New York Post,* damp from the rain, on his kitchen counter, quickly leafing through it until he found what he was looking for on page nine.

The headline read:

ACTOR FOUND DEAD IN THEATER
VICTIM OF ROBBERY.

There were two photos. One was Alex's headshot. In it he was young, handsome and promising. Next to it was a photo of the Jubilee stage floor with a large bloodstain on the center of it.

Pike poured what was left of Kestrel's bourbon into a small glass and looked out the tiny kitchen window at First Avenue as the rain came down.

— • —

Ronnie's subway pulled into the 51st Street IRT station. She was eager to get to Newman's apartment and finish with all this. Hurrying off the train, she bumped into a pregnant blond woman.

"I'm sorry," Ronnie said to the woman and walked quickly toward the station's exit. But something about the pregnant woman seemed familiar and, when Ronnie got to the stile, she stopped and turned back to the train. The pregnant woman with short white hair stood in the still-open door of the train and stared back at her.

It was Shelby.

Ronnie didn't move as a million things raced through her mind. Shelby looked at Ronnie and shook her head slowly as if she knew where Ronnie was headed and she was telling her not to go there. The train's doors shut and, through its grimy window, Shelby grinned at Ronnie and shrugged. It wasn't unlike the look Shelby gave her when she got out of the cab with her designer bag full of cash earlier that morning.

Ronnie never left the station. She got on the next train going in the opposite direction and went home.

MONDAY NIGHT

Louis Pike stood in front of his New School classmates, all but two of whom were younger than him. One gentleman appeared to be in his fifties and a woman in the front row was older than that.

Earlier that afternoon he'd decided against telling the class his theory about the classic novel. Instead, he'd toe the traditional line. He'd point to Dorian Gray's descent into madness and murder as a symbol of the decadence Wilde believed was hidden beneath the proper surface of Victorian life.

But as Pike stood at the front of the room he recalled the side-by-side photos in *The Post*, the 8x10 showing Alex in all his youthful freshness and the other of his blood pooled on the stage floor. The hell with it. He'd tell them his own take on the book.

— • —

Ronnie spent the weekend settling her mother into her new life at Ledgewood Gardens. The buildings and its grounds were stately and impeccably kept. The furniture was elegant and on the walls were prints of artists like Rembrandt and Vermeer, paintings that suggested a world of order and civility. The staff was unfailing friendly and immediately took care of any request Ronnie or Carlotta made.

Ronnie sat with her mother in her private room. Carlotta had fallen asleep watching a British cooking show.

Since Friday the discovery of a man's body in an apartment at The Maxwell was all over the news. At first the police called his death suspicious. But most opinions now leaned toward the man dying by accidental electrocution in his bathtub. This was not unheard of. A newscaster mentioned three other instances that year in New York State alone in which the victim died the same way. One was a drug user. Another was a suicide.

But most perplexing to the authorities was that the man couldn't be identified. No records of Martin Newman, the man who'd rented the apartment, or at least the name he'd used on the lease, could be found. None. Anywhere. And in a time when people can be tracked by their credit cards and cell phones and so many other ways, this was unusual.

But Ronnie knew who the man was and how he'd died. The expression on Shelby's face through the grimy subway window told her everything. It kept Ronnie from going to Newman's apartment and she was grateful to Shelby for the warning. She wished she could sit down with her and talk about everything that had happened. Obviously, Shelby had been Lance's accomplice. Ronnie doubted from the start that Lance could have managed it all himself. But it also meant that Shelby was partially responsible for Alex's death and Ronnie blamed her as much as she blamed Lance or Pike or herself.

But the girl from Atlanta, if that's where she really was from, was excellent at what she did. She'd played Ronnie perfectly over the last ten months and her performance in the cab during the ransom delivery was nothing short of brilliant.

Ronnie assumed that Shelby, like Pike, had made sure they'd left no trace of themselves in Newman's apartment. And even if the police did find Alex's fingerprints at The Maxwell they weren't on file anywhere and would soon be gone along with the fingers that left them.

Ronnie took the remote from her mother's lap and lowered the volume so as not to wake her. She channel surfed. She stopped at the Bloomberg Business Report when she saw that the news conference that morning announcing the merger of Boundary and Salient was being rebroadcast.

Tom Bowden stood on a small stage in the Boundary lobby with Barry Kestrel at his side, the two men very different in age and style. Behind them were several Salient directors and next to them stood Natalie Jenkins and Walter Shaw, both with wan smiles on their faces.

"We at Salient Industries are great admirers of what Mr. Kestrel has accomplished here at Boundary over the last twenty-seven years," Tom Bowden said.

Kestrel leaned into the microphone. "The feelings are mutual, Tom, and I'm certain this move will benefit everyone involved." It was called a "move" rather than the takeover it really was to give respect to Kestrel, but he wasn't going to have any power. He didn't want any. He had money.

— • —

"For me," Pike said to the class, "Oscar Wilde's novel isn't a horror story."

"What is it then?" Ms. Rosen asked him.

"I think it's a riddle, ma'am."

"Explain to us what you mean by that, Detective."

"I don't think it's a painting that Dorian Gray locks in his attic," Pike said.

"What do you think it is?" a young lady in the second row asked Pike.

"I think it's a mirror."

"What kind of mirror?" Ms. Rosen said.

"Any mirror. Every mirror," Pike said. "Dorian Gray never looks at it because he doesn't want to see who he is or what he's become. That's how he convinces himself that he's still young. And still beautiful. And, most importantly, that he's still good."

212

The women in the class sat up when he said this. Was it because they knew more about mirrors than the men did?

"And it works for him, too," Pike continued, "because if we believe something ourselves it's easier to convince other people of it. And that only works if we don't look in the mirror and see what we really are." From the looks on their faces, it was clear that most of the students didn't understand what Pike was saying to them. Of course they didn't. They were too young.

"In the end Dorian Gray has no choice," Pike said. "He looks in the mirror and has to accept what he sees, what he is. Like all of us are forced to do eventually. When he does that, when he looks at his true, horrible image, the monster, himself, he's overwhelmed by it and he dies."

Pike finished and the class, led by Ms. Rosen, applauded politely after a long pause. Their reactions varied. The young men were not persuaded by Pike's take. Like Alex had, they preferred the horror elements of Wilde's story and relished the power of the evil painting and Gray's final graphic transformation. The young women were not so certain. But the oldest student, the woman in the front row, nodded her head knowingly.

Pike sat down and took notes on what Ms. Rosen said about the next book they'd be reading: William Golding's *The Lord of the Flies*.

— • —

On the TV in her mother's room, Ronnie watched both Salient's and Boundary's employees applaud enthusiastically when the news conference ended. A few even cheered.

Reporters shouted questions at the two executives, but Tom Bowden held up his hand. "Thank you, ladies and gentlemen. That will be all."

Several reporters yelled their questions at Kestrel. Barry Kestrel shrugged. "Sorry, guys, but Kestrel has left the building," he said with a smirk. He walked off the stage, disappointing the reporters who'd always been able to count on him to say something terse, often comic and unfailingly quotable.

Ronnie shut the TV off and looked out at the large garden. She wondered how much Kestrel, Natalie and Walter would make from the Salient deal and how many Boundary employees would lose their jobs because of it.

Ronnie went over the events of the last week, the same way she'd take notes on a performance, notes she'd give the cast and crew after the curtain came down. The kidnapping was, after all, an improvisation that she'd devised, perfected and performed. But it wasn't about make-believe characters with imaginary results forgotten as soon as the audience left the theater. What she did was real and maybe that's why she enjoyed it so much. She was ashamed at how much she missed the high that she'd felt this last week.

But why shouldn't she feel proud? The scheme she'd come up with was a solid one. She managed to hold it together even after the deranged wannabe, Martin Newman, showed up out of the blue. She'd played him successfully. And she was able to keep everything under control when Pike entered the picture and when Shelby wormed her way into it, too.

Was it done perfectly? Of course not. No performance is. Especially an improv like this. There were times she was frightened, unsure and eager to end it. Luck, both good and bad, played a part, too. When she failed, she failed badly. Alex died because of that, something she'd regret for the rest of her life. But there was a charge, an excitement to it all that no rehearsed play could ever have.

And what if Alex's death was not a reason to avoid doing it again? What if his sacrifice was exactly why she should do it again? A way to make sure that he didn't die in vain. He'd want her to do it again, wouldn't he? Together they'd outplayed a prominent Wall Street figure and had a million dollars in cash to show for their work.

Could she concoct another scheme like the Newman kidnapping and pull it off as successfully? And what would happen if she tracked Shelby down? Would Shelby feel cornered? Or flattered? A grifter's a kind of actor, too, conning their marks like an actor cons the audience, so Ronnie guessed that Shelby would be intrigued. Maybe she could learn from Shelby and possibly even work with her.

Ronnie smiled at these Robin Hood-like notions of hers. They were childish; they were absurd. Or were they?

It was too dark to see the forsythia that had started to bloom in the garden, but in the glass's reflection, Ronnie saw that her bemused smile had been replaced by a more determined expression. Alex used to tease her, saying this was the look she always wore on the first day of rehearsal.

ABOUT THE AUTHOR

CHARLIE PETERS

Charlie Peters is a playwright and screenwriter who was raised in New York City and educated at Stonyhurst College in England, the University of Connecticut and Carnegie-Mellon University. His plays have been produced at La Mama E.T.C., Playwrights Horizons, The Edinburgh Festival, The Actors Theatre of Louisville and Primary Stages. Twelve of his screenplays have been produced and the casts in those movies include Sally Field, Bob Hoskins, Renee Zellweger, Burt Reynolds, James Caan, Morgan Freeman, Jeff Bridges, Michael Caine, Claire Trevor, Richard Dreyfuss, Diane Keaton, Frances McDormand, Jude Law and Maureen Stapleton.

MORE GREAT BOOKS FROM

VEIL OF SEDUCTION by Emily Dinova

1922. Lorelei Alba, a fiercely independent and ambitious woman, is determined to break into the male-dominated world of investigative journalism by doing the unimaginable-infiltrating Morning Falls Asylum, the gothic hospital to which "troublesome" women are dispatched, never to be seen again. Once there, she meets the darkly handsome and enigmatic Doctor Roman Dreugue, who claims to have found the cure for insanity. But Lorelei's instincts tell her something is terribly wrong, even as her curiosity pulls her deeper into Roman's intimate and isolated world of intrigue.

THE LAST STAGE by Bruce Scivally

Dying in a small Los Angeles bungalow with his Jewish wife, Josephine at his side, famed lawman Wyatt Earp imagines an ending more befitting a man of his reputation—returning to his mining claims in a small desert town, tying up loose ends with his wife, and—after he strikes gold—confronting a quartet of robbers in a showdown.

THE MAN FROM BELIZE by Steven Kobrin

Life-saving heart surgeon Dr. Kent Stirling lives in paradise, diving his time between two medical practices in the exotic Yucatan. Deeply in love with the woman of his dreams, he has everything a man could desire...until enemies from his secret past as a government hitman convene to eliminate him, including a death-dealing assassin known as the Viper.

HENRY GRAY PUBLISHING

PAPA ROCK'S ROMANCE MOVIES WORD SEARCH
by Rock Scivally and Jeffrey Breslauer

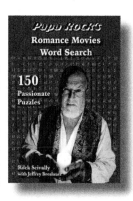

Here are Word Searches for 150 classic Romance movies made between 1921 and 1999, including *Gone With the Wind, Casablanca, Roman Holiday, Breakfast at Tiffany's, The Way We Were, When Harry Met Sally, Jerry Maguire,* and *Titanic,* among many others. Just remember—if this book closes before you've finished working a puzzle, you'll regret it, maybe not today, maybe not tomorrow, but soon and for the rest of your life.

PAPA ROCK'S HORROR MOVIES WORD SEARCH
by Rock Scivally

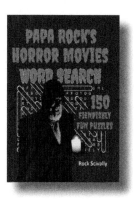

Sharpen your stakes - er, pencils - to solve these unique puzzles designed for anyone who loves classic horror films from the first Frankenstein film in 1910 to the giant bug movies of the 1950s. If you grew up watching scary movies presented by a local horror host, or collected plastic model kits of monsters or read monster magazines, then this is the Word Search book for you!

PAPA ROCK'S SON OF HORROR MOVIES WORD SEARCH by Rock Scivally

The 1960s and '70s. Two decades that saw a shift in screen horror from Dracula, Frankenstein, and giant insects, to Blacula, Dr. Phibes, Regan, Damien, Carrie, a killer baby, and a rat named Ben. Pick up your pens, your pencils, or your blood-red highlighters and literally find all your horror film favorites from 1960 to 1979 within these pages.